PRAISE FOR *SCARS OF SILENCE*

'A horrific, baffling crime startles a small Swedish community. This is perfect Scandi Noir, dripping with atmosphere. The writing shines, and the story is impossible to resist. Gustawsson is a master'
Shari Lapena

'A shockingly cold slice of Scandi noir that combines the darkness of folk horror with a sharp-eyed exploration of consent'
Sarah Hilary

'Johana Gustawsson is an extraordinarily talented storyteller, with a beautiful, eloquent writing style. *Scars of Silence* unfolds at a breathless pace, and the climax is devastating ... Gustawsson richly deserves all of the accolades she has won in recent years'
Kate Rhodes

'Relevant and timely, *Scars of Silence* is compulsive whodunnit, with a strong and important message, tackling issues of great relevance in today's world. Once I started reading, I couldn't stop – utterly addictive' Sam Holland

'A page-turner full of twists and turns, told with devastating tenderness; I felt bereft when it ended. *Scars of Silence* is a masterclass in Nordic Noir' Heidi Amsinck

'Haunting, human and wholly unputdownable ... *Scars of Silence* grips you from the first page: unforgettable characters caught in the web of a chilling mystery, set against the stark, mesmerising backdrop of Sweden. Few writers balance heart and horror so masterfully – this is Scandi Noir at its finest' Thomas Enger

'*Scars of Silence* is incredible – powerful, timely, superb – with layers of emotion even in the darkness. Such a talent!'
Louise Swanson

'Magnificent! So chilling and atmospheric ... I was utterly gripped. Johana Gustawsson gets better and better with every book'
Lisa Hall

JOHANA GUSTAWSSON
WINNER OF...

Livre de Poche Readers Award
Cultura Ligue de l'Imaginaire Award
Gujan Thriller Readers' Prize
St Laurent du Var Festival Novel of the Year
Peur sur Jean Bart Novel of the Year
Plume d'Argent Award
Balai de la découverte Award
Balai d'Or Award
Prix Marseillais du Polar Award

SHORTLISTED for the CWA International Dagger

Also by Johana Gustawsson
and available from Orenda Books

The Roy & Castells Series
Block 46
Keeper
Blood Song

The Bleeding
Yule Island

ABOUT THE AUTHOR

Born in Marseille, France, and with a degree in political science, Johana Gustawsson has worked as a journalist for the French and Spanish press and television. Her critically acclaimed Roy & Castells series, including *Block 46, Keeper* and *Blood Song*, has won the Plume d'Argent, Balai de la découverte, Balai d'Or and Prix Marseillais du Polar awards. Johana's gothic historical thriller *The Bleeding* was a number-one bestseller in France and worldwide, shortlisting for the CWA Crime Fiction in Translation Dagger in the UK. *Yule Island* – the first in the Lidingö Mysteries series, and based on a true story – has followed suit, winning the prestigious Livre de Poche 2024 Readers award, the Cultura Ligue de l'Imaginaire Award, the Gujan Thrillers Festival Readers' Prize (Crime Novel of the Year) and Crime Novel of the Year at the Saint-Laurent-du-Var Polar Festival, hitting number one on the bestseller list, and reprinting five times in the first two months after publication. A TV adaptation of *Yule Island* is currently under way. Winner of the 2025 Maison de la Presse prize for *Scars of Silence*, Johana is also the author, with Thomas Enger, of *SON*, featuring Oslo police consultant and body-language expert Kari Voss. Now published in more than forty countries, she lives in the Stockholm archipelago with her three sons. Follow her on X @JoGustawsson, Instagram @johanagustawsson and facebook.com/johana.gustawsson.

ABOUT THE TRANSLATOR

David Warriner grew up in deepest Yorkshire, has lived in France and Quebec, and now calls British Columbia home. He has translated Johanna Gustawsson's *Blood Song, The Bleeding* and *Yule Island* and Roxanne Bouchard's Detective Moralès series for Orenda Books. His translation of Roxanne's *We Were the Salt of the Sea* was runner-up for the 2019 Scott Moncrieff Prize for French-English translation. Follow David on X and Instagram @thewarrinerd and on his website: davidwarriner.com.

SCARS OF SILENCE

JOHANA GUSTAWSSON

Translated from the French by David Warriner

ORENDA
BOOKS

Orenda Books
16 Carson Road
West Dulwich
London SE21 8HU
www.orendabooks.co.uk

First published in the United Kingdom by Orenda Books 2025
Originally published in French as *Les morsures du silence* by Calmann-Lévy 2025
Copyright © Calmann-Lévy 2025
English translation © David Warriner 2025

A catalogue record for this book is available from the British Library.

ISBN 978-1-916788-92-3
eISBN 978-1-916788-93-0

Typeset in Garamond by typesetter.org.uk

Printed and bound by Clays Ltd, Elcograf S.p.A

For sales and distribution, please contact info@orendabooks.co.uk

For Maximilian, William and Alexander,
my three little dragon hearts.

Silence is my secret lover
We meet whenever we can
I crave her. An unbendable urge to sit in her embrace
Letting every fibre in me be caressed by her presence.
—Sussi Louise Smith,
'If You Must, Sing', in *Seachanger – Wave Weaver*

1

Anna had put an ocean between herself and her mother. She wasn't the one who came up with that image. It was the woman who gave birth to her. Anna didn't have the imagination. That was something her oh-so cultured family never let her forget. But it was hardly an ocean, this mere strip of sea. A moat, more like – cutting Lidingö off from the life of the Stockholm mainland. A ghost-infested moat surrounding a poisoned island, where that all-powerful matriarch still reigned supreme, in spite of all that had happened.

Shaking – more with infuriation than from fear – she drove over the bridge connecting Lidingö to the capital, past the shabby stacks of the cement factory that greeted you as you reached the island, and followed the road that hugged the shore, where those lucky enough had once built holiday homes. Those shacks were now luxury villas clad in white, yellow or pink wood. Each had its own slipway and sweeping views over the bay of Stockholm.

Anna pulled over for a moment to gaze at the glassy depths. There was some strength to the sun that morning. It had none of its spring pallor and all of its summer swagger. It wasn't enough to warm your blood, but it was turning the leaves green and tinting the sea a bluer shade of grey. June was when day devoured night and put smiles back on faces. When the Swedes were drawn to the light just as strongly as they avoided conflict.

Driving on, a shiver ran down Anna's spine as she passed the golf club. She had been there so many times with her grandfather, arriving at dawn during the summer months, when it was easier to get away from her mother. She had ended up becoming an excellent caddie, despite her lack of talent for anything else. Especially for the sport itself, which reeked of old money, even in Sweden. Goosebumps broke out on her skin as she continued towards the neighbourhood of Sticklinge – the light at the end of a green tunnel.

The school was coming up on her left, on the crest of a hill by the edge of the forest. It was straight out of a Montessori brochure (printed on recycled paper, of course) – a series of small red buildings grouped around a central courtyard, plus a football field, swings and a slide snaking down the natural contours of a rock face.

Anna parked near the bus stop and zipped up her down jacket. Then she set about climbing the twenty or so steep steps that spiralled their way around a cemented-in boulder up to the school playground. Through the windows of the classroom, she saw the students in 5A sitting at their desks. Lukas, their teacher, was sitting at his, too, one leg crossed over the other, gesturing with his hands to get his point across.

Anna entered the building through the cloakroom, where trainers, coats, backpacks and rain boots were strewn all over the floor as if they had been torn out of the lockers and off the coat hooks by a tornado.

Keeping her shoes on she stormed into the classroom.

Startled, Lukas shook his head and gave her a bemused smile. Then he blinked a few times and slowly got up from his desk.

It was as if he had flipped a switch. Anna's anger turned to rage. She slammed the door and sat down with her back against it.

Then she pulled out the gun.

The children started screaming even before she pointed it at Lukas. Some of them curled up in fear. Others hid under their desks. Lukas froze, his mouth gaping but making no sound. There was a first time for everything.

'Now all of you, gather around Lukas. Sit down. On the floor.' Anna drew an oval in the air around all the children with the barrel of the gun. 'Now!'

Chairs scraped and socks slipped and slid across linoleum.

'I don't want to hear a peep out of you, do you understand? Not a sound. Not a word. And don't even think about crying.'

One of the twenty or so pre-teens in the class stood out to Anna – a blonde girl who was sitting cross-legged with her hands clasped between her thighs. Her lips were moving silently. The centre parting in her hair looked like it had been drawn with a ruler. The collar of her polo shirt was starch-stiff.

'You, with the pearl headband and the stripy-blue polo shirt,' Anna said. 'Go and close the blinds.'

All eyes turned to the girl, who looked down at her chest as if she needed to remind herself what she had put on that morning.

'Now!'

The girl stood and bit her lips, which were as pale as her skin. Keeping her eyes glued to the floor, she made her way to the nearest windows, behind where her classmates were sitting. The first blind put up a fight, one side of it fanning downwards with a screech that made some of the children scream.

'Sssh! Not a sound, I said.'

The girl tried again. This time she managed to get the slats horizontal and lower the blind to the window sill with a thunk. The girl did the same with the next two windows, then went across to the other side of the room, her fingers trying to pull imaginary sleeves over her wrists.

After closing the blinds on the three windows overlooking the playground, she hurried back towards her place on the floor.

'Come here.'

The girl stopped and looked at Anna, terrified.

Lukas opened his mouth and hesitated for a second before he spoke. 'Anna, please, don't—'

'Shut up. Shut up! I don't want to hear another word out of you. Is that clear? Is that clear?!'

'Her name is Louise Dahl, Anna. Don't...'

Anna strode across the classroom.

Lukas dropped to his knees and put his hands in the air.

She pressed the gun to the crown of his head.

'I don't give a shit what her name is!'

'Alright, Anna. I'm sorry—'

'I said, shut up!'

She drew herself tall and reached into the pocket of her parka for her phone, then unlocked the screen with a quick swipe of her thumb.

'Come here,' she barked again at Louise, who was still standing in front of her classmates, not daring to move.

Her skinny shoulders shaking, the girl took a few steps forwards.

Keeping the barrel of the gun pressed to Lukas's head, Anna leaned down and pinched the girl's chin between her thumb and forefinger.

Louise closed her eyes as tightly as she could.

'Look at me,' Anna said.

Louise opened her eyes again. They were streaming with tears.

'You're going to film us, alright? And don't even think about using that phone to make a call, do you hear me?'

Louise nodded frantically and clenched her jaw in an attempt to stop crying.

'Be careful, it's filming already,' Anna said, handing the device to the girl. 'Go and stand over there, in front of the window.'

Slowly, Louise stepped backwards, holding the phone with both hands like it was something precious. Then she raised it in front of her face.

Anna moved her hand so the gun was pointing at the back of Lukas's head. Then she started to speak:

'My name is Anna Hellström. On 28 May, my son Gustav hanged himself.'

She bit the inside of her lip to stop herself from shouting.

'But it was you – all of you – who drove him to suicide. All your accusations. All the harassment. You all have my son's blood on your hands.'

She swallowed the tears that caught in her throat.

'No one. No one tried to find out what really happened. You all sentenced him to death. You all sentenced my son to death. And you, Lukas, more than anyone,' she said, never taking her eyes away from the unblinking lens of the phone camera. 'You really had it in for my son. You took everything away from him. And now I'm left with nothing.'

Anna moved the gun away from Lukas's head. For a few seconds, her arm hung by her side. She blinked. Then she put the barrel of the gun in her mouth and fired.

2
Maïa Rehn

31 October 2023

I had to create some rituals.

Keep myself to a strict, almost military, routine. Tame my thoughts by organising my days like a production line. One thing after another. An email. A meeting. Lunch. An arrest. A court hearing. Dinner.

Writing, too. Actually no, journalling isn't the same as writing. Scribbling about where your life is at doesn't make you a writer. Writing means daring to dream and flirting with fancy. Letting go a little. Seeking revenge.

A routine forces you to accept that grief isn't something you can rush. You can't just skip a stage. *Seriously? I can't? No, not even you can, Maïa.* Five, that's how many there are, apparently. According to the specialists – and all the crappy websites I've combed in search of advice. Personally, I've counted seven. Resignation and rebuilding seem to be missing from the usual list.

For a long time I was stuck at stage two: anger. That anger was nothing like my usual outbursts. I'd always been such a hothead. But then, suddenly, I wasn't. This new anger was like gangrene. No, that's not right. It was like cancer. I was rotting from the inside out. So, I had to suck it up and spill my guts to a therapist, because – spoiler alert – friends aren't actually that great at listening. And because writing, working out and wallowing in denial are only sticking plasters that end up peeling off and exposing the wound. The gaping, festering wound that's never been treated.

Eventually, it was talking to a psychologist friend of mine that helped me see how getting away didn't mean running away. And it was something I had to do.

That's how I've found myself here. In the far North. In Sweden. The country where the tips of my fingers freeze in winter. The country where Krisprolls come from, as my friends used to tease when I first got together with Ebbe (whose name is pronounced 'eh beh,' not 'ebby,' by the way). This corner of Scandinavia where my fabulous husband was born; a statistician who could never be enough of a talker for my liking, but who's always known how to listen, which isn't so bad, I suppose – you can probably imagine which of us, the Swede or the French, is more of a thinker. Our Sweden, the place I fell in love with the very first time Ebbe brought me here, two months after we met and a few days before a New Year. I saw a swan gliding between sheets of ice on the frozen Sticklinge sea and thought, one day, I would plant my own roots not far from this beach.

Twenty-five years later, that thought has gone from prophecy to reality and our life in Paris is now a thing of the past. For just shy of a month now, I've woken up in the Falu-red-painted house Ebbe grew up in. Every morning begins with a steaming mug in the cold and the dark, and with long breaths of autumn drawn in the sloping garden beside the bay at Rödstuguviken, the sea lapping at my feet. The first intake of air, with its whiff of coffee and damp earth, lasts mere seconds. It's the only breath of the day free from any thoughts. Because as soon as I exhale, the pain and the pictures flood back into my mind.

Christian, that psychologist friend, has taught me to consider every thought without judgement. To accept it as an uninvited guest and let it sit there painfully and awkwardly. He's taught me to accept my scattered mind, my moments of absence, the times I wallow in memories. 'Grief is a unique, personal process for everyone.' That's what I read on some funeral home website. It's true.

It's not even five o'clock in the afternoon when this place

plunges into darkness. It sneaks up on me every time. I've spent most of today sanding the kitchen worktop. It's funny, you know. For the past twenty-five years I've been poking fun at the Swedes for doing it all themselves, IKEA-style, and only now, by calling this place home, have I realised that working with one's hands is the best way to busy the mind. I suppose it's not the only way – working out is another – but I can't spend my life lifting weights. Basically, this house needs some love, and that's all I have to give.

I've taken a quick shower and written a list of all the projects I want to do around the house, putting off getting dressed and doing my makeup. I knew in a heartbeat what I was going to wear tonight, though. The little black dress. Always my go-to, never a hassle. I hate getting all sweaty and dishevelled trying on dusty old outfits from the back of my wardrobe, only to be reminded why I haven't worn them in a while. Once I've put it on, I reach for some old-school pearl earrings and pick out an evening bag. Now I'm ready – and unrecognisable.

'You know, I had no desire whatsoever to get dressed up to the nines, but it does feel good.'

Ebbe doesn't say a word, obviously. My monologues are essential to the stringing out of our dying relationship. But as much as I need them, they do weigh on me. I don't turn around. I'm content with the picture of him, lying in bed, computer in his lap, glasses on the end of his nose. His combed-back fair hair the only part of his appearance he gives any thought to.

I smile, and yet I feel a lump of sadness rising in my throat. I'm about to ask him if he's sure he doesn't want to join me, but I bite my tongue.

Making my way downstairs to the hallway, I realise I'd better put trainers on and carry my stilettos, in case I have to walk half a mile when I get there. The Swedes are always full of surprises. Their idea of comfort is not the same as mine. Twenty years ago, the thought of wading through mud in an evening gown to get to a party would have horrified me. But not anymore. Experience and plenty of stories to tell have taught me otherwise. Better safe than sorry, I figure, slipping my heels into a tote bag. Thank goodness my dress isn't long enough to drag on the ground.

Headlights sweep across the vestibule and my phone beeps. It's Christian. My carriage awaits.

I put on my coat and gloves, but snub the woolly hat that would ruffle my hair beyond repair. Then I grab both bags and step out into the night, my heart hammering in my mouth, ready as I'll ever be to face the world for the first time in eleven months.

3
Maïa

Ellery Beach House is a place I know by name only. Christian's told me he treats himself to a writer's retreat there every time he starts working on a new book. An all-inclusive stay at a luxury spa hotel with a sea view. Maybe I should become a writer too.

The hotel is in Elfvik, at the eastern tip of Lidingö, and opened during the pandemic. I've never set foot there myself. In the past, we would holiday in Sweden in the summer and, when Ebbe's parents were still alive, every other Christmas. I remember being horrified by how many layers of clothes I had to wrap Alice in before she went outside. But I was the only one complaining. The Swedes have an eternally optimistic saying that my mother-in-law never let me forget: 'There's no such thing as bad weather, only the wrong clothes.' That was how I ended up with an outfit and gloves for every kind of shitty weather.

During our Swedish escapades, we lived the opposite of our life in Paris. Gone were the exhausted parents who spent more time working than sleeping, couldn't survive without a nanny and nourished their family with takeaway dinners and supermarket ready meals. In Sweden, we could take the time to do everything. To cook, explore nature and love one another.

'So, you're going to lug those muddy shoes around with you all night?' Christian teases me as we walk down the paved path to the hotel. 'How very un-Parisienne of you. Just think how disappointed our hosts will be. You do know that French women have a duty to be chic, don't you, Maïa?'

'And scoff croissants without gaining weight – I know.'

'It's more polite to say "savour" not "scoff." Everyone has a secret crush on French women. Even Swedish women.'

With a hot flush that has more to do with apprehension than my age, I leave my shoe bag and my shame at the door and follow Christian through the lobby.

To our right, the space opens into a restaurant with a view over the gardens that flow down to the pebbled shoreline, the whole ensemble accented by the subtlest of spotlights. The tables are pale wood. The chairs and benches are upholstered in a vintage shade of pink velvet. The music is jazzy. And my sole desire is to return to Ellery Beach House without a man on my arm. It's no wonder I'm hot and sweaty. The room is packed. I must have been crazy to say yes.

Christian is accosted by a woman in a dress with sleeves so puffy they're all but tickling her ears.

I leave them to it and find my way to the far side of the room, drawn by the sight of an illuminated gazebo in the gardens. This folly of sorts, perched on a rock, lends the place an air of romance. I find myself picturing a wedding taking place inside, an exchanging of vows, a promise of eternity.

I shake my head to keep the feelings rising in me at bay, and observe the other guests gravitating politely towards the champagne. Seeing them all with their apple-green and ruby-red velvet cocktail dresses, the creative knots in their hair, their suits with patterns way bolder than Christian's subtle beige and chestnut check, I can't help but feel somewhat naked in my little black dress.

There he is now, carrying two champagne flutes.

'Sorry, it's a bit like a Disneyland parade here tonight. You're rubbing shoulders with all of Sweden's literary elite, I tell you. Not bad for your first time out on the town, eh?'

'The only authors I'd recognise are Annie Ernaux and Stephen King, so I'm afraid we're doomed.'

A hostess offers us canapés on a silver platter. Christian gives her a smile and reaches for a fancy meatball with what looks like a strip of beetroot on top.

'Ooh, I could scoff ... I mean *savour* a few of these,' I say, before plucking a tiny salmon and dill creation from the tray.

A tinkling of crystal hushes the conversations.

A woman whose face seems frozen in time is standing on a low podium in front of the bay window, glass of bubbles in hand, smiling at the crowd. Her gaze sweeps across the room, taking in all the faces.

'*Hej, välkomna.* Out of respect to our overseas authors here this evening, I'll continue in English. Good evening, everyone, and welcome. My name is Leonor Andersson, and it's a great pleasure for me to manage Akerman Editions. Sophia Akerman,' she says, motioning to someone in the audience, 'has asked me to speak to you all this evening, on behalf of the company.'

All eyes flit to a woman with a time-weathered face, sitting tall, graceful and alone at the back of the room. She raises a hand to thank the spokesperson, who nods and carries on.

'It's heartwarming to see so many of you here. Thank you for joining us to celebrate the bicentennial of our fabulous publishing house. Two hundred years of making history, publishing bestsellers, defending our independence ... and a few flops thrown in for good measure.'

Peals of laughter reward her honesty.

'And that's what helped – and still helps – us grow, don't you think? Making mistakes and trying again.'

She pauses to embrace the audience with her gaze.

'We share our birthday with Halloween. Even though there's no shortage of dead bodies in our catalogue, the date of our founding is a pure coincidence, I assure you.'

This time, the laughter is less generous.

'The books we've published over the last two centuries all have one thing in common – they were written by passionate people with passionate stories to tell. These people are doctors,' she says, with a nod to a man in the front row. 'Teachers, lawyers,' she continues, making eye contact with others in the audience.

'Criminologists,' she adds, raising her glass to Christian, 'and novelists, who play and dream with the small but mighty written word. Thank you all for investing your talent for us, so we can share it with the world.'

Murmurings of approval ripple through the room.

'Now, let's raise our glasses to the good health of Akerman Editions. Here's to the next two hundred years! *Skål*!'

The crowd responds with a hearty cheer of *skål!* Then chins start wagging again around the room.

A woman with tomboy hair and lipstick as vivid as her earrings immediately strikes up a conversation with Christian in Swedish, every damned word of which escapes me. I've never learned the language. Not really. I've picked up enough of the basics to get by from day to day, but there's no way I could keep up with the storyline of a movie, make sense of the TV news or hold a conversation of any depth.

As I sidle away from them, my gaze is drawn to Sophia Akerman. I imagine she must be a descendant of the company's founder. She's still sitting in the same spot. Still alone, her champagne untouched, unless one of the hostesses has topped up her glass. There's something magnetic about her. I feel a sudden urge for the two of us to share our solitude.

'Good evening. I wondered if you might like something else to drink,' I lead with. 'Or perhaps I can offer you some company? I'm sorry, I don't speak Swedish, though.'

'I like the idea of champagne and what it symbolises,' she replies in perfect English. 'I just can't bring myself to let a drop past my lips, however. I don't have the palate to truly appreciate it ... And you are?'

'Maïa Rehn. I must admit, I'm not one of your authors.'

'Oh, I knew that already. I know all the authors in my publishing house, even the ones who hide behind those silly pen names. As if one should ever be ashamed of what one writes. Are you a ... budding writer yourself?' she asks, making little circles in the air as if to conjure the right words.

I smile. Nothing could be further from my reality right now.

'No, I'm a detective.'

'Oh yes, of course,' she replies, slapping a palm on the table. 'You're Christian Bergvall's friend from France, aren't you? He mentioned you'd be joining us. You live in the old ferryman's house in Lidingö, I believe? I seem to recall it was the Rehn family that bought the place. I live in Brevik, in the south of the island. Did you know that your in-laws' property has such a storied history?'

I nod, transfixed by the clarity of her voice, which sounds thirty years younger than her face suggests.

'Are you here on holiday?'

I hesitate, wondering how to label this indefinite leave I've taken. I suppose I could call it a de-maternity leave.

'I'm on sabbatical for a year.'

Now it's her turn to smile – or at least give me the hint of one. I'm not sure if she's smirking because she can tell that's not quite the truth, or if she's making fun of me. Either way, I immediately regret my honesty and start to seriously question these stupid good intentions of mine.

'Too many bad guys wearing you down, was it, Detective?'

I try to swallow the lump I can feel growing in my throat. I remember the promise I made to myself. To own my grief. To use the right words, the real words. To tell it like it is.

'My daughter died.'

'Mine too.' Her quick retort feels like a slap in the face.

We exchange a glance imbued with a whole new intimacy. As if we've bared our wounds to each other, comparing our pain.

'You know what I found out when I lost my daughter?' she suddenly blurts, breaking the silence. 'There's no word in Swedish, or in English for that matter, to describe a parent who's been widowed – or orphaned – from their child.'

'There's a word for it in Sanskrit: *vilomah*. It means "against the natural order".'

Sophia Akerman locks her gaze on mine. She's clinging desperately to me with her eyes. Like a lost soul in a foreign land finally finding someone who speaks the same language.

'Against the natural order,' she repeats, tightening her grip on her glass, not realising she isn't quite holding it straight.

A few drops of champagne spill onto the table.

She nods a few times without releasing me from her gaze.

'Thank you, Detective, for giving a name to my pain. Thank you so much.'

4
Aleksander Storm

Two quick sips are all it takes for me to down my espresso.

Fanny is already waiting by the door for me, raring to go. It's only two minutes past four in the morning, but I know there's no point trying to get back to sleep.

I don't sleep as soundly as my wife does. I don't snore like she does, either. The slightest sound bothers me. In the early hours, I was woken by a group of drunken youths – well, I assume they were youths – laughing and singing in our street. The racket they made, so unusual for a mid-week dawn in our sleepy neighbourhood of Sticklinge, cut my night short by a good two hours.

I give Fanny's head a rub. She's wide awake and wagging her tail impatiently. Then I pull on my hat, gloves and head torch and venture out into the ice-cold air.

Snow's coming, I think to myself. I hope I'm right. It brings the light that autumn steals from us. I hate this in-between slice of the season. November, when the days are grey and darkness descends in the middle of the afternoon. If it weren't for our colourful wooden houses, we'd be wading through a world of brown when the trees drop their leaves.

Jogging down from the porch, I give the neighbours' garden a sideways glance. It's filled with skeletons and cobweb-covered pumpkins. Ah, how could I have forgotten? Last night was Halloween, which explains the drunken revellers making their way home.

I pause for a moment in the street and hop from one foot to the other, wondering which way to go. Since I have the time, I decide to head down to the beach and hug the shoreline. The moon is hiding behind a curtain of cloud. I won't see the sea, but I will hear it.

I've been running for the last forty years. I started with my father when I was eleven years old. What seemed like a chore in the beginning became an addiction. Neither of my two daughters has been bitten by the bug. Nor my wife. She's too smitten with her bike. Birgitta is one of those die-hard Swedes who rides in all weathers. She even puts studded tyres on her bike in the autumn so she can ride on the ice and snow.

And so the only other runner in the family is Fanny. She was supposed to be my eldest daughter's dog, but the shine wore off caring for a puppy after three days of picking up poop. That was four years ago. Our snarky pre-teen named her golden shepherd Fanny after the character in the film *Fanny and Alexander*, so it was only fitting, she insisted, for me to look after her from now on and take her along on my morning runs. How could I say no to a kid who's a Bergman fan?

Suddenly, Fanny stops and barks. She's staring at something in the bushes downhill from us. Immediately I stop and sweep the beam of my head torch around us.

Last winter, a wolf ventured onto the island. Someone spotted it crossing the frozen sea. Lots of islanders and holidaymakers took videos of the wolf as the year went on, but no one has seen it for months.

Fanny barks again. I'm breathing too heavily to hear any ambient sounds. The head torch illuminates the forest ahead, projecting pools of yellow wherever I look. For a split second, I see something, but it's just a fleeting glimpse because I've turned my head too quickly. I repeat the movement, more slowly this time. And freeze. There it is. A shock of fur, and grey eyes staring at me from between two trees. Then before I know it, it's disappeared. I try to track the silhouette, following the sounds of snapping twigs and rustling bushes, but to no avail. Was it a fox? A wolf? I'll never know.

Fanny takes off again, and I run after her. The first breath of air after the brief pause stings in my lungs. I've just set foot on the Sticklinge beach when my phone rings, scaring away in a chorus of quacking a family of ducks who were gliding towards the shore.

I reach into my pocket and see the call is from Dominic, one of the boys on the football team I coach.

I stop running and answer the phone. Sounds of heavy breathing and childlike crying fill my ear.

'Dominic? Are you there?'

'Holy shit. Holy shit, Coach. Shit, shit, shit.'

'Dominic, what's wrong?'

I hear something rustling, as if an object or a piece of clothing is covering the phone's microphone, then I hear a few sniffs and short, sharp breaths.

'Holy shit, Coach. There's a ... a ... girl. She's dead! Fuck. Her head ... there's blood everywhere!'

'Where are you?'

'Abborrparken. In the woods. Behind the school.'

I change direction and start running around the edge of the marina, Fanny at my heels, phone glued to my ear with the sound of crying still in the background.

'Who else is there with you?'

'Annette ... my girlfriend. We were ... Holy shit.'

'Are you both alright? You're not hurt in any way?'

'No, no, we're OK, Coach. Just ... Fuck.'

'Listen: don't touch anything, alright? Wait for me in front of the school. I'll be there in five minutes.'

5
Aleks

When I get to Abboren primary school, my lungs and throat are burning from the effort and I'm sweating in spite of the cold.

I can see Dominic and Annette sitting on the pavement, in the yellow pool of a street lamp. They spring to their feet and hurry towards me. I switch off my head torch, not wanting to dazzle them.

Dominic is holding a ghost mask, like the one from the *Scream* film. His girlfriend's face is painted white, with two black circles around her eyes and a black cross on her right cheek. The hem of a torn white dress or skirt and a pair of fishnet stockings are sticking out from the bottom of her puffer jacket.

Fanny dashes towards Dominic.

'Fanny, heel!'

My dog turns around straight away and comes back to nuzzle my leg.

'I'm going to take a look, alright? You two, wait here. Are you going to be OK?'

They nod.

'Where is she, exactly?'

'Follow the path behind the school,' Dominic explains, pointing somewhere in the distance, past the fence. 'And when you get to the gazebo, where the barbecue is, go left. You'll see the light.'

'The light?'

'Yes. From her Saint Lucia crown.'

'OK. Fanny, stay.'

I point to the pavement in front of the school gate. She whimpers in resignation and goes to sit down.

Starting up the rocky path, I skirt around the side of the school, taking care to walk in a straight line so I can retrace my steps on the way back. I'm using the light on my phone as well as my head torch to see where I'm going. I usually love striding into the night on my runs, but now, as the darkness swallows my every step, I feel uneasy.

I dread to think what I'm going to find. Trying to shake the thought that it could be one of my daughters, I tell myself that they're safe at home, tucked up in bed. That all this is just a cruel prank, because it's the perfect night for kids to toy with death and give their friends a fright.

Before long, I spot the glow through the trees ahead. I switch off the light on my phone and keep my head torch on. The beam is high and bright enough to light my way without overpowering what looks like flickering candle flames.

Another ten metres or so down the path, the beam reveals a white dress. And a body lying face up on the ground, between a rock and a tree stump. Moving closer, I realise that what I thought was a dress is actually a tunic. A crown of greenery planted with five LED candles sits askew on the head, obscuring half of the face and highlighting a bashed-in section of skull.

Twigs crack beneath my feet as I circle the body to the left. I'm acutely aware of the silence of a forest consumed by night. Not a hoot, not a chirp, not a rustle of leaves trampled by deer or fox. Nothing but the sound of my own shallow breath as I contemplate this poor girl, whose one uncovered eye stares lifelessly into the darkness, flickering in the glow of these tawdry plastic candles.

It suddenly strikes me that this is the first time I've been alone, face to face, with a dead body. Suddenly, I feel like I can't breathe.

I take a few steps back, place my hands on my thighs and bend forwards, trying to find the space I need. Eventually, the breath comes with the sensation of a bubble bursting between my lungs and my heart.

Drawing myself upright, I decide to take off my head torch and use it with my hand. A spatter of blood on the rock next to the dead body is the first thing the beam sweeps over.

The second is the rest of the victim's face.

And I realise it isn't a girl lying there in a Saint Lucia costume with her head caved in.

It's a boy.

6
Aleks

Retracing my steps along the path I took to get to the crime scene, I take out my phone and call the cavalry.

I can hear Fanny barking as I come down the slope towards the school.

Dominic hurries towards me. Fanny stays, pawing at the ground until I signal for her to come too. She soon catches up with him. Annette, whose name has just come back to me, isn't far behind, eyes still glued to her phone. She quickens her step and soon puts the device away in the pocket of her puffer jacket.

'So?' Dominic asks.

I simply nod, not wanting to get into any of the gruesome details.

'Holy shit,' he says, bringing a hand to his face as if to scratch an itch, before realising his fingers are gloved.

'What's that?' I ask, pointing to some reddish streaks on Annette's dress.

She follows my finger with her gaze, not quite sure what I mean, then shakes her head. 'It's ... it's nothing. It's part of my costume, that's all. Fake blood. We didn't go anywhere near her.'

'Hell no. We didn't dare.' Dominic smooths a hand across his forehead as Annette clasps hers around his waist and clings to him.

'And you didn't cross paths with anyone out there, or here, by the school?'

They both shake their heads.

'You didn't see any shadows or hear any voices? What about the sound of a car or boat engine? You didn't hear any footsteps?'

'No, Coach, nothing at all.'

'Right. I'll need you to stay here with me until the police get here. Have you phoned your parents?'

They look at each other sheepishly, then stare at the ground.

I should have known. For a couple of teens, there's nothing normal about being out at four in the morning, even if it is Halloween.

'Sneaked out of the house, did you? I suppose you were at a party?'

Annette turns to Dominic, who breathes a shaky sigh and nods.

'My dad's in Bergen for work. He gets home tomorrow morning. And the plan was for Annette to...' He scratches his nose. 'She was going to sleep over. Her parents think she's staying at her friend Camilla's house tonight.'

'And I suppose your dad doesn't know, either – that Annette was going to spend the night at yours?'

He shakes his head.

'Where was the party?'

Dominic's mouth twitches with a nervous tic.

'Over in Stockholm ... Well, no, Djursholm, actually,' Annette replies, drying her eyes with a trembling hand.

'We took my dad's boat,' Dominic adds.

'Is that why you phoned me instead of calling 112?'

Dominic sniffs. 'No ... I honestly thought of you first, Coach. I ... we were worried that the police would think it had something to do with us ... and arrest us. But we didn't do anything. I swear, Coach, we had nothing to do with this.'

He wipes his eyes before the tears have time to flow.

'We left my dad's boat at the dock in Rödstuguviken at about four, and we were taking a shortcut through the woods when we came across that ... light. We wondered what it was. We thought it might be some kind of Halloween decoration, so we went to have a look. It never even crossed our minds that we might stumble across a real ... Holy shit...'

He pauses and bites his lip.

'I knew that if I called you, Coach, you'd believe me. And anyway, you *are* the police, so it's almost like I phoned 112, isn't it?'

7
Aleks

The headteacher gets out of her mustard-coloured Volvo in a hurry and tugs a woolly hat over her ears.

Agneta has been in charge of the school since before my daughters came here. Every day for seven months, my youngest would refuse to let go of my leg and scream bloody murder when her despicable dad insisted on abandoning her at drop-off time. Agneta would crouch down and whisper gently in her ear to reassure her. Not once did she lose patience or raise her voice.

'*Hej*, Agneta! Thanks for coming so quickly.'

She looks surprised to see the area around the bottom of the hill cordoned off. The crime scene is up the hill, in the woods, but marking the perimeter down here will keep the gawkers away. Of course, the blue-and-white tape won't exactly reassure the parents and their kids, but you can't have it all.

'God almighty, Aleksander, what's going on? On the phone, you said there's been a death, but ... was it accidental, or...' Hands out in front of her like two sides of a scale, she looks like she's weighing up the possibilities.

'We don't know yet, Agneta.'

Her mouth forms a silent 'o'. 'So who's investigating, then?' she asks.

'What do you mean?'

'Well, there's no police station in Lidingö anymore, is there?'

'That's right; we're attached to Stockholm now.'

'Ah, OK. Do you think I should close the school?' Her voice is quivering with panic. 'What I mean is, are the children in danger?'

I shake my head. 'No, not at all, Agneta, I assure you.'

'Dear Lord, thank you.' She presses her hands together in prayer then places them against her heart and lifts her gaze to the sky.

'Nothing will happen to the children, Agneta, I promise.' I mean what I say.

She bobs her chin a few times in approval.

What I don't say is that we've already erected two tents up the hill. The forecast is calling for the first snow of the season this morning, so the NFC – the forensics team – put up the first one in record time to preserve the scene. The second tent, where I'm about to go, is up by the gazebo, on the only level ground in the vicinity of the body. That one is for us to store equipment and change into and out of our coveralls. None of the children, parents or teachers need to see a bunch of crime-scene technicians clad in white suits coming and going. What an ominous and disturbing sight that would be for them.

My phone vibrates in my hand. A quick glance at the screen tells me I have an incoming call from Siv Nord, who's recently been promoted to chief of section. My model of resilience, as my wife would say. I'll call her back later.

'One thing you could do, Agneta, is send a message to all parents to let them know there's a police presence in the woods at Abborrparken. Explain that it's related to an incident that has nothing to do with the school. I'd also appreciate it if you would ask them to bring their kids to school on foot or by bike, if possible, to lessen the traffic today.'

We both know they won't get the message until it's too late. In the morning rush, wrapping their tired, cranky, wriggling little ones in three layers of weather protection, none of them will have a second to check their phones. But at least the information will have been sent, and no one will be able to say that this remarkable woman didn't do her job.

'Alright, yes ... of course, Aleksander.' Her gaze flits left and right like a moth stirred by light.

I walk with Agneta to the school gate, promising to keep her abreast of the situation. Then I carry on past the playground towards the crime scene, where Alvid, the head of the forensics team, is waiting for me.

My phone vibrates again.

'*Hej*, Siv...'

'What the hell, Storm? Do you have two arseholes for eyes? Do you have any idea what a shit storm you've caused?!'

'Siv, what are you talking about?'

Her voice is really hitting the high notes, but I keep my tone calm and measured. This throws her off a bit, I think, as she responds with a second or two of silence. I've never heard Siv raise her voice, other than to call Arnold, her old dog, who's getting hard of hearing, or to make herself heard while she's preparing another liquid breakfast with her handheld blender. For herself, not the dog.

'Are you serious? What am I *talking about*?'

I've just arrived at the tent where I'll be donning my crime-scene suit.

'Siv, please stop shouting at me. What's got into you?'

'What's got into me, Storm, is that the editor-in-chief of TV4 just phoned me to ask if I could confirm that the dead body of a minor has been found near a primary school at the north end of Lidingö.'

'Oh, shit.'

'You can say that again. You're the one who left it steaming, but I'm the one who has to scoop it up! That witness of yours, Annette Lykke, had the bright idea to "Snapchat" – that's her expression, not mine – a friend, who then posted something on bloody TikTok. You can imagine the rumours, I'm sure. Apparently, there's now a bloodthirsty Halloween killer on the loose in Lidingö, hashtag bloodandgore. For fuck's sake, Aleks, you do know what teenagers are like, don't you? How the hell could you screw things up this badly?'

If I believed in being hard on myself, I'd curl up into a ball and die right now. I'm the father of two teenage girls. Why the hell didn't I remind myself that young people don't talk to each other, they message each other? News doesn't spread by word of mouth anymore. It goes from phone to phone. I didn't react quickly enough, or strictly enough. I should have got Dominic and Annette to give me their phones.

'I did tell them not to talk to anyone besides their parents, and not to put anything on their socials. But you're right, it's my fault.'

'Bloody Generation Z. Look what good conquering space has done us. We launch satellites into orbit so these kids can watch stupid things that make them even stupider.' Siv heaves a crackling sigh. 'I hate this job,' she says, this time without raising her voice. 'I'm going to have to feed some info to the press. So you'd better get a move on. Because before the morning is out, Sticklinge is going to be like the red carpet at Cannes.'

Suddenly, I hear barking on the other end of the line. Arnold sounds happy about something.

'No, no, no. Arnold, come here. Good boy ... Aleks, are you still there?'

'Yes.'

I can see Alvid waiting for me by the entrance to the tent. I hold up two fingers to let him know I won't be long.

'Another thing ... As you know, safety is at the top of the agenda right now, so if the mayor decides to throw us under the bus – make scapegoats of us by saying we're being too slow and ineffective, or whatever – in a bid to deflect any media criticism coming her way about the surge in violent crime, then it would be ... well, let's say it would be counterproductive.'

She pauses. I know where this is going.

'Do you think...' she continues, her tone as smooth as silk now. 'Do you think you could have a word with your wife and let her know how wonderful it would be should the mayor grasp the idea that working with us would be better than trying to trip us up?'

My wife is in charge of communications at Lidingö Town Hall. She works closely with Esther Lind, our mayor, who has her sights set on running for parliament in the next election. But I'm not supposed to know that.

'I'm sure the mayor will grasp that idea easily enough on her own, Siv.'

'I think the only thing she cares about is covering her own behind, like the rest of us. I'm counting on you to pass the message on, Aleks.'

'Understood, Siv.'

She hangs up.

I close my eyes for a moment, thinking that it's not even seven in the morning yet, that a kid is dead, that I reek of sweat and that I still haven't had my second coffee.

I follow Alvid into the tent. He hands me a plastic pouch.

'Any updates?' he asks me, pulling the hood of his coveralls over his bald head.

'The chief of section wants me to make full use of my personal connections,' I reply, zipping up my own protective suit.

Alvid smiles and we step out of the tent.

We follow the markings on the ground to approach the crime scene, which is just metres away. It strikes me now how much longer the distance seemed earlier this morning, in the darkness.

Suddenly, my thoughts turn to the parents of this boy, whose identity we don't yet know. They must be so worried about him. Little do they know that the worst has happened.

Alvid pokes his head into the crime-scene tent and says a few words, which are promptly drowned out by a phone ringing. We slip on our overshoes, pull down our face masks and enter.

The uneasy feeling I had earlier this morning has gone away. The crime scene is more like the kind of thing I'm used to seeing – a hive of muted activity around a floodlit corpse. The oppressive silence of the middle of the night has been replaced by a quiet of much less depth. Coveralls swish, brushes sweep and tools clink. These layers of sound are like soothing white noise to me. They mean that I'm not staring at death alone.

A triangle of floodlights cast the victim in a raw, dehumanising light. The forensic technicians have removed the crown. Now I can see the boy's broad forehead, the arch of his eyebrows, his blue eyes, his hairless chin. I don't know if it's the pure-white tunic or his cherub-like features, but something about him makes me think of a choirboy.

Good God, what happened to this kid?

I move closer to his body and squat beside his head. The injury is on the right side, towards the back of the skull. A crater filthy with matted hair and dried blood.

'Did you find any impact marks or blood on the crown?' I ask, looking up at Alvid.

'No, not a trace,' he replies, his voice muffled by the face mask.

I shift position and turn my attention to the collar of the tunic and the skin on the neck below the wound. Blood is conspicuous by its absence.

'As you can see, there's nothing on the tunic, either,' Alvid adds. 'I have to admit, it's an unconventional choice of costume. Plus, anyone dressing up as Saint Lucia on Halloween would probably tear the fabric to shreds and splash fake blood all over it, wouldn't they?'

'You're probably right. But even if the murderer dressed the victim in the tunic after killing him, I would expect there to be some traces of blood on the collar. But there's nothing at all. And you haven't moved the body?'

'Not by a millimetre.'

'May I?'

'Wait a sec. Bertil?'

'I'll be right there,' one of the technicians replies.

Alvid crouches beside me.

Bertil is ready and waiting with a large sheet of white fabric to collect any dirt, gravel, twigs and leaf debris that might have stuck to the victim's neck and tunic.

'Ready?' Alvid asks me.

I put one hand on the boy's shoulder and the other on his forearm. Even through my gloves, the feel of the icy skin gives me goosebumps. I still hate this part of the job, even after twenty years.

'Here we go,' Alvid says.

Together, we gently lift the torso off the ground.

'Well, here's your answer, Storm,' the head of the crime-scene team confirms, as Bertil places the sheet on the ground under the victim's back.

The tunic has been split apart like a hospital gown. The back is open all the way from the collar to the hem.

'Looks like the perp thought of everything,' Alvid says.

8
Maïa

The conservatory door sticks for a second, but with a push it gives way. We ... no, *I* really must get around to sanding it one of these days, so it won't be such hard work every time I go out to the garden this way. It's almost like this door has a voice. For twenty years I've heard it creak and squeak, as if to betray anyone who tries to sneak out undetected.

I retrieve the cup I left on the coffee table and step outside. After a moment's hesitation, I leave Ebbe's where it is, the one I filled by force of habit. The things you do automatically when you live together and wake up together every day. Since I returned here, I've resolved not to set an alarm. I don't have to get up and go to work, so I might as well let my body decide when it wants to get up. But putting this into practice is another thing entirely. Since trying to make this house my own, I've hardly been sleeping at all. Talk about my body giving my newfound freedom the middle finger. I typically manage to grab a few hours of sleep between midnight and three or four in the morning, then my eyes are open again.

I've put my parka on over my pyjamas to keep the chill in the air at bay. I can barely feel any warmth from my coffee cup through my alpine gloves. I wonder what I'll have to wear when the temperature drops another fifteen degrees. Probably the heated fishing gloves Ebbe gave me for Christmas a few years ago. We got a good laugh out of those.

The door doesn't make a sound. Still, I know he's here.

'Call me crazy, but I think my Iron Man gloves will finally come in handy,' I say. That's what Alice called them, because they flash when the battery is full or about to run out.

I close my eyes and lose myself in his warm, familiar embrace, remembering everything that life here is not.

My coffee's already getting cold. I take a long swig and force that healing breath, which I've somehow forgotten to do while struggling with the stubborn door and my skittish soul-searching. I appear to be forever at the mercy of the powerful current of my thoughts, which seem to go back and forth between my daughter toddling around this very garden on her little legs more than twenty years ago, and her empty rooms – the one in Paris and the one here, too. I have thought about storing boxes in the one here, but I've not mustered the courage. I can't bring myself to set foot in there anymore. Her room has all the lightness and nudity of a pied-à-terre. A place where you live out of a suitcase, where everything that would seem so passé at home oozes 'chic' and 'vintage'. It pains me that her absence isn't more conspicuous.

'I'm sorry, but I need to be alone,' I blurt to Ebbe, as I feel the tears starting to rise again. 'Would you mind giving me some space?'

It takes him a while to leave. In the silence left by his departure, I wonder how I'm going to survive in this house. It's really more his than mine.

Suddenly, I see a stream of headlights on Braxenvägen, about three hundred metres up the hill towards Abborrparken – the forest that hugs the shore. I can't make out anything else. Dawn is still far away on the horizon. But even in the daytime, I've never seen so many cars on such a narrow street, where two vehicles can barely pass each other. A few seconds later, the lights disappear into the forest and darkness descends on the beach once more. The moonless sky is contemplating itself in the sea, I think.

When the tips of my fingers and toes go numb and it feels like ice is running through my veins, I head back inside.

I spend the morning sanding the door and cursing Ebbe's absence and the cold, not to mention the door itself.

At noon, I switch on the TV to get my daily dose of Swedish

while I make a sandwich and brew myself another ration of coffee. I've made a habit of watching the news in the middle of the day, something I could never do in France. I keep TV4 on in the background, even though I only catch the occasional word here and there. But the images give me context and I get to practise my passive listening.

I'm only half watching the screen when I notice the words on the banner at the bottom: *Ett mord på Lidingö*. It takes me a minute to find my phone – under a tea towel beside the coffee machine – and tap the phrase into Google Translate to make sure I've understood.

No, I'm not mistaken. In fact, it's worse than I thought. It doesn't say 'Death in Lidingö'. It says 'Murder in Lidingö'.

The newsreaders in the studio hand over to a reporter, who's talking to the camera from the bridge connecting Stockholm to the island. Then the reporter is replaced by a video montage showing police vehicles parked on the fringe of the forest at Abborrparken, beside the primary school, and some uniformed officers standing guard in front of a security cordon.

Finally, the reporter comes back on screen, with a man who stands a good head taller by her side. The banner below them says *Kommissarie Aleksander Storm*. The reporter spends a minute or two interviewing him, then hands over to her colleagues in the studio. Next, the screen shows a young man – somewhere between fifteen and seventeen years old, I'd guess – being bundled into the back of a police van in handcuffs. This must be archive footage, judging by the grainy video and the style of people's clothes. Next, the report shows a shot of a building and a plaque on the wall bearing the name 'Akerman'. Standing next to it, with about a dozen microphones in front of her, is a younger, stony-faced Sophia Akerman, giving what looks like a press conference.

Then the report is over, and it's back to the studio.

I think about telling Ebbe what I've just seen, then the voice of reason reminds me of the desire to be alone I expressed this morning. I can hold out for a few more hours. Maybe I'm finally reaching the point where I can grieve without him. The thought of that should be freeing, but it makes me feel sick.

I pour myself some more coffee and pick up my phone.

I'm going to call Christian. I know he'll be able to tell me what's happening right here on my doorstep.

9
Aleks

I make a quick pit stop at home to shower, change and scarf down some breakfast. But I savour my sacrosanct coffee like the first sip of a cold beer in the height of summer. On my way back out, I find a Post-it note stuck to my car keys:

You've got this. Luv U.

B. x

My wife knows how to make me smile. This is the first one of my day – smile, that is – and I'm sure it will be the last, too. Because no matter how positive I try to be, a day that starts with a murder can only be shitty.

Erik Brink, age forty-one, the manager of an office-supply shop on the eastern tip of Lidingö, where he also lives, called the police this morning to report his son Daniel missing. Daniel, age seventeen, was last seen late yesterday afternoon, heading out to celebrate Halloween somewhere on the island with his friends. Daniel Brink is now lying on the autopsy table under the keen eye of Paola Holm, our medical examiner.

Now I'm standing in front of the door of their apartment at 25 Merkuriusvägen, one of many characterless three-storey buildings in the Käppala neighbourhood. I know that as soon as I introduce myself to Erik Brink, life as he knows it will be over. So I make the in-between moment – the tipping point – last a little longer to give this father just one more measly scrap of time. I've done this so often – walked a tightrope, stretching out hope like an elastic, before the knock on the door replaces life with death.

Take 29 December 2004, for example. That was when I had to tell a mother that both her sons – eighteen and twenty-one years old – had perished in the tsunami that ravaged the shores of Thailand. That mother, Maria, froze. It's not just an expression. She really was incapable of moving. She was like a robot. I had to help her husband sit her down on the sofa. Her eyes were open, but *she* wasn't there. Her body was an envelope of flesh and nothing else. Her soul, or her consciousness, whatever you want to call it, had checked out. Her brain couldn't handle the shock, so it short-circuited the rest of her body, leaving her in standby mode. So she could focus on the one thing that really mattered: survival.

I ring the doorbell.

Close my eyes.

And wait.

I'm following protocol to the letter. I learned that the hard way. One day, when I was a cocky new recruit, I broke the worst possible news to a father on the doorstep of his home. I meant well. I wanted to spare him both the agony of waiting and the frustrating formalities. He crumpled to the ground as if he'd been shot.

There's a sound of soft, swift footsteps before the click of the lock. A man with a short, greying beard opens the door. Part of the collar of his white shirt is sticking out from his sweater.

'Erik Brink?' I ask.

He responds with a subtle nod.

'Commissioner Aleksander Storm,' I announce, flashing my warrant card. 'May I come in?'

He steps to one side, waits for me to enter, then closes the door behind me.

He ushers me down a narrow hallway to a living room where a pale-yellow sofa sits facing a gigantic TV screen that takes up two-thirds of the wall.

Erik Brink sits down on the sofa. His eyes are pleading with me. Then as soon as I sit beside him, they abandon hope.

'I'm afraid I have some terrible news to tell you.'

His shoulders sink.

'Daniel was found dead this morning.'

He buries his face in one hand.

'I'm sorry, Erik.'

The silence that grips us both is more treacherous than quicksand. Time has taught me there's no sense feeding this silence with words. It'll only spew something worse later. You just have to let it run its course.

After a few minutes, Erik Brink raises his head with a sniffle. He blinks and wipes the snot from his nose.

'Would you like me to get you a glass of water?'

He shakes his head, then gets up and looks at the room around him.

'No, thank you,' he eventually replies. 'I'll go make some coffee.'

'Why don't you let me take care of that?'

'No, I ... I need to move.'

I follow him through to the kitchen.

He takes a few steps towards the kitchen cupboards, then staggers backwards and collapses into one of the two chairs at the table.

I switch on the Nespresso machine and open a few cupboards before I find the cups and the coffee pods. I've lost count of how many kitchens like this I've made coffee or poured whisky in.

'What happened to him...? Is it ... Was he taking drugs? Or ... something else?'

'We don't know the exact circumstances of his death yet,' I reply, pressing the button to pull a shot of espresso. 'But we should know more soon.'

There's something both reassuringly and disturbingly normal about the whirring of the machine. How can life just keep on playing its everyday soundtrack?

I sit down across from Erik. He reaches for the cup I hand him and starts twirling it around by the handle.

'I must have fallen asleep around ten o'clock,' he says, staring into the void. 'I was completely exhausted. I woke up at six-thirty and made breakfast like usual. At seven, I knocked on his bedroom door, because he was going to be late.'

He purses his lips. Grief furrows his chin.

'It never crossed my mind that something could have happened to him, you know? Not even for a second. I saw his empty bed right there...' he says, gesturing to the space between us, 'and I thought he must have left for school early. It didn't even occur to me that he hadn't come home last night. Can you imagine?'

'It's alright, Erik. I understand.'

'I thought he must be on his way there,' he carries on, his voice wavering. 'Or maybe he had an early class, or ... I don't know. I texted him, but he didn't message me back. So I tried calling him. I tried again and again for about half an hour. Then I phoned Thea, his girlfriend. She told me Daniel never showed up at the Halloween party and she hadn't seen him all evening.'

He closes his eyes and runs his thumb around the rim of the cup. Perhaps there are memories resurfacing. Or regrets.

'Can I ... When can I see my son?' he asks, opening his eyes again.

'Later this afternoon. Someone will call you.'

'Thank you. Sorry, I can't remember your name.'

'Storm. Aleksander Storm.'

'Right, yes. Of course.'

Silence descends on us once more.

'At some point soon, we'll send a team out to look at your son's things and pick up a few of his personal belongings, if you don't mind.'

He nods silently.

'I imagine he would have taken his phone with him?'

'Yes, always.'

'Do you track his location?'

'No, not since last year. He pays his own phone bill with the money he earns from coaching the little kids at the football club.' He shrugs. 'I didn't want to insist too much.'

'Daniel was coaching kids at IFK?'

'Yes, he had the six-year-old boys on Tuesdays and the eight-year-old girls on Thursdays.'

I've never crossed paths with Daniel Brink, but the local football club here in Lidingö has hundreds of members, so it's impossible to know everyone.

He takes a sip of coffee, licks his lips and grimaces.

'Is ... the body they're talking about on TV ... the one they found in Sticklinge ... is that Daniel?'

I nod.

'They said something about a murder back in 1999. What does that have to do with Daniel?'

'Journalists tend to make connections they shouldn't. Not at this stage of the investigation, at least. For now, we don't know anything about that. But as soon as we have anything to report, Erik, I'll call you, or I'll come and see you.'

10
Maïa

It's snowing on Kottlasjön – Kottla Lake.

It's been years since I last saw snowflakes falling in Lidingö. The few days we used to spend here at Christmas tended to be cold, but were rarely white. And now, sitting in the window at Vattenverket, the cafe in the old converted waterworks, I see Mother Nature knitting her winter coat. The flakes are coming down thick and fast, plunging like arrows into the inky water, which will be frozen solid a few weeks from now.

What I love about snow, besides the fact that it cloaks and lightens nature's nudity, is its immutability. The flakes always seem to fall consistently, following the same trajectory, whatever their size, whatever the wind strength, whatever the temperature and whatever obstacles they encounter.

I'm waiting for Christian, who's fashionably late.

Personally, I can't *not* be punctual. I always arrive early or – worst-case scenario – right on time. It's almost like I'm resisting something hereditary. In Paris, whenever I was planning how long it would take to get somewhere, I would always build in a subconscious buffer. I'm not hard to psychoanalyse. I'm an anxious person who needs to be in constant control. So what? At least I never keep anyone waiting.

I met Christian fifteen years ago at Europol, in The Hague; I was doing some training there with some colleagues in the Brigade Criminelle. Christian was speaking about the use of clinical criminology in preventing criminal relapses. When his talk was over, keen as he was to practise a language he speaks fluently, he joined us French for a drink in the bar. The two of us bonded over our mutual Swedish connection. He was born a Viking; I married one. When he was in Paris a few months later, he came over for dinner and that sealed the friendship – not just with me, but the rest of the family too. We soon made a habit of catching up whenever he was in the City of Light or we were in Lidingö.

When Alice died, 'Uncle Chris', who called my daughter his 'Rehn de coeur' – his Queen of Hearts, in a sophisticated play on words – was the only one who found the words that could help me accept my loss and show me the way forwards. For me, he's also the only person who appreciates the power of silence. I don't know how many times I've picked up the phone for him to listen to me and the memories I refused – and still refuse – to let go.

'*Madame la commissaire.*'

His voice startles me. Christian is standing in front of me holding a tray with two steaming cups and a plate of pastries. I can't help but smile. With the upturned collar of his fitted Burberry jacket and the faux-casual loop of his grey scarf, he is as far from the common image of a criminologist as he could be. Next to his elegance, I always feel like a sack of potatoes.

'Dr Bergvall,' I reply, nodding my head with discreet reverence.

He sets the tray down on the table. 'Let me guess, you were cursing me because I'm two minutes and twelve seconds late, am I right?'

'You absolutely are.'

I offer him a cheek, and he bends down and kisses first that one, then the other. Giving each other *la bise* is a Gallic thing. Vikings prefer a heartier embrace. I've grown used to their hugs, but sometimes, when I'm not thinking, my inner Frenchwoman comes out.

'Here I am with three saffron buns, a coffee and a matcha latte. I'd say that was worth waiting for, wouldn't you?'

My nose wrinkles. 'Tell me that green insult to the taste buds is for you. Matcha looks like tea made with seaweed. And milk, too? Honestly, I don't know how you can stomach the stuff. It's too much for my educated palate to handle.'

'Relax. The seaweed tea is mine.'

'Why three buns, though, may I ask? Are we expecting someone else?'

'No, not at all. But these are the best on the island and, trust me, one each is simply not enough. But two is just unreasonable.'

He doffs his jacket, undoes his scarf and sits down.

'Thanks,' I say, taking the cup he hands me. 'So, what's going on?'

'Have you not read anything at all?' he asks, greedily licking the sugar from his sticky fingers.

I put my cup on the table. 'No, I called you straight after I saw the news. You can't imagine how sick I am of typing everything into Google Translate. And I can't exactly ask Ebbe to keep translating for me, can I?'

'Ah, I understand.'

He gives me a long look. A look that says: *I won't ask how things are going at home. I'll leave it to you to decide whether you want to talk about it.*

I lower my gaze and take another sip of coffee.

'Right,' Christian says. 'I'll start with the bone of contention. In 1999, sixteen-year-old Jenny Dalenius was found dead, here in Lidingö. She had been raped. Her ex-boyfriend, Gustav Hellström – the young man you saw on the TV4 news report this lunchtime – went down for her murder on the strength of irrefutable DNA evidence. He spent more than twenty years in prison, insisting he was innocent. And a few days before he was due to be released, he hanged himself in his cell. Seven days later, his mother, Anna Hellström, also died by suicide – which she live-streamed on social media.'

'Oh, my god.' I gasp.

'Wait a second. Do you know Sophia Akerman?'

'Yes, the owner of the publishing house.'

'Whose acquaintance you made at that literary soirée. Well, Sophia is Anna Hellström's mother. And that makes her Gustav's grandmother.'

Leaning back in my chair, I recall Sophia's words that evening. About the death of her daughter.

'What's the connection to the murder this morning?' I ask. 'The crime scene?'

'Are you familiar at all with Saint Lucia?'

'Vaguely. It's a religious festival, isn't it? Something to do with choirs and a song?'

'Oh, it's much more than that. Saint Lucia's Day, the thirteenth of December, marks the beginning of the end-of-year celebrations in Sweden, and you know what a song and dance we make of Christmas here. All the schools, colleges and parishes put on a concert where they sing that song you mentioned, "Sankta Lucia". It's a beautiful song, by the way. Everyone knows it by heart. I'll take you to a concert this year, if you like. Curiously, the most famous Saint Lucia's Day concert of all is the one at St Paul's Cathedral in London.'

Christian pauses to take a sip of matcha.

'Anyway, for the concert, all the girls dress up as handmaidens, in a white tunic with a red sash and a crown of candles – although these days, they're all LEDs, thank heavens. I can't imagine how many accidents there must have been with real candles. And the boys, they dress up as *stjärngosse*, or "star boys", in cone-shaped hats. Or they dress up as gingerbread men carrying lanterns. It's a great honour for a girl to be chosen to represent Saint Lucia herself, who guides the procession when the choir comes into the church, singing. But to answer your question, finally, Jenny Dalenius was killed on Saint Lucia's Day – the thirteenth of December – 1999. And, like the victim this morning, she was found in the woods at Abborrparken, wearing a white tunic and a crown of candles.'

11
Aleks

'Aleks!'

I turn around and see Siv standing at the other end of the corridor.

'Do you have a second?'

'Absolutely.'

A moment later, I walk into her office and shut the door behind me.

Siv is sitting at her desk in stony silence, staring down at her steepled hands. Her fingers are shaking. I sit down across from her.

'Siv, are you alright?'

'Can I be brutally honest?'

'Yes, of course.' I lean forwards in my chair, worried all of a sudden.

'Listen, I ... What I'm about to share with you is a bit personal, but I think it's best to be transparent. I'm ridiculously perimenopausal and it's just unbearable. I feel like I'm on a battlefield, fighting my alter ego. The worst thing isn't the physical stuff – I mean that's unpleasant enough – but really, it's this...' She waves her hands around her head like a magician who's about to make something appear out of nowhere. '...This constant fogginess. That, plus the sluggishness, the sadness and ... good grief, Aleks, the ... the anger,' she says, gritting her teeth. 'I've never felt anything like this before. Not even when I was pregnant. It's like I'm turning into a dragon. There's something so volatile about it. I'm not in control at all. When it comes over me, it feels like I'm about to explode, you know? It can happen at any time.

There's no rhyme or reason. One minute I'm fine, and the next I'm screaming my head off because someone left a Mars bar wrapper on the kitchen counter. I swear, it's exhausting just thinking about it. I mean, for fuck's sake, I've been undercover to fight organised crime, I've been a hostage negotiator and I've spent my whole life working with men. I know how to keep a lid on my bloody anger!'

Biting her lip and shaking her head, she dusts something imaginary off her impeccably tidy desk.

'At first, I thought I had something neurological going on – it was that bad. When the doctor told me it was actually my hormones screwing everything up, I burst out laughing. But seriously: it's not easy, getting old.' She releases a long sigh. 'So basically, all that is to say I'm sorry I flew off the handle at you this morning.'

'It's OK, Siv. You should call Birgitta. She finds the hormone replacements have really helped.'

'Really?'

'Yes, give her a ring. She can put you in touch with two or three gynaecologists who know what they're talking about too.'

'Thanks, Aleks.'

Only now does it dawn on me how quiet it is in her office right now. Unusually so. 'No Arnie today?' I ask.

'He's out in the yard. Having the time of his life in the snow. I asked Pålsson on the front desk to bring him in as soon as he starts barking.'

It occurs to me that I've just changed the subject, as if talking about hormones being out of whack makes me feel uncomfortable. It doesn't. With a wife and two daughters at home, I've learned to speak their language. I'll be honest: I do feel outnumbered sometimes, especially with all the talk about empowerment and bringing men down. But when push comes to shove, I just play the cards I've been dealt: I pretend I didn't hear or don't understand, and I make a swift exit from the room when things get dicey.

Siv breaks the silence. 'So, how did it go with Daniel Brink's father? What kind of family are they?'

'His wife died from a stroke nine years ago, and he's been raising his son on his own ever since. The small business he runs in Käppala is doing alright, and the apartment looks well kept. So no dark shadows in the picture as far as I could tell. And he didn't break down when I broke the news. He was almost stoic.'

'Must be in shock.'

'Oh, a hundred percent. I asked the officers who were going over there to search Daniel's room today to keep an eye on him. I'm worried that at some point he'll either blow a fuse or just lose his way. Before I left, I offered to call someone to come and keep him company. But he declined.'

'Sounds like you're on top of things. I'll leave that with you then.'

I remember that Paola's finished the autopsy and is ready to share her findings. I know she's waiting for me.

'I'll be there when he comes to identify his son's body. The team that's at his place right now can always bring him to the morgue, unless I go and get him first after I've seen Paola.'

'That sounds like a good plan,' Siv replies, opening the middle drawer of her desk and pulling out a packet of dates. She offers me one with a tip of her chin. I shake my head. 'Did you see the news at lunchtime?' she asks, munching away. It looks like hard work.

'Yes, I watched a recording of the TV4 report after it aired.'

'All the other channels followed their lead, you know. The story is everywhere – on SVT, Channel 3, you name it.'

'According to the headteacher, the school's turned into something of a shrine.'

'I know, I saw that on X. Mostly young people, it seems. That's the power of the hashtag for you. How many officers did you leave on site?'

'Two.'

Siv nods, but adds nothing. I get up, preparing to take my leave.

'I was wondering,' I say, 'did the editor-in-chief of TV4 tell you they were going to bring up the Jenny Dalenius murder and the Akerman scandal?'

'Of course she did. She wanted to see what she could get out of me. I told her that first of all, it's unprofessional to make that kind of connection while Daniel Brink's body is still warm. Plus, it's ridiculous to draw a line between the rape and murder of a girl and the death of a boy more than twenty years later – not to mention how shameful it is that the media is all about bringing in the viewers and the money, and finding the angle that will keep the most people glued to their screens. Anyway ... you'll call me once you've seen Paola, will you?'

I nod, one hand on the door handle. 'I asked her to dig up the autopsy report for Jenny Dalenius.'

Siv smiles. 'I know that already, Aleks. I asked her the same thing.'

12
Aleks

Erik Brink has come to meet me at the morgue. We're sitting, waiting, in one of the brown imitation-leather chairs. Elbows on knees, hands in prayer, he's pinching his lips between his fingers.

'Erik Brink?'

I hear the voice of the medical examiner, Paola Holm, before I see her. When I do, the look in her eyes speaks to how tough our jobs are, even after decades of peeling back layers of horror. Times like this are, predictably, heartbreaking.

Erik gets up with determination. Paola leads us into a small, rectangular room equipped with a flatscreen TV on one wall, a table and two chairs.

Erik looks from the TV to the box of tissues on the table, then turns to Paola.

'Are ... are you going to show me my son on a ... on this screen?' His breathing quickens and comes shakily. 'Do you seriously think I'm going to sit here like a ... like a stranger? I'm supposed to be in there with Daniel. Not out here!'

He tightens his jaw. His body stiffens. He clenches his fists.

Paola gives me a brief glance. She knows as well as I do that it's important to defuse his anger.

'Of course, Erik,' I chime in. 'I understand. He's your son and this is your choice.'

Paola makes her way to the door.

'Where does she think she's going?' Erik says, with a sneer of disdain.

'I'm taking you to see Daniel, Mr Brink,' Paola replies calmly. 'Please, come with me.'

It takes Erik Brink a moment to react. He wasn't expecting this change of tack.

The three of us walk down the corridor side by side, with him in the middle. Paola pushes open a swing door to our left and leads us into a room with pale-green walls and dark-green linoleum on the floor. It seems so vast compared to how cramped the last room was.

Daniel is right there, laying on a stainless-steel table. There's a camera on a tripod filming him from above. His body is covered by a sheet from the base of his neck to his toes. There's another sheet around his head, hiding the wound.

For a second, Erik Brink freezes. Then he strides across the few metres that are separating him from his son. He stops when he gets to the steel table and reaches for the sheet by Daniel's arm, not daring to actually touch it. He hesitates for a few seconds before placing a trembling hand on his child's face. I see that it startles him at first – he'll be feeling how cold and hard the skin is, like it's been wrapped around a block of ice. Then he leans forwards and plants a kiss on Daniel's cheek – the kind of kiss we parents give silently while our child is sleeping. The kind of kiss that seals our unconditional love at the end of a day by their side, no matter how pleasant or unbearable it's been. I know he won't recognise the texture or the scent of his son's skin, but still he leaves the trace of his lips, applying that unconditional seal one last time.

When he detaches himself from Daniel, he turns around and bends forwards, one hand on his thigh, the other still on the steel table. I wonder if he's about to throw up, but his movements are too slow for this to be nausea. No, I realise, as the tears start to flow and his body shakes with hiccups, this is grief taking him by storm.

13
Aleks

Paola is sitting at her desk, where two glasses and a bottle of Kilchoman are also waiting.

I shut the door and collapse into the chair across from her.

'Five-year-old single malt, matured in oloroso sherry casks from Jerez,' she says, pouring us each a wee dram. 'If you keep harping on at me about beer after tasting this one, you're a lost cause.'

I smile and raise my glass.

'*Skål.*' We clink glasses half-heartedly, repeating a ritual we've developed over the years to mark the passing of children who end up in the morgue – as if a shot of the strong stuff can somehow hasten the process of forgetting, wipe away the memories of grieving parents' tears and their wails of desperation.

'Did one of your officers see Brink home?'

'No, he wanted to be alone. He needed to walk, he said.'

Paola nods, twirling her glass. I sense her drifting away for a moment as she contemplates the whisky rolling gently around the base.

She sets the glass down on the desk but keeps it cupped in her hands. 'Right, where do you want me to start?' she says.

'Time of death.'

She scratches her forehead, then disciplines a few strands that have dared to stray from her strict bun.

'You know that rigor mortis sets in around the head first, before moving down the body to the feet, right? Well, the muscles in Daniel's face were barely starting to stiffen. His eyes were open, but the corneas hadn't turned opaque. What's more, the cool temperature last night – two degrees below zero in Sticklinge, will have slowed the decomposition process. So, I would estimate the time of death at between midnight and two in the morning. Actually, what complicated things for me a bit – even threw me off a little – was that his stomach was empty.'

'As in, he hadn't eaten?'

'No, nothing at all. Not for a long time. His last meal was about ten hours before he died.'

I nod, savouring a sip of Kilchoman, thinking I could easily get used to this stuff.

'And the murder weapon?'

'Ooh, I feel like we're playing *Cluedo*. Or *Inkognito*. Do you know that game? I used to love it when I was a kid. The hammer!'

'Are you joking? ... Or was he really killed with a hammer?'

'Yes, I'm serious. The murder weapon was a hammer.'

'Really? I didn't recognise the impact marks.'

'Well, the killer did use the face of the hammer – that's the flat part you use to hit the nail. But because there were two points of impact on the skull, one above the other, the wound didn't look like it was caused by a hammer, at least not to the naked eye.'

I put my glass down on the desk and lean back in my chair. 'I'm guessing the first blow came when he was standing up, and the second when he was on the ground?'

'Yep. The first blow was to the right temple, and from the angle it looks like the assailant was behind him. Daniel must have lost his balance and fallen onto his back, judging by the cuts and scrapes on the back of his head. The second blow, which aggravated the first, was fatal. But you didn't find the hammer at the scene, Alvid said.'

I shake my head. 'No, and I don't think the body was moved either, was it?'

'That's right, there was nothing to suggest it had been moved. No scratches or abrasion post mortem. The body showed clear livor mortis – that's pooling blood – around the back and buttocks, and contact blanching – paler skin – on parts that were in contact with the ground.'

'No defensive wounds?'

'None at all.'

'Any other DNA?'

'Yes, I found traces of saliva on his penis. Apparently, someone was really into him before they *laid* into him.'

'Really, Paola?'

'Oh, don't be such a prude, Storm.' She rolls her eyes. 'Let's chalk that up to the single malt, shall we? Oh, and one more thing, which struck me as quite unusual for a young man of his age. I found traces of sildenafil citrate in his blood. There are two main uses for that drug. One is to treat pulmonary hypertension, which can cause shortness of breath during exercise – but Daniel was very athletic and his lungs were in excellent condition, so that doesn't make sense. The other is to treat erectile dysfunction.'

'What? Are you saying this kid took Viagra?'

'Yes, that's exactly what I'm saying.'

14
Aleks

I came home last night to a quiet house, while everyone was sleeping, and I left again this morning right after Birgitta's alarm went off. I kissed her on the neck, and her blonde hair, which smelled like summer, brushed against my cheek. She groaned and sighed before kicking off the duvet, eyes still closed.

I arrived at the police station before seven, at the same time as Siv. I had my second coffee in the darkness of an early-autumn morning, reading Paola's detailed autopsy report. We're still waiting for forensics to get the crime-scene blood-spatter morphology tests back to us. And our IT experts are still examining Daniel Brink's computer, iPad and cloud storage. We haven't found his phone, but we should be able to piece together his call history pretty quickly.

At nine-thirty, after my fourth coffee, I drive back to Lidingö. The road I take splits the island down the middle. The last part of it weaves through fields and forests. The scenery here is so spectacular that after a mere quarter of an hour's drive, I almost forget the reason why I'm traversing this island of mine. The fresh snow has turned the plains into seas of white. It's outlined trees' skeletons and dusted their bare branches. It's powdered the tops of bushes, buildings and rocks.

It's a few minutes to ten when I park in front of the house where Thea Andersson, Daniel Brink's girlfriend, lives. Her family's place is on the eastern tip of the island, in Elfvik, a place separated from the suburbs of Stockholm only by a narrow strip of sea. As I ring the doorbell, my gaze is drawn to the Baltic and the grey rollers crashing onto the shore below the Anderssons' yellow-painted home.

A woman in a chestnut-brown hoodie and matching leggings opens the door.

'Commissioner Storm,' I announce, flashing my warrant card.

'Yes, yes, please follow me,' she says, ushering me inside hurriedly. 'Thea's downstairs in the TV room. Do I need to be here for this?' She twirls the end of her ponytail around her fingers. 'I have a call starting in two minutes.'

'Well, if you give me permission to talk to your daughter in your absence, then there's no problem.'

'OK, great! Let's go.' She bounds down the hallway in front of me, ponytail swinging from side to side. 'The TV room is just down there,' she adds before vanishing.

I try to quiet the voice inside me that's bad-mouthing Mrs Andersson for thinking a phone call is more important than her grieving daughter. Maybe she's spent the morning mopping up Thea's tears, and now she has a business meeting she really can't afford to miss. Unless she's just desperate to share how her intermittent fasting is going with her friends on FaceTime.

I head across the living room to the stairs she pointed to and descend a dozen or so steps to the basement.

The TV is on, but there's no sound. Thea is lying on the sofa with headphones over her ears. Her eyes are glued to the screen of her phone. It's a scene I see all the time at home.

I move around the sofa to subtly enter her field of vision. Still, Thea is startled and sits up quickly when she sees me. She takes off her headphones and smooths the blonde hair cascading over her arms.

'Good morning, Thea. I'm sorry, I tried my best not to sneak up on you, but I think that was a fail.' I offer her a sheepish grin, but I'm sure it must look more like a grimace.

She responds with a polite, elusive smile.

'I'm Commissioner Aleksander Storm. We made plans for me to come here and talk to you at ten o'clock.'

'I know. Mum said you were coming.' She stretches her legs and moves to the edge of the sofa, fingers still clenched around her phone.

'May I?' I ask, pointing to the sofa beside her.

She consents with a nod.

I take a seat next to her, leaving enough room between us so as not to intrude on her personal space or make her feel any more uncomfortable.

'I'm sorry about Daniel, Thea,' I say, after a few seconds of silence. 'I really am.'

She puts her phone on the armrest and stares at her feet, which she's flexing the way a cat kneads its paws. She puts her hands on her thighs and tugs at her joggers.

'You know, Thea, in situations like this, there are two types of victim: those who pass away, like Daniel, and those who are left behind, like you and his dad. It's very hard for those who are left behind. Sometimes, it's easy to think you're coping, but then the sadness wells up and gets so overwhelming, you feel there's no way out. If that happens, it really helps to talk to someone. Just saying what's going through your mind, even if it's harsh, shocking or shameful, can be very liberating.'

Thea looks at me. Her eyes are pooling with tears. Her jaw is trembling.

The father in me is desperate to give her a hug. The cop settles for a quick squeeze of her hand.

'Someone will be coming to the school to be there for anyone who wants to talk about Daniel's death. I'll also give you the number for a therapist who works with us in the police. She's amazing – you'll see.'

Thea nods.

'I have a few questions to ask you. Your mum told me she had to be in a meeting. Do you mind if we talk without her being here?'

'No, it's OK.'

'Alright. Can you tell me how long you've known Daniel?'

'Since middle school. We went to Torsvik together. And now we're in the same class at Hersby. I guess cos Torsvik is the only middle school on the island, and Hersby is the only high school.'

'Were you together, or just hooking up?'

Thea's mouth gapes in surprise.

I asked the question without really thinking about the words I was using. When my daughters started raving about how sick something was and ranting about something else that was cringe, I knew I needed to get with it if I didn't want to be left behind. So I started a glossary – a real, old-school one in a notebook – so I can at least understand all the *lits*, *bruhs* and *weshes* my girls throw into conversation, without thinking too much about it. I never thought I'd need it outside of our family setting, but here I am.

Thea crosses one leg over the other. 'We were a couple,' she replies, looking me in the eye.

'Had you been together long?'

She lowers her eyes. 'Since the eleventh of February this year.'

I nod. 'And when was the last time you saw Daniel?'

'We were together yesterday, in the afternoon. He came over here.'

She pauses, bites her lip, then carries on.

'He left just before five to go and train the little kids. We were supposed to meet up again later, at a party.'

'And where was the party?'

'Here, in Elfvik, at one of our classmates' places.'

So, it wasn't the same party that Dominic and Annette went to, I note.

'Almost everyone in our class was going. Daniel had promised his dad he'd help out at the shop with some stocktaking, so he'd join us later. But he never ... he never showed up.'

Erik Brink didn't mention anything about stocktaking. I'll have to check with him about that.

'When did Daniel find out he had to help his dad with the stocktaking?'

'Only a few days ago. It was kind of out of the blue.'

'Do you remember when he told you about it?'

She furrows her brow and rubs her temples with her fingertips. 'I remember we were at school, but I don't know what day it was.'

'When was the last time you spoke to him?'

Thea picks up her phone and unlocks it with a swipe of her finger. 'At two minutes past ten last night,' she replies, holding her phone out to show me.

I take it from her and read the message on the screen: *Sry. Let u no when I split* – followed by a heart emoji.

'And did you speak at all between the time he left your place and sent that text?' I ask, handing the phone back to her.

'No, but the weird thing is, we normally message each other on Snap – Snapchat, I mean. But that message, the one I just showed you, was on iMessage.'

'Why do you think he contacted you that way instead of on Snapchat?'

'Maybe because I couldn't see his location that way? That's the only reason I can think of.' Thea tugs at the sleeves of her hoodie and tucks her hands into the ends. 'But that doesn't add up.' She looks up at me. 'It doesn't make sense, because Daniel wasn't a liar. He was super loved-up. He was the one who asked me out. No, seriously, he wasn't the type to go looking somewhere else.' She shakes her head. 'I know what you're thinking,' she says, 'you're wondering how I can be so sure.' She twists her lips into a shape that's somewhere between a smile and a sneer. 'I'm sure because my dad cheated on my mum before he took off and left us. I knew exactly when he was hooking ... when he was with someone else, I mean.'

'I understand,' I say, imagining how brutal it must be for a child to catch on to her father's lies.

'It was written all over his face. You could see it in the way he walked. It was like he was flaunting it, but trying to hide it all at the same time. So that's how I know Daniel wasn't seeing someone

else. I'm certain he wasn't … But having said all that, he had been
acting a bit bizarre for a while.'

'Bizarre? How so?'

She looks away, then, keeping her hand inside her sleeve,
smooths a lock of hair that's fallen over her arm.

'He wasn't … um… on top form. He wasn't quite himself, I
mean.'

I think about the Viagra Paola found in Daniel's blood and the
saliva on his penis.

'And when did you first notice that he wasn't quite himself, as
you put it?'

'A few weeks ago. I couldn't tell you exactly when.'

'What do you think was going on for him?'

She shrugs. 'Dunno.'

I'm trying to find the right words to keep this going. But
nothing comes to me, so I decide to bite the bullet.

'I'm sorry to have to ask you this, Thea, and if it makes you feel
uncomfortable, you don't have to answer, OK?'

'OK.'

'Unless you'd rather your mum be here?'

'No, no.'

'Alright. Did Daniel have trouble getting an erection?'

Thea hangs her head and stares at her sleeves, which she twists
and turns like tentacles before bringing them to rest on her thighs.

She nods a yes.

'OK. And … was that something new?'

'Yes … only for the last few weeks.'

'And was this something he talked to you about?'

'He said he was going to find a way to sort it out. He said it had
nothing to do with me. My besties kept telling me he was such a
lame-o, but I believed him. He told me he was just on a bit of a
downer. He said he missed his mum and thank goodness I was
here.'

Her gaze drifts to the TV screen and the image of a young

blonde woman in a blue sequinned dress, dancing on a stage with a male ballet corps behind her. It strikes me that, for once, the men are the more naked ones.

'And what do you think?' Thea now turns and asks me.

'I think you're right, Thea. Daniel wasn't in a good place, but that had absolutely nothing to do with you.'

What I also think, but don't say, is that something must have happened to this boy – something traumatic enough to make him impotent. I think that he had a plan to meet one or more people on the evening of Halloween. And I think that it was something he couldn't tell his father or girlfriend about.

15
Maïa

I've spent the last four weeks fending for myself, and what scares me more than anything else is that I didn't see the time go by. But the first anniversary of Alice's death, which I was dreading so much, is finally behind me.

I was jittery as the dark day approached, as I remembered in the minutest detail what I had been doing the week before, the weekend before, and the morning of the fateful day when my daughter smashed into a tree. Many parents describe their experience of the moment of no return as a feeling of terror or deep uneasiness, as if they had suddenly developed telepathic powers and could sense that their child was departing this world, as if they could hear them take their last breath.

But not me. When my daughter died, I was taking a shower, feeling overjoyed to have the house to myself for once. The triviality of that moment weighed heavily on me for a long time during the grieving process. While my daughter was quite possibly crying my name, the way soldiers are rumoured to do before they die, all I had ears for was my own desire to be alone.

Alice is buried in Paris, at Père Lachaise Cemetery. When it came to deciding her final resting place, I simply picked the closest cemetery to home. Still, I've never visited her grave. Not once. But I did pay my respects in her room. In the gardens at the Parc des Buttes-Chaumont, where she took her first steps. In every memory that surfaced, as I recalled her whims, the faces she pulled, the laughter we shared, the words she misused at two years old, the spontaneous hugs, the misbehaviour that was always forgiven. The worries, the sickness, the sadness, our smiles. There's none of that at Père Lachaise. Apart from which, as cemeteries go, this one is steeped in a far more storied history than my daughter's life, so I just couldn't picture myself facing crowds of tourists on my way to grieve my child.

Ebbe and I could not have taken more different approaches to our loss. Every time we travelled to Sweden, he would always insist on leaving flowers at his grandparents' grave, and later, at his parents'. If we were there for a while, he would go every week to leave a bouquet, a candle or one of Alice's drawings. I'm not like that at all. I don't need a grave to feel connected to those I've lost. My daughter is everywhere except six feet underground.

However, Alice had two parents. And it's just as important to honour Ebbe's wishes as mine. And so, I gave in to that sense of duty and did, in fact, plan to go to Paris to lay flowers on our daughter's grave on the first anniversary of her death. But when I got to the airport, when I was sitting in the departures lounge, I couldn't bring myself to go. I just couldn't submit to what my husband wanted. I couldn't bring myself to grieve our daughter his way. Was I in medical distress? the agent at the airline counter asked me. No. Did I have a family emergency? Yes, I replied, feeling now as if I was adrift, out of my depth, my heart crying out with shame.

And so I returned alone to Sticklinge.

Ebbe still hasn't come back and he hasn't spoken to me since. What surprises me the most is that this solitude isn't weighing on me. Quite the opposite. After making it through November and overcoming this new stage of grief, I managed, alone, to celebrate my daughter's life the way I wanted to.

Sometime before I took this sabbatical and said goodbye to Paris, while I was filling my days with noise so I wouldn't hear my inner monologue or Ebbe's voice, I stumbled upon an interview on the radio that sealed my decision to leave France. A science journalist was explaining that pregnancy is a two-way journey: the foetus not only gains cells from its mother, it also gives some back to her. Every embryo that populates our womb – not just those that end up being born, but also those we lose or choose not to keep, every one we conceive – during the life it spends inside us, gives us cells we make our own. These stem cells, called microchimeras, will even protect us when our body gets sick, migrating toward the organ that's suffering and working with the rest of our body to heal us. What that journalist was saying, and what I needed to repeat out loud, was that Alice was living on inside me. Suddenly, this was more than a poetic image. It was a scientific fact.

This morning, I woke up obsessed with this idea, as if a dream had just reminded me about it. I felt a sudden urge to go out into the garden to breathe in the end of autumn, to listen to the snow protesting beneath my boots, to warm my cold, numb lips with a sip of coffee. And that's what I did. It turns out that feeling winter's frigid embrace, sipping steaming coffee and coming back to the present moment are not as painful as remaining stuck in the past.

A few hours later, reconnecting with my routine, I switch on the TV while I'm cobbling together a meal from some leftovers I've found in the freezer. When I sit down to eat, I muster the courage to wade into the sea of notifications on my phone. Then I turn the volume down on the TV and check my voice messages. I let them play one after another, while I'm clearing up, but just as I'm opening the fridge to put the butter away, I freeze at the sound of the unmistakable voice.

Sophia Akerman is inviting me over for dinner this weekend.

16
Maïa

It's 4.39 pm on a Saturday. I'm standing outside the metal shutters at Systembolaget, fuming in disbelief and only just managing to stop myself going on an extended rant about this whole country. The state-owned alcohol-store chain is the only place in Sweden permitted to sell wines and spirits. And every single one of its outlets across the nation shuts up shop for the weekend on Saturday at three o'clock. Seriously. Three in the afternoon. I know the Scandinavians dine early, but still.

Sweden, a country at the cutting edge of so many social policies, decided in the 1950s to fight the scourge of alcoholism by introducing the most tightly controlled of monopolies. So be it. And yet today, nearly three generations later, despite the powers that be having evidence that restrictive opening hours have the opposite effect – Swedes tend to buy more alcohol than they need, which leads to excessive consumption – the state insists on maintaining its monopoly and closing its stores at a time when most Spaniards would be sitting down to lunch.

Walking into Coop, the supermarket next door, to pick up a bouquet of flowers in lieu of a bottle of red, I feel a pang of nostalgia for Jérôme, the wine merchant on the corner of our street in the 10th arrondissement. It suddenly occurs to me how intolerant and embittered I have become. The timing of this evening's invitation couldn't be better for drawing me out of my unhealthy isolation.

Sophia Akerman lives in the south-west of the island, in the historical area of Brevik, where the heart of Lidingö started beating in the fourteenth century.

I follow the road that runs along the south side of Kottla Lake, then, as Sophia instructed, keep on going until I reach the marina in Brevik, where the hook of the wharf is lined with stone pontoons. The Akerman house is around three hundred metres further on, by the waterfront, beside a park and a deserted beach. On a smooth rock, a man sits waiting for his dog – boisterous and oblivious of the biting cold – to get tired of running through muddy puddles and across the wet sand.

Bouquet in hand, I breathe in the perfume of the night, which is laced with salt and fresh snow, and walk up three steps between the columns of the porch. Then I ring the doorbell.

A young woman in a black dress and a white apron opens the door while the bell is still echoing. For a moment, I'm taken aback. Ebbe's always boasted about Sweden being a classless society – not that I've ever believed that, of course. 'See what I mean!' he'd say with a wink, if he were here.

'Welcome,' the woman murmurs shyly in English.

She ushers me into a hall decorated with beige wooden mouldings from floor to ceiling. At the far end is a wooden staircase painted in the same muted tones.

'Please allow me to make you more comfortable,' she says.

I set my bag at my feet and hand her my coat. But I hang on to my flowers.

'I can take care of those if you wish.'

I hesitate for a second, then acquiesce.

I change out of my boots and into the flat shoes I slipped into my bag before I left the house. Then I follow her upstairs, trying not to be fazed by the opulent decor.

She leads me into a huge drawing room with a bay window – aptly named, I think, as it looks out over the illuminated garden towards the sea.

Sophia Akerman sits facing the window, in the middle of a sofa flanked by two armchairs. Her centre-parted white hair is tied in a low ponytail that kisses her neck. Hearing us arrive, she sets her laptop down on a side table and stands up gracefully to greet me with an amenable smile. There's something familiar about this woman. Something I can't quite explain. Perhaps I can see something of myself in her – the aging portrait of another mother who's lost her daughter. Or maybe I just want to see myself in her because even though her loss is more recent than my own, she carries it with a restraint I envy.

Sophia invites me to join her, as the young woman slips away discreetly.

My shoes are sliding on the waxed parquet floor and I thank myself for remembering to bring them. In socks, I would have gone flying.

'Commissioner Rehn,' she says, giving me a firm handshake. 'What would you like to drink?'

'What are you having?' I reply, eyeing the whisky glass on the coffee table.

'A Negroni.'

'Perfect. Same for me, please.'

'Do sit down,' she says, gesturing to the sofa.

Sophia takes a seat in the armchair to my left. I sit down in turn and marvel at the view.

The garden is fringed by a strip of snowy beach. To the right, leaning against a rock as round as a turtle's shell, a lonely pontoon straddles the inky sea.

The young woman, whom I've neither heard nor seen approaching, sets down a glass topped with a twist of orange peel on the coffee table in front of me. Next, on a pedestal by the window, she places a midnight-blue vase with my flowers in it.

'Thank you.' Sophia reaches out towards the bouquet, then seems to change her mind. Instead, she touches her liver-spotted hands – first one, then the other. 'At the risk of sounding a little abrupt,' she continues, 'I'd rather get straight to the point.'

I freeze, suddenly acutely aware that this meal is not going to be one between two mothers grieving their daughters. No, Sophia

Akerman has summoned me here for another reason entirely. And my instincts have been so numbed by these weeks I've spent cut off from the world, I didn't see it coming. She did nothing to deceive me. I just misinterpreted her invitation.

I wait for her to go on. Sophia doesn't seem like the kind of person who asks for permission to open her mouth. If she has something to say, she just comes out with it.

'I have an idea that I'd like to share with you,' she says.

I nod, wondering now where this conversation is going.

'Twenty-four years ago, my grandson was arrested for the rape and murder of his ex-girlfriend, Jenny Dalenius. Perhaps you're already aware of that.'

'Yes.'

'In that case, you surely know that a few weeks before he was due to be released, Gustav – that was my grandson's name – died by suicide. And that my daughter took her own life shortly after that.'

I bob my chin by way of confirmation.

'What else do you know?'

'That he claimed he was innocent, but the evidence against him was damning.'

'Indeed. You've probably also heard what the media have been saying these past few weeks, since the death of Daniel Brink – a case that remains under investigation.'

'I have: they've suggested there's a connection between the two cases, because Daniel, like Jenny, was wearing a Saint Lucia crown and tunic, and his body was also found in the woods at Abborrparken.'

'That's right.' Sophia reaches for her glass, takes a sip and sets it down again before continuing: 'My daughter spent more than twenty years fighting for her son's freedom. She fought alone, because I always thought Gustav was guilty.' She looks me straight in the eye. 'I refused to have our name associated with the scandal. But still, as I'm sure you can imagine, there were irreversible consequences for my family and for Akerman Editions, so I had to step back from the business for a while.' She thins her lips, making the corners of her mouth wrinkle. 'It doesn't escape me that, other than the Saint Lucia costume and the scene of the crime, if indeed Abborrparken was the scene, the murders have nothing in common and happened more than two decades apart. But since Daniel Brink's death, something has been niggling at me. And I believe that when something is stuck in your mind, it's important to hammer it out.'

Now I see where this conversation is headed. My pulse quickens, but I don't know if it's from anxiety or excitement.

'Sophia, I have neither the means nor the authority to reopen this case.'

'Oh, but you do. You have both, Commissioner. And you also have neutrality, objectivity and experience on your side. Don't tell me your title doesn't open doors. And – no offence intended – you're my last resort. No one has agreed to reopen this case. And it hasn't been for lack of trying on my part. But no one will help. This matter is far too sensitive, it seems. And the question I'm always asked is why dig up a closed case when the murderer was the heir of an influential family, was convicted on irrefutable evidence – and ended his own life, to boot? On top of which, why would I advocate for a re-examination of the facts at a time when the country is legislating for tougher penalties for rape? My timing couldn't be worse, I'm told.' She pauses and looks away from me for a moment. 'But it seems to me – and don't get me wrong, I'm no criminologist – that the parallels between the two cases are striking enough for someone to at least explore the possibilities. Don't you agree, Maïa?' She looks back into my eyes. 'Of course, you can name your price.'

I look down at the glass I still haven't touched. The ice has melted and the orange peel is floating in the amber liquid, which suddenly looks to me like stale cooking oil.

'I do wonder whether I was wrong, Maïa – whether my grandson was actually innocent.'

Then her mouth twists in disgust.

'And I also wonder whether it was my silence that drove my daughter to suicide. I cannot regret my actions – or rather, my lack of action – because regret is meaningless. You can't bring the past back to life. There's no sense in wasting time and energy lamenting something that was never done. But I can right the wrong I did, if indeed I did something wrong. I'm not trying to clear my grandson's name, Maïa. I just want to know the truth.'

17
Aleks

I step through the door to our bedroom balcony and close it behind me. There's a real chill in the air. It must be close to minus ten degrees, but that doesn't faze my wife. Birgitta has put a down jacket on over her pyjamas. She's out here smoking a cigarillo, contemplating a sliver of the Baltic between two roofs.

She hands me the box of Davidoffs.

I raise the hood of my parka to cover my ears. Taking one of the cigarillos from the box, I lean towards her and she lights it for me. I take a first drag, and it's divine.

November has felt like it's never going to end. It's unbearable. It seems like the darkness just doesn't want to let go. It's like an endless set of waves that keeps battering the shore. And the investigation has gone nowhere. Cases that become stagnant like this make me feel nervous and impatient.

The crime scene has failed to yield any clues likely to lead us to the killer. The partial footprints aren't enough for us to piece together a picture of their movements. That said, at least the blood-spatter morphology tests were consistent with Paola's findings, confirming the trajectory of the hammer and the killer's position at the time of the assault. Nothing has come from canvassing the neighbourhood, though. No one saw anything whatsoever in the vicinity of Abborrparken. The night Daniel Brink was killed, most people headed for bed earlier than usual, exhausted from running after their trick-or-treating offspring all evening long.

Then, there's the Saint Lucia tunic Daniel was wearing when he was found. We were hopeful that we would find at least a fingerprint or some DNA evidence on the fabric, because the killer must have cut it along its entire length before dressing the body in it. But no, we've found nothing on the garment or the crown. As for the provenance, it's one of those mass-produced costumes from Turkey, the kind of thing you can buy online or anywhere in the country.

By trawling the cloud and Daniel's browsing history, however, we've been able to build an accurate, albeit shallow, picture of a teenager like so many others his age, who are into football, *Call of Duty* and online porn. But there were no calls, messages or chats to indicate who he might have been planning to meet before he died.

We have managed to clarify two points, however: contrary to his son's claim, Erik Brink has confirmed that he didn't do any stocktaking on Halloween night; and the saliva found on Daniel's penis belonged to his girlfriend. Thea Andersson agreed to a DNA test with her scandalised mother present. Obviously, the forensics team didn't go into detail about where exactly her daughter's saliva was found on Daniel's body.

Meanwhile, we're still in the vice-like grip of the media. The period between Halloween and Saint Lucia's Day is typically slow on the news front, so the timing of this national drama has been perfect. It keeps feeding the headlines and filling the front pages. How could any journalist resist? There are so many angles from which to approach the story. If you believe everything you see in the media, you'll think a serial killer is still on the loose, Gen Z-ers are the lost generation, insecurity is rising and – the icing on the cake – the saga that shook the Akerman dynasty on the eve of the new millennium is far from over.

I'm jolted from my thoughts by a sound from Birgitta that isn't quite a laugh, but is something like a snort and a sneer rolled into one.

'Are you OK? What's going on?'

She swivels her head my way in surprise, as if she's forgotten I was here. Then she knocks the ash from the end of her cigarillo into the terracotta cup she's holding, which was a gift from one of our daughters for Mother's Day.

'I was just thinking how, here in Sweden, no matter how close we are to gender parity, we have to keep up the fight. Changing mentalities didn't exactly follow a smooth curve, of course. It took a fair few kicks of the anthill to change the game and give women more attractive roles in society than just being nannies. There's more equality with things like housework now, and gone are the days when we had to apologise for being mothers if we wanted to take on the same responsibilities as men. But still, you blokes, there's something about you that reeks of ... atavism, is that the word? I don't know. It's like one of your genes is somehow resistant to the idea of gender equality.'

I inhale another puff of my cigarillo, sure that everything's about to be my fault again.

'Sometimes, it seems like a stealthy thought that you don't dare to voice,' my wife continues. 'Other times, it's like a cry from the heart. We may well be in 2023, but bias against women is still deeply entrenched. It's like a layer of grease. There's just no escaping some people's instinctive reactions, and that makes me seethe with rage. For instance, there are some situations, where, if a man makes a certain decision, he's "thinking strategically", but if I make that same decision, I'm "being manipulative". And that's just one example. If the mayor bangs her fist on the table, she's "hysterical". But if her deputy mayor does the same thing, well then, he's "standing his ground"'. She turns to me. 'Don't look at me like that,' she says, crushing the butt of her cigarillo.

'What do you mean?'

'Like you're thinking, "here she goes again, on one of her feminist rants"'.

'Because that's not what you're doing?'

'No, I am.'

'Well, here I am. I'm listening. Tell me about it.'

'I just spent all day in meetings preparing for the election, building an image for Esther as not "just" the mayor of Lidingö, but also as the country's future minister of gender equality. But the whole time there were men digging their heels in and bending the truth. You should have seen them...' Birgitta shakes her head. 'You know, I almost wonder if there's something political about that murder.'

'Which murder? Daniel Brink's?'

'Yes. Maybe Esther is ruffling feathers. Maybe she's breaking down too many doors, too quickly. She's standing up for two feminist bills that the pillars of the party are grinding their teeth about. Maybe someone wanted to put a dead body in her way – quite literally – to slow her down a little.'

'Killing a teenager to burst your precious mayor's bubble? Don't you think that's pushing it a bit?'

18
Maïa

When I get home, I realise I probably shouldn't have driven. The blood-alcohol limit in Sweden is so low that no driver drinks a drop.

After quickly taking off my coat and boots, I hurry upstairs to our bedroom to look for my work bag and end up finding it in the wardrobe. I sling the strap over my shoulder and walk across the hallway. Then I take a deep breath, as if I'm about to go underwater, and enter Alice's room. My daughter set up the printer in there when she was writing her dissertation. She finished it here, during the kind of miserable summer only the Nordic countries can concoct, with the wind and the rain conspiring to keep the temperature below fifteen measly degrees.

Once I've unplugged the printer, I grab the pack of A4 paper beside it and carry my loot downstairs to the kitchen table. Salivating at the thought of a glass of the cognac I wish I had in the house, I fill a glass with water instead and set up my new office. As I'm waiting for the test page to print, I press my palms to my jumpy heart and heave a deep sigh, short and loud. It brings a smile to my lips. I haven't felt this kind of energy, or motivation, since the day of the accident. I don't miss work. I miss the job. I could say I chose this career to satisfy a keen sense of justice, but that wouldn't be true. The truth is nowhere near as noble and is far more embarrassing. I joined the police to satisfy my obsession with order. Not military and dictatorial order, but domestic. As in, the opposite of disorder. Whenever something seems out of place in a situation, be it a fact, a word, an action or whatever else, I find myself obsessed with that detail. And until I've found an explanation for it, I scrape away, deconstruct, dissect and reconstruct until everything slots into place. My guess is the feeling that's niggled at Sophia Akerman since Daniel Brink's death is just this: that something is out of place.

I never imagined my evening would take such a turn. There I was, thinking two grieving mothers were going to dine together, and now here I am, bringing home two murders, a USB key and the login details for a special translation software program. Sophia Akerman has thought of everything. Well, almost: there are still Gustav's belongings. Sophia has no idea where they are, but she has promised she will find them somehow. The prison must have sent them to Anna, I suppose.

I plug the USB key into the port on my laptop. On it are the contents of the file put together by the law firm that defended Gustav Hellström, along with some photos, added by Sophia, of the various protagonists in the case. I upload the documents into the software program, which superimposes the translation over the original text. That will make it much easier for me to make sense of the drawings, photos and diagrams, as I won't have to jump between those images in one window and the text in another. When I worked with Interpol for a couple of years, we had access to a program like this for translating investigation findings, witness statements, forensic reports and other documents from the various countries a case might lead us to. The mistranslations were amusing sometimes, and the constructions were often a bit convoluted, but it wasn't like we were translating literature.

As I send the translated versions to the printer, I cross my fingers that it won't run out of toner.

The printer whirs into life and gets down to work.

I've always had a hard time working on a screen. I need space to scribble on the documents in front of me. I like to be able to think, make notes and use colours to classify things. Sometimes I even print multiple copies of the same page so I can let different theories play out. The problem is, my notes are illegible to anyone other than me. They're a cryptogram to which only I have the key.

As the printer spits out paper, I take the first few sheets over to the sofa with a pen, a block of Post-it notes and a highlighter.

Jenny Dalenius had long blonde hair, delicate features and a pale-green gaze. She was sixteen years old and went to the high school in Hersby, at the centre of the island, where she and her family lived. That year, she had been chosen by the parish of Lidingö to play Saint Lucia. On the evening of 13 December 1999, she led the procession and sang the solo in the annual concert at the church on the island.

After the concert, around eight o'clock, she went with some of her classmates to a house party organised by Gustav Hellström, her ex-boyfriend, in the home he shared with his mother.

Jenny was found the next morning, around seven-thirty, in the woods at Abborrparken, by a thirty-eight-year-old man walking his dog. She had been raped. Her skull had been bashed in with a rock. She was still wearing her Saint Lucia tunic and crown of candles.

Gustav Hellström, whose semen and DNA were found on Jenny's body, was arrested and locked up on 8 January 2000.

I get up to fetch the list of witnesses who gave evidence in Gustav's trial from the printer. As I leaf through the stack of paper, something jumps out at me – a document I wasn't aware Sophia had also given me. It's the police report about the suicide of Anna Hellström, Gustav's mother. Skimming through it, I can't help but notice two names, both of which I immediately recognise. But one of them, I wasn't expecting to see there at all.

19
Maïa

Like most primary schools in Sweden, the one in Sticklinge doesn't have a gate, or a fence around it. It's a necklace of little red huts, draped around a huge central courtyard – an open space on the edge of the forest.

One day, when we were out for a walk with my in-laws, Alice saw the swings and insisted on going to play on them. She must have been two or three years old at the time. I had walked past the school in Sticklinge dozens of times before becoming a mother, but somehow I had never noticed there was only a flight of steps separating the playground from the road below.

'Can you imagine? Any lunatic can come in here if they decide to,' I said to my mother-in-law while my father-in-law was pushing Alice on the swings.

As far as my mother-in-law was concerned, the only monsters in Sweden were the trolls from the Nordic folk tales and whoever murdered Olof Palme, the Swedish prime minister, who was shot dead in central Stockholm while walking home from the cinema with his wife, in 1986. At the time, ministers didn't have bodyguards. And they still didn't when the country's foreign minister was stabbed to death in NK, a luxury department store in the capital city, in 2003.

My mother-in-law shrugged. 'Who would ever come and cause harm to children, Maïa? That doesn't happen in Sweden. We don't have those kinds of crazy people here.'

If she were still alive, I wonder what she would have thought about the Utøya massacre in Norway – the sister country Sweden shares a border with – during which sixty-nine young people lost their lives and hundreds more were wounded, some of them playing dead to evade the killer. I also find myself wondering what she would have made of Anna Hellström's suicide in front of some twenty schoolchildren, leaving them traumatised by the horror, smell and colour of death.

Now I'm striding up those same snow-kissed concrete steps to the oval courtyard. The snow is fresh – undisturbed and unsullied by children's boots.

In Sweden, the school day finishes early. *Fritids* – a period of leisure time that's something like a children's day camp – fills the gap between the early afternoon and six o'clock to help out those few parents who have to work late.

Cursing my need to always be early, I walk across the courtyard and sit down on a bench near classroom 5A, where I have an appointment in about ten minutes' time. I couldn't stop thinking about the case last night. I only managed to get a couple of hours of sleep in the early hours of the morning. I spent most of the night piecing together Jenny's murder and outlining the victimology. Every new snippet of information I gleaned from the investigation report was another impressionistic brush stroke on my mind's portrait of this bright young woman – the kind of canvas you need to take a step back to appreciate.

I'm supposed to be meeting with Lukas Dalenius, Jenny's brother, who's a primary-school teacher in Sticklinge. His name is in the police report about Anna Hellström's suicide, because it was in his classroom, and in front of his students, that Gustav's mother took her own life.

I found his email address on the municipal website and sent him a message just before midnight to ask him if he would be open to talking to me about his sister's murder. I signed the email with my professional title, which, in the circumstances, was neither particularly honest nor deceptive of me. It lent some weight to my request, I thought, or at least a certain legitimacy. Early this morning, Lukas Dalenius replied to my message, saying that he would be finished for the day at two-thirty. He suggested I meet him shortly after.

The door to the building opens to reveal a man dressed in a grey wool vest over a pale-blue shirt with an Italian-style widely spread collar. He holds the door open for me without venturing outside.

'Commissioner Rehn?' he asks, greeting me with a broad smile.

'Hello,' I reply, getting up, keen to be inside in the warm.

'Please come in,' he says, still smiling from ear to ear.

I step inside the hut, which is far more spacious than its façade suggests, and find myself in a cloakroom that looks like a bomb has hit it.

I take off my boots, unbutton my parka and follow Lukas into his classroom. I wonder if this is the same room Anna Hellström killed herself in. And if so, what the school authorities had to do to erase the imprint of the drama.

He gestures for me to sit down at a table by the window. The feet of the chair I pull out slide silently over the linoleum floor in their tennis-ball slippers.

'I'm curious,' he says, sitting down across from me. 'How come the French police are taking an interest in the case? I have to admit, I found your email intriguing.'

His eyes are the same shade of green as his sister's. But there's something hard about the look in them, like he's still carrying a flag for his pain.

I give him a smile. 'Sophia Akerman is a friend.' I figure it's probably going to be simpler and more productive if I play up our connection. 'She's asked me to take another look at your sister's murder case, in light of recent events.'

Lukas Dalenius shakes his head with a sneer. 'That old bat? I thought she had the sense to stay out of all this and see past her daughter's obsession.'

'She ... has some questions.'

Planting his elbows on the table, he opens his palms to the sky. 'What questions? Gustav was guilty. Who cares if he spent his life claiming he was innocent? He was hoping his family's reputation would tip the scales of justice in his favour – and probably counting on it. But, believe me, I did my damnedest to make sure it never did.'

I'm about to ask him what he means by that, but he's not finished yet.

'I mean, for God's sake, the guy had already been violent towards my sister. That's why she broke up with him.'

I don't recall reading anything about that. 'What do you mean, violent?' I ask.

'One night, Jenny came home with bruises on her arm. I could see the finger marks. She broke up with Gustav a few days later.'

'Did she tell you that Gustav had assaulted her?'

'No, not explicitly. I did ask her, but she didn't want to say anything.'

'How long was this before she was killed?'

'Two, three weeks.'

'If she was afraid of him, why did she go to the party?'

'Because her whole class was invited. She was Saint Lucia that year, so she didn't want to miss any of that evening. She couldn't.'

'I understand,' I say with a nod. 'Just now, you said something about making sure the justice system wasn't influenced by the Akerman family. What do you mean by that?'

'Gustav was every bit the predator with power. One hundred percent. If he were on trial today,' he says, tapping his index finger on the table, 'there'd be far more witnesses coming forward. Gustav Hellström was used to taking what he wanted, when he wanted. He sexually assaulted other young women before my sister, I'm sure of it. And if he had been released from prison, he would have carried on doing the same. So we made sure he stayed behind bars as long as possible.'

'We?'

'The RVSA – the rape victim support association I'm a member of. Sweden is ahead of the curve on many things, but our legal system is lagging behind. Criminals getting out after serving twelve years of a life sentence; don't tell me that's not scandalous. Gustav deserved every one of those twenty-three years behind bars. And he knew he couldn't keep lying when he finally got out. So he killed himself. Simple as that. I mean, just take a look at his family. His mother came right here, into this very room, to blow her brains out in front of a class of children.'

He pauses to purse his lips and furrow his chin in anger.

I blink, and feel like I can hear their screams of terror. What a brutal act of cruelty, I think, for a mother who had lost her child to subject other people's children to a sight like that.

'Can you imagine?' Lukas goes on. 'I had to yell at my students to get down on the ground and curl up in a ball. I said to keep their eyes closed until I – and only I – told them they could open them again. One of my students, Louise, was covered in blood and ... Well, I'll spare you the rest. The poor girl still can't sleep in a room in her own. She screams every time a motorcycle roars by or she hears a gunshot on television. We have some headphones here for her to put on when she goes out to the playground, because she has panic attacks when she hears another kid squeal. Do you realise how much damage Anna Hellström has done? All that to stand up for her monster of a son? And do you know, Detective, what was even more tragic than Jenny's death? What it did to those of us left behind. My mother died of cancer less than a year later. She was gone before the next Christmas. My other sister died by suicide. She couldn't live without her twin. And my father ended up moving out of the country.'

I have so many more questions to ask this man, but I can't find the words. I can't stop thinking about this decimated family. I can see what remains of it eroding before my eyes. Until there's nothing left. Like a body ravaged by disease, gradually shutting down.

A lump is forming in my throat. A lump so big, I feel like I'm going to choke. That's what grieving a child is like. It's a contagious disease. And for some, it's deadly.

VI

Do you remember that night, when I opened up to you and told you how terrified I was of silence?

You asked me to close my eyes.

You told me you were taking me on a journey to Woodstock, in New York State, on a damp, sultry evening in August 1952. There, at the end of a muddy track, is the Maverick Concert Hall, a makeshift theatre built at the turn of the century by a poet with more than a dash of whimsy. The place is more like a barn than a venue for the performing arts. Two trunks reach skyward from the heart of the space – forming the backbone that holds up the wooden framework and the moss-covered roof. The walls are a patchwork of crooked branches and lime-washed planks. Studded with stained glass, the pediment looks out over the parterre of wooden benches beneath the forest canopy.

A pianist walks out onto the stage. His name is David Tudor. Stopwatch in hand, he sits down at the piano, closes the lid over the keyboard and starts a timer. For thirty seconds, he waits, not playing a single note. Next, he resets the timer for two minutes and twenty-three seconds and, once more, sits motionless at the keyboard. Chairs creak. Rickety benches squeak. The audience is losing patience. There are whispers and rumblings in the crowd. Tudor adds another minute and forty seconds. Then, the concert-goers begin to hear the wind toying with the branches, the rain pattering on the mossy roof. They hear the whispering of discontent and surprise. A rustling of leaves. The warbling of a bird. A swishing of cloth. They're listening to 4'33". That evening Tudor is performing this silent piece composed by John Cage – Tudor is playing the music of life we call silence.

After you took me on that journey, I was no longer afraid of silence.

Not until that day. The day when you forced me to listen to a silence filled with noises and sounds I should never have heard. The silence you condemned me to.

20
Maïa

I ring the bell, and the door is answered almost immediately by the man I saw on the TV a few weeks ago, on the day of the murder in Abborrparken: Commissioner Aleksander Storm. Like Lukas Dalenius, his name was also in the police report about the suicide of Anna Hellström.

'*Hej*,' he says. The word seems to dance from his lips.

A dog comes yapping along the hallway behind him. It presses its snout to its master's thigh, gives it a sniff, then zooms back down the hallway and up the stairs.

Commissioner Storm wipes his hands on a tea towel draped over his shoulder and gives me a polite smile.

'Good evening,' I say, returning the smile. 'I'm Maïa Rehn. We're neighbours. I live in the house down on Rödstuguviken bay.'

'Ah, yes, Rehn. I knew Leif well. I'm guessing you must be his French daughter-in-law who's in the police?'

I nod. 'That's right.'

Leif, my father-in-law, was a long-standing president of the Sticklinge residents' association. He knew most of the people in the neighbourhood and was as chatty as my mother-in-law was reserved.

A tall, slender woman joins the detective at the door. Tired brown curls hang over her shoulders.

'You remember Leif who lived in the old ferryman's house, don't you?' Storm says to her. 'This is Maïa, his daughter-in-law.'

'Oh yes, of course! Hi, I'm Birgitta, Aleksander's wife.'

Crow's feet fan out from the corners of her eyes. Her friendly smile bears none of the usual Scandinavian reserve. There's a lightness to it that reminds me of home, as if my country had followed me here to return a bag I'd left behind.

'I apologise for disturbing you at home,' I say. 'I was planning to contact you at the station, but then I thought, we live so close by ... Perhaps I'm interrupting your dinner, though.'

'No, no, we've finished,' Storm replies. 'I was just doing the washing up. Please, come inside.'

I hesitate for a second. I've never had to justify my reasons for asking questions before, and now here I am, doing it twice in the same day. I decide it's best to be straight with him before taking up the invitation.

'Sophia Akerman has asked me to look into the Jenny Dalenius case, and I read that you worked alongside Commissioner Bodin at the time.'

'Sophia?' Storm's wife looks surprised. 'But she's always been so adamant that her grandson was guilty.'

'Well, she's been having doubts, since the murder in Abborrparken and how that body was staged. She's beginning to wonder if she should have listened—'

A shrill cry mutes the rest of my sentence.

'Sorry about that,' Birgitta says before turning around and calling up the stairs: 'Girls, please keep it down, will you? We have company!'

More shrieking and heated words come from above.

'I'll go,' Storm says.

'No, no, it's alright. I've got this,' his wife insists. 'Just a normal evening of bickering with two teenagers,' she adds with another friendly smile before dashing up the stairs what looks like four at a time.

'It's funny – this reminds me of the terrible twos.'

I regret the words as soon as they're out of my mouth. Because they beg the inevitable question, *Do you have kids of your own?*

Storm laughs. 'I'd never thought about it, but you're absolutely right. There's just over a year between them and it's...'

He lets out a sigh that deflates like a balloon.

'So, you're going to take another look at the Dalenius case,' he says, steering the conversation back on track. 'You have a bit of time on your hands, then?'

I'm relieved by his reaction. 'Yes, I do.'

Voices are raised upstairs. The argument sounds like it's a tough one to settle.

'I'm intrigued to hear about Sophia Akerman's change of heart.' He smiles and pulls the tea towel from his shoulder. 'Would you like some coffee or tea?'

'No, thank you.'

'Just a second.' He disappears into a room on the left, probably the kitchen, before reappearing without the tea towel. 'Follow me. We'll be more comfortable in the living room. You can leave your coat here if you like.' He gestures to a white wooden coat stand.

I hang it up, take off my shoes and follow him down the hallway, which opens up into a generous room overlooking the garden, furnished with two deep beige sofas overflowing with brightly coloured cushions. The coffee table is heaving with books, candles and a collection of remote controls that would drive Ebbe – always the minimalist when it comes to decor and technology – around the bend.

We sit down facing one another, and I attempt to pull my feet under my chair, curling them up as if to hide them. I've never got used to the Scandinavian habit of being shoeless indoors, so I always feel almost naked in other people's houses without my footwear, in what is pretty much a professional setting.

I try to ignore my discomfort and pick up where I left off. 'I think the suicides of her daughter and her grandson are weighing heavily on Sophia Akerman's conscience. She's struggling with guilt – she feels she could have done a better job of listening to them. And now the similarities between Jenny's case and this new killing have given her food for thought.'

Storm raises his eyebrows. 'These crimes have nothing in common besides the location and the Saint Lucia costume.'

'And the type of injury.'

'True, but not the murder weapon. Jenny's rape was a crime of opportunity. That wasn't the case with Daniel Brink's murder.'

'Which means that Daniel Brink's costume wasn't a Halloween thing.'

He smiles and clasps his hands in his lap.

'Sorry,' I say, 'that was something that seemed obvious to me. I know there are limits to the answers you can give me. But I'd be grateful to know what you are able to share.'

'Thanks, I appreciate your understanding. You worked for Interpol, as I recall?'

'For a number of years, yes. I'm on the crime squad now.'

'And you're here on holiday?'

'In a way. Well, not anymore, I suppose.' I smile, thrilled to have sidestepped a tearful explanation of the grief, the unpaid leave and the move to Sweden. 'You seem to remember the Dalenius case well.'

He uncrosses his seemingly endless legs. 'That case had enormous repercussions. I was immersed in it for months. It was a heinous crime that involved a widely respected and admired family falling from grace. And it really opened people's eyes to the fact that Sweden can create monsters just like any other country. As a sociologist said at the time, "For Swedes, it's like Saint Lucia has died all over again." I'll never forget those words. I think that crime tarnished our values as a people at the deepest level. And we have a small population – no more than London and its suburbs. That's why Gustav Hellström spent more than twenty years behind bars. He paid the price for everything we had to grieve.'

I hear a scurrying of light, quick steps on the stairs. Perhaps it's Birgitta.

Then, the sound of a door swishing open and shut.

'Gustav Hellström's defence hinged on his claim that Jenny hadn't been raped,' Storm continues. 'He explained the bruising on her inner thighs and the scratches on his neck, as simply the result of them having rough sex, like they sometimes would, at his home on the night of the party. According to him, Jenny must have then been attacked by a stranger.'

'The injuries to Jenny's back could have been caused when her attacker pinned her to the ground.'

'Yes, but no DNA other than Hellström's was found on her body,' Storm counters.

'There's nothing unusual about that, if she was attacked by someone wrapped up against the weather like most of us are in Sweden in December. If I'm not mistaken, the murder weapon – the rock that was used to bash her head in – was never found. Nor was any clothing stained with her blood recovered from Gustav's home.'

'That's correct. But we only found his blood – no one else's – under Jenny's nails, and it tallied with scratch marks on his neck.'

'Which could very well have been inflicted during rough sex, like he claimed.'

'Certainly. But what do you make of his history of violence? The kid was impulsive and had a short fuse.'

'Lukas Dalenius said the same thing, but there's nothing about that in the file. Any reason for that?'

'Because we had no proof. It was just hearsay. Jenny had apparently had some bruises and didn't mention them to anyone, but her brother said he noticed them ... Wait, you've been to see Lukas?'

'Yes, I went this afternoon, after I learned that Anna Hellström died by suicide in his classroom. She must have really flipped her lid when her son died. When you've been holding it together for so long, it doesn't take much to push you over the edge. Maybe this was her taking revenge on the society that condemned her to her fate by condemning those children to theirs.' I release a deep sight. 'Those little ones are going to struggle to bounce back from that trauma. I can't begin to imagine the impact it's had on the community.'

The next few seconds stretch out in silence and respect. For those children – and for Anna, who, in my eyes, was above all a mother consumed by her pain.

Storm's gaze travels to a photo on the wall above the piano. A portrait of two four- or five-year old girls who look so alike, they could almost be twins. They have their mother's dark hair and their father's light eyes. My thoughts turn to Ebbe, Alice and me. To our family that was.

Storm opens his mouth and tilts his head to one side, but the words are slow to come. I'm hoping they will take away the sadness I feel welling up inside me.

'You've read the file, Maïa. What's making you doubt Hellström's guilt?'

'I'm not doubting anything right now. I'm just pointing out what bothers me.'

'And what is it that bothers you?'

'That a murder has just been committed and staged to look like another one that happened more than twenty years ago. The same tunic. The same crown placed the same way on the head. The same fatal wound. The same place.'

'Assuming there's something to this idea, why start killing again after all these years? And why go after a boy and not a girl this time?'

'Jenny's killer might have left the country or served a long sentence for another crime or crimes. Or maybe they were physically incapacitated for some reason and couldn't kill again – until now. People's fantasies, needs and frustrations change over the course of twenty-four years. This could even be the passing of a torch from one killer to another. And if it is, Daniel Brink's murder could be an initiation.'

21
Aleks

The wind came in squalls all night long. It whistled around the flagpole in our neighbour's garden, slamming the cord against the pole in time with the fifty-knot gusts.

This morning, our snow-covered lawn was littered with fallen branches and dotted with paw prints from the animals that darted across it to seek shelter in the woods at Abborrparken, a few metres above our house.

I'm standing in the living room, drinking my coffee and looking out at the barren garden. There are no snowmen out there, no backyard bobsleigh tracks, no snow forts.

We bought our house thirteen years ago with the enthusiasm of a couple of city-dwellers who had heard the green space calling. We were obsessed with finding somewhere for our children to run around and say goodbye, once and for all, to those dreaded work parties when everyone in the apartment block had to roll up their sleeves and help out with whatever maintenance needed doing. We wanted an outdoor space to fill with a swing set and one of the inevitable trampolines that plague the Swedish suburbs like weeds. But for the last three years, our girls have done none of the running around they used to. The trampoline, the swings and the plastic paddling pool have all disappeared, and I find myself wondering why, from May to September, we pour blood, sweat and tears into mowing a lawn no one ever sets foot on.

On my way to work, I drop Birgitta off at the mayor's house for another crisis meeting. These have been occurring weekly since Anna Hellström's suicide in June. Esther Lind receives hate mail by the bucketload. It doesn't help when the media blames her brand of local politics for shattering the safety of the community. The murder of Daniel Brink has only prompted more poisonous messages, coming more regularly and in greater quantities. For someone who aspires to hold higher office, this is disastrous publicity. It's my wife's job to constantly fend off the blows, defuse the bombs and turn public opinion around. This morning, however, the problem has become more personal in nature. A heated family argument broke out last night and is threatening to spill out of their home if Esther's son decides to take the battle with his father onto social media.

I leave Birgitta at the gate of their villa and drive away. Her perfume, a blend of caramel and a heady-scented flower whose name I can never remember, stays with me all the way to the police station.

At the front desk, Otto Pålsson, sporting a cap over his thinning hair, beckons me towards him.

Making my way over, I plant my elbows on the counter.

He's deep in a phone conversation. Well, no; he's trying to get a word in edgeways with the person on the other end, who seems to keep cutting him off.

'No, no, no, no, no, whatever you do, don't do that,' he eventually manages to say. 'Hold tight, madam, we're on our way.'

He hangs up, doffs his cap and sighs as he wipes a giant hand over his face.

'Were you on the night shift?' I ask.

He nods. 'It was dead as a doornail until that old bat over in Djursholm phoned me with her knickers in a twist. I tried to tell her, we're not the bloody coast guard.'

'What's going on?'

'Her neighbours are away in Dubai, apparently. And through her binoculars – which she probably uses to spy on them – she saw a boat that wasn't theirs banging up against their jetty. She says there's someone in a Saint Lucia costume lying on the deck. I'm sick to death of kids playing pranks, I tell you. If you ask me, it's just another bloody blow-up doll. But because you said you wanted to know anytime something like this came up, the old bat's all yours.'

'I'm on my way. Tell Siv I'll call her if it's worth the bother. Can you text me the info?'

'Will do.'

I get back in my car and drive out towards the bay. Harriet Windberg, the woman with the binoculars, lives on Skärviksvägen, at number thirteen.

I'm halfway down the driveway when the front door opens.

'Don't move!' a gravelly voice orders as an elderly woman in a white down jacket steps out onto the porch. 'We'll go through the garden,' she adds, tugging a fur-brimmed hat over her ears. Harriet locks the door behind her and slips her keys into her pocket.

'And you're Commissioner...' She tends an ear like a schoolteacher waiting for a pupil to finish their sentence.

'Storm.'

'Right, well that's that sorted. That's the name they gave me on the phone. Follow me. We have to go all the way down there, to the shore. You won't see a thing from up here.'

She leads me down the garden path, so to speak, along the side of her house. Her skinny pins in her black leggings make me think of a heron's legs.

'Careful, it's slippery. You really should get some non-slip grips for your shoes. They have some very good ones at the chemist's,' she says, pointing to her trainers. 'They're amazing. Just slip them on over whatever you're wearing. Just look at me. I could do Zumba out here in these things and still I wouldn't fall ... I must say, he wasn't very friendly, that colleague of yours I had on the phone. You'll never believe how many times I had to repeat what I told him. You know, it's terrible, this grey curse. As soon as you're past seventy, no one believes a word you say anymore.'

'When did you first notice the boat?' I ask her, watching where I put my feet to keep my balance on the icy paving stones.

'Early this morning. It was the noise it made that woke me up. It must have been three or four o'clock. *Thunk, thunk, thunk* – that was the kind of sound it was making. I was only half awake, so I told myself it was something blowing around in the storm and I went back to sleep. Anyway, when the wind calmed down later on, I could still hear it. I'm surprised no one else has called you about it. Or maybe they have?'

I shake my head.

'This morning, when I got up, I had a look with my binoculars and saw this boat sitting at a strange angle to the jetty, down at the Olssons,' she continues. 'And I know their yacht's in dry dock because they're in Dubai for the winter. So, I came out into the garden to get a closer look – still with my binoculars – and that was when I saw this Saint Lucia. Just like the one in Lidingö.'

We're at the end of the garden now. I step out onto Harriet's dock. To my left, in front of her neighbour's property, I see a small motorboat, about four or five metres long, swaying back and forth between the beach and the jetty. Its cockpit is open to the elements, and it isn't moored up, which is concerning.

I carefully retrace my steps and return to where Harriet is waiting on the beach.

'Is this the only way to get to your neighbours' place from here?' I point to a narrow opening between a garden shed and some bushes. It can't be more than a foot wide.

'Yes. It's a good job you're not any wider. Or else you'd be swimming there.'

'Wait here for me, please.'

Harriet nods stoically.

I pull my hood up and squeeze my way through the opening, holding one arm in front of my face for protection as the bushes scratch at my coat and shake snow on me. Emerging on the other side, I walk across the neighbours' garden, skirting along the edge of the snow-kissed beach.

When I get to the boat, I see that the port side is beached on the shore and it's the bow that's knocking against the jetty. And then I see it. The sopping-wet white tunic. The right sleeve soaked with blood. The crown of faux candles, none of which are switched on this time, perched on a bashed-in head. I move closer to the bow for a better look.

I stifle a gasp and take a few steps back.

My chest tightens. My throat constricts. I find myself struggling to breathe.

I know that face.

22
Aleks

My wife is the first person I see. She's standing in the hallway, speaking in hushed tones with a young man who's taking notes on an iPad. Birgitta looks up at me for a second. Her lips form the beginnings of a smile, but nothing more.

I walk down the hallway to the living room.

All three remaining Linds are sitting there on the main sofa. Esther is in the middle. Peter, her husband, is on her right. And Sixten, their youngest son, who's nine, is on her left. He's curled up in a foetal position, eyes closed, head in his mother's lap.

Esther's stroking her son's cheek, but there's something robotic about the gesture. Her other hand rests limply by her side, unmoving, palm facing up. She's the image of a puppet with a broken arm.

Peter sits staring straight ahead, inky bags under his eyes, hands on his thighs as if he's about to get up. Esther's eyes are on Sixten. A painting takes up the entire wall behind them. It depicts a sleeping girl in a white tunic amid a horde of wild animals. That child is doomed, I think every time I see that scene – she just doesn't know it yet. It strikes me that the painting, a fore-shadowing of death, has always been a bit of an omen for what this family is going through now.

Alvid, the head of the forensics team, signals to let me know he's going upstairs to the bedrooms.

I've been to the mayor's house a few times for the occasional fundraiser or reception, but there's always been an element of work to my visits. Since Esther started to venture into politics, every step she's taken has been calculated to lead her closer to government – and power in general. Everything has been calibrated and curated to project a family image that's more honest than wholesome – one that's not without its flaws, because people aren't stupid. Everyone knows model families are the most dysfunctional of all.

Working so closely with Esther, Birgitta has developed a bond with her that goes beyond the professional. Birgitta shapes Esther's image and spends more time protecting her from herself and those close to her than she does Esther's critics. Like a psychotherapist, she knows all the nooks and crannies of her client's soul – including, most likely, all the secrets about her marriage and her family.

When he emerges from his daydream, Peter gets up and opens his arms. His face has aged with grief. He gives me a brief hug and sits down again. Esther lifts her empty gaze towards me for a moment before it falls to Sixten again. She gently plucks the thumb her son has started sucking from his mouth. Sixten closes a fist and presses it to his chin, suddenly seeming far younger than his years.

The Linds are only taking up three-quarters of the sofa. To Peter's right, there's an empty seat. A void where Roland, their eldest, should be sitting. Their sixteen-year-old son, whose body I found this morning.

I sit down in one of the armchairs beside the sofa.

Esther opens her mouth, but her lips and jaw just wobble. She closes her eyes for a few seconds before she tries again.

'Sixten doesn't want to be left alone,' she says in a hoarse voice, without taking her eyes off her son, whose hair she's stroking. 'So, if you need to talk to us, it will have to be here at home, with Sixten present. And I'd rather you be the one asking the questions, because he knows you.'

Sixten's eyelids still haven't budged. It's like he's delaying the moment when he has to open them again and face a world without his big brother in it. The last thing I want to do is tear him away from his parents when a pillar of his family has just crumbled. Plus, I think coldly, it might be useful for me to observe their interactions. In any case, it's either this or nothing, it seems.

'I'd like to ask all three of you a few questions about yesterday, if you don't mind.'

Esther nods and her face creases as something contracts inside her. Peter starts blinking, like he's just woken up.

'Can you tell me when you last saw Roland?'

As if relishing the memory, Esther tips her head to one side and smiles. It's a smile tainted with sadness and pain.

'Yesterday morning,' she slurs. 'Before I went to work at seven. I woke him up. I gave him a hug. He smiled. Then I opened the curtains and left the house.'

'When was the last time you heard from him?'

'Yesterday afternoon, around three o'clock. He messaged me to let me know he wouldn't be at football practice because he had a science test to revise for.'

Esther interlaces her fingers with her son's, clinging to him so she won't lose him too.

'I didn't know Roland played.'

'Yes, at IFK Lidingö. Mostly to make his dad happy.'

Peter's eyes glaze over. He takes his wife's hand in his, or rather, latches on to her. Seeing this man and boy like limpets on a rock, I can't help but wonder, if Esther herself comes unstuck, will the whole family be set adrift?

'And after that message...?'

'That was the last one,' she replies.

'What time did you get home last night?'

'Around eleven. There was a dinner at the Ukrainian Embassy.'

'What about you, Peter?'

'Peter and Roland had an argument last night,' Esther says. 'About football, as it happens.'

The reproach brings a rough edge to her voice. I don't let on that Birgitta has already shared that detail with me.

'Do you feel able to tell me what happened, Peter?'

Eyes glued to the floor, he starts talking. 'Roland was home when I got back, around half past six or twenty to seven, something like that. I was surprised to see him. He was supposed to be at football. And we...' He stops, heaves a staccato sigh, then carries on. 'We argued. About football, like Esther said. He went up to his room and didn't come out again all evening. It was only ... when I woke up this morning that I realised he had taken the boat out.'

'Do you know when he left the house?'

No, Peter signals with a series of quick, barely perceptible movements of his head. 'No idea. I didn't hear a thing.'

'As the evening went on, you didn't go up and see him? You didn't ask if he wanted something to eat or ... check how he was doing? Even if he didn't open his door?'

He looks up at me anxiously. He's going to replay those final moments with his son in his mind on a never-ending loop.

'No, I ... He and Sixten had already eaten dinner by the time I got home.'

Sixten opens his eyes. Tears are streaming down his cheeks and onto Esther's thighs. She wipes them away absent-mindedly.

'So, the last time you actually spoke to him was at what time?'

'Around seven last night, I think.' He massages his left palm vigorously.

'What time did you go to bed?'

'Around nine-thirty.'

'Do you think you would have heard the boat, if Roland went out before you went to bed?'

'Maybe, but I wouldn't have thought much of it. We often hear boats out on the water, even in the middle of winter.'

'Was Roland in the habit of taking the boat out?'

'No, not without us.' Peter presses his lips together. He coughs, trying to suppress a wave of tears.

'How about you, Sixten?' I ask, letting Peter catch his breath.

Sixten sits up on the sofa and settles cross-legged. Then he wipes the wetness from his face with the back of his hand.

'I went and knocked on his door after he argued with Dad,' he replies with a sniffle. 'I stayed in his room for a bit with him.'

'What did you talk about?'

'Nothing. We just...' Sixten shrugs. 'We just watched some stuff on his phone.'

'Do you know what time you were there until?'

'I didn't stay long. Until about eight, I think.'

'And you didn't talk to him after that? He didn't send you any messages?'

'I sent him some messages, but he didn't write back.'

'Alright. Did he tell you he was planning to go out at all?'

Sixten shakes his head, then snuggles up against his mother and draws his knees to his chest.

'I'll need you to tell me the names of his closest friends, and his girlfriend, if he had one.'

Esther and Peter exchange a sheepish look.

'He didn't have a girlfriend,' Sixten says, but without sitting up again. 'He had a boyfriend.'

23
Aleks

Standing behind her desk, legs shoulder-width apart and hands on her hips, kitted out in something that looks like a life jacket held in place with clips at the chest, Chief of Section Siv Nord shifts her weight from left to right.

I'm sitting across from her, drinking coffee and eating a late lunch of a meatball sandwich and beetroot salad while she does her workout.

'So the mayor of Lidingö's son was gay,' she says, waving her arms in a circular motion. 'Was he out?'

It takes me a second to swallow my mouthful.

'Yes. Esther and Peter knew.'

'How did they take the news?'

'It must have been easier for her than for him. He's a bit strait-laced.'

'Have they known for a while?'

'A couple of weeks,' I say, taking a sip of my coffee.

Siv nods, then winces as she rolls her shoulders backwards.

'It was super fresh, then. What about his friends at school and in the football club? Did they know, or not?'

'His parents weren't able to tell me. We've had a quick look at his TikTok and his Insta, but there's nothing about it. I'll find out,' I add, between two bites of my sandwich. 'It's quite possible his little brother knows more than he said. They seemed close.'

'We should have thought about the homophobic angle straight away,' Siv says with a sigh. 'It just doesn't add up, a teenager like Daniel Brink taking Viagra. That should have tipped us off.'

'I don't see how we could have made that leap, Siv. Plus, I don't agree with you. At the football club, we have kids who are gay who've never had any problems with bullying or harassment.'

'Still, not so long ago, I remember hearing some of the pros talking about needing to hide their homosexuality from their teammates.'

'Yes, but those guys must be at least ten years older than my juniors. Mentalities have changed in the last decade. I don't see any reason why Daniel had to claim to be straight, and go as far as to prove it physically. He didn't have to go out with anyone. And even if he had a girlfriend, that doesn't mean they had to sleep together.'

'Or maybe he felt he had to live up to his dad's expectations – fit the stereotype. Single dad, only son, you get the picture. Maybe Erik Brink isn't very forward-thinking.'

I shrug. As I'm taking a sip of lukewarm coffee, there are two sharp knocks at the door. In comes Paola.

'So?' Siv asks her.

'Good grief, what the heck is that? It looks like a bulletproof jacket you found on Amazon. Or a fishing vest. I'm not quite sure.'

'Go ahead and laugh. You'll change your tune when you're old like me. It's a weighted vest.'

'A weighted vest? What's that for?'

'It weighs twelve kilos. It's good for my bone density.'

'Your *what*?' Paola has to bite her lip to stop herself from laughing. 'Don't believe all the health advice you see on TikTok, Siv. All that thing's going to do is throw your back out.'

'Well, you know what, I haven't had any angry outbursts since I've been wearing it.'

It's true. I haven't seen the dragon in Siv for a while.

'No shit, Sherlock. You're far too tired for that.' Paola grins and sits down in the chair next to mine.

'Alright, Holm, what do you have for me?' Siv asks, sitting down in turn, but without taking her vest off.

'Roland Lind died between midnight and half past one in the

morning. No evidence of sexual activity before death. He ate his last supper around five o'clock. Hawaiian pizza washed down with Coca-Cola. And the killer used the same hammer as the one in the Daniel Brink case.' She looks at me. 'Any lab results from the boat yet?'

I shake my head as I swallow another mouthful of my lunch.

'They'll have had to take the family's prints to compare them against what they found aboard the day cruiser,' I eventually say. 'So that'll have slowed things down a bit. But what with the wind last night and the waves washing over the boat, there's not much chance we'll find anything, if you ask me.'

'Any idea which way the boat went?' Paola asks. 'Was there a GPS log, for instance, or is that something you can calculate based on the wind strength?'

'You know what Alvid would tell you?'

'That he's not a bloody magician. Believe me, our place would be a hell of a lot cleaner and tidier if he was. Ugh, beetroot. I've never been able to stomach the stuff,' she says, giving the salad in my sandwich the stink eye.

I savour the last bite with a smile.

'So, is this going the way I think it is?' I say, wiping my lips with a napkin. 'Even though, technically, we only have two crimes, and not three?'

'Yes,' Siv replies. 'With the crown, the hammer and the tunic slit all the way down the back, I think it's safe to say we're dealing with a serial killer, not just any old murderer.'

24
Aleks

The numbers on the dashboard tell me it's minus five degrees, but the temperature has been as low as minus seventeen these past few days. The snow is tenacious. Undeterred by the relentless wind, it somehow clings on to the branches and treetops – an immaculate icing.

I park at the sports complex, which is next to the church and the yacht club. Vallen is not just a gathering place for islanders, it's the heart of Lidingö that never stops beating. There's always something going on at the stadium, football pitch or tennis courts – or the skating rink in winter. Training, competitions and matches happen every day of the week, sometimes until late at night. When it's snowy out, we rarely use the football pitch, but the athletics track is open all year round.

I get out of the car, zip up my parka and head into the stadium, drawing breaths of icy air that make me want to go for a run myself. Jackets and scarves hang from the gate as if it's a drying rack. There are three people out here, warming up on the track. After a few seconds, one of them jogs over to me.

Sixten has given me the name of Roland's boyfriend – Stefan Wolinski, one of the rising stars of athletics on the island. I coached his younger sister at the football club a few years ago before I started coaching the juniors instead.

'*Hej*, thanks for coming out here, Coach,' he says, unscrewing the lid of his water bottle to quench his thirst.

'*Hej*, Stefan.'

He rubs his forehead under his thin running hat, then tugs the hat back down over his ears. You'd never know he was just running around the track. His breathing is already back to normal.

'Would you like to go inside and talk?'

Stefan shakes his head. 'I'd rather we stay out here, if you don't mind.'

I smile. In this situation, I thought I'd be wearing my detective's hat, not my coach's cap. But it makes sense that he'd feel more comfortable talking to someone he associates with sports, rather than law enforcement.

'How are you feeling?' I ask, as he grabs his down jacket from the gate.

'It depends. I've had some ups and downs. When I run, it's OK.'

He takes a long swig from his water bottle and waves at his two teammates on the track.

'Had you and Roland known each other for a long time?'

Stefan nods. 'Since primary school, in Sticklinge.'

'And how long had you been together?'

'Since August. Four months.' He swallows. A film of tears forms over his eyes.

I wait a few seconds before I go on.

'Who knew about your relationship?'

He clears his throat. 'Not a lot of people. This whole thing was new for us. We were basically learning as we went along.'

'Could you tell me who did know?'

He sniffs. 'My sister. Roland's brother, Sixten. His parents as well, but only for the last two or three weeks. Some of my friends at athletics, too.'

'How did Roland's parents react?'

'He told his mum we were seeing each other. Esther is very open-minded. For her, love has no gender. She's always been pro-LGBTQ+, and not just to get votes. She's really supportive. But he didn't want to talk to his dad about it.'

'Why not?'

'Because his dad's a dick.'

'Homophobic, you mean?'

'I don't know if he's homophobic, but he had some very

specific ideas about what Roland should and shouldn't do and even how he should be. He wanted Roland to play football and music. He wanted him to be good at maths and be comfortable with people – so basically, everything Roland wasn't. It was like he wanted him to fit into certain boxes. So Roland didn't say anything to him.'

'He asked Esther to keep it a secret?'

'No – the opposite. He asked his mum to talk to his dad about it because he didn't want to. They barely said a word to each other, anyway. Whenever they did, it almost always led to an argument.'

Stefan tucks his water bottle under his armpit and zips up his jacket.

'How about at school? How did your classmates react?'

He shrugs. 'Nobody cares. I mean, there are a couple of clowns. The same ones who think it's funny to mime blow jobs in front of girls. Not exactly the crowd we liked to hang out with, so it wasn't a big deal...'

'And did Roland hang out with Daniel Brink at all?'

'We weren't friends with him. But we knew who he was, obviously. Lidingö isn't that big a place.'

'What about Thea Andersson?'

'Who's that?'

'Daniel Brink's girlfriend.'

He shakes his head.

'Why do you think Roland waited several months to tell his mum about your relationship?'

'Because ... we didn't really know if it was serious. We were friends for a long time before. He told her when we realised ... when we knew it was for real.'

Stefan's face tenses. His mouth forms a thin line. Hanging his head, he presses his fingers to his closed eyelids.

I put my hand on his back, between his shoulder blades. Slowly, he wipes away his tears.

'If you need a minute, or if you'd rather we talk later instead...'

'No, no, I want to do this now,' he replies, drawing himself upright.

His lips are trembling as he pulls himself together.

'I was going to call you, Coach. I saw online that you were leading the investigation, and Iris said so too, when we were talking about the news in class earlier.'

Iris, my eldest daughter.

'Roland wasn't in a good place. He hadn't been doing well for a while. He was … I don't know … absent, somehow. It wasn't anything to do with us. I wasn't worried he was going to break up with me. It was something more general. The last time I talked to him was yesterday, about four in the afternoon. He was in his room and he couldn't stop crying. We were on FaceTime and I could see how distraught he was. But he didn't want to talk about it. He just said it was something that couldn't stay under wraps, and he'd tell me when he had the proof. Whatever it was, he said it would mean prison for sure. And if anyone ever found out, his mum could kiss her career goodbye.'

25
Maïa

I set my glass of Burgundy down on the coffee table, mindful of the deep grooves that might topple it off balance, then I jam another cushion behind my back.

There's been a second murder on the island.

A second boy dressed as Saint Lucia.

Sophia called to let me know, but I had already seen the news on TV and the images spoke for themselves. Only the victim's identity had escaped me. Sophia filled me in. Roland Lind is the son of Lidingö's mayor.

The case has taken a whole new turn. A turn that may well leave me behind, because my French police badge carries no legal weight here. I'll have to get creative. And careful, to make sure I don't ruffle any feathers.

The doorbell rings.

I glance at my phone, wondering if Christian has decided to drop by, though that wouldn't be like him at all. There are no messages to suggest he's going to stop in and see me. And Swedes are not in the habit of paying visits unannounced. I still remember the panic – and I'm not exaggerating – on Ebbe's face when I invited some Parisian neighbours we didn't know to join us for our New Year's party, nearly twenty years ago. One of those neighbours became a brother from another mother, and he was one of the pallbearers who carried Alice's coffin.

I get up to answer the door.

Aleksander Storm is standing on my porch in the inky darkness.

'Good evening, Maïa. I hope I'm not disturbing you?'

Despite the surprise, I shake my head to say no, not at all, and step aside to invite him in. He looks at me as a few unpleasant seconds of silence tick by, the cold seeping in from outside.

'I'd like to express my condolences,' he says.

I gape at him, caught off guard.

'I imagine that if you came here, it's probably to avoid people doing this.' He gives me a brief, embarrassed smile.

An immense wave of fatigue washes over me. It's sadness, I know – manifesting like this, weighing so heavily on my body, I can barely stand.

Instead of inviting him to follow me into the living room the way I normally would, I find myself inching backwards towards the sofa, trying to maintain the façade of a smile, although I have no idea whether my lips are doing what they're supposed to.

'I called the crime squad in Paris to check ... to find out why...'

'...Why I took a holiday that isn't really a holiday.' I finish the sentence with a bigger hint of bitterness than I intend.

His mouth twists into an awkward pout. 'These two murders are a delicate matter that's taking a complicated turn. It crossed my mind that Interpol, Europol or the French police might have sent you to follow a trail. The killer here might have struck before ... in your country ... I figured.'

He sits down beside me. I didn't invite him to, but it doesn't bother me. There's something strangely pleasant and comforting about his presence.

He wrings his hands one way, then the other, before reaching them out towards me.

'I'm so sorry, Maïa ... I have no words.'

'There aren't any.' I swallow, but the nausea keeps rising. I need a crutch. Right now.

'So, do you want a drink?' I ask him, falling back on the wrong way to heal the wound and realising I've also forgotten my manners. 'Sorry, that was a bit abrupt. Can I offer you something to drink, I should have asked.'

'Don't worry, no offence taken. And yes, I'd love a drink, thanks.'

I navigate my way around the sofa, hoping my legs won't give way beneath me. Then I open the china cupboard and take out another stemmed glass.

I put it down on the coffee table and start pouring the wine without thinking.

'Sorry, I didn't ask. Is red alright?'

'Red's perfect,' he replies, smoothing his trousers with his palms.

His knees are touching the coffee table. I can't believe how tall he is.

'It's a Burgundy,' I say, handing him his glass. 'Gevrey-Chambertin.' I finally made it to Systembolaget before they closed. Thank God.

I grab my own glass and take a swig, forgetting about the sense of ceremony that comes with alcohol here. People see it as an experience to share by clinking glasses all round. It's something I usually enjoy.

Detective Storm doesn't seem offended. He takes a sip. His cheeks hollow as his lips form an 'o'. Then he swallows with appreciation.

'Isn't it just?' I say, wetting my own lips again.

The effect is immediate. My crutch is holding me up and I have to be careful not to lean on it too heavily. Drowning my sorrows in alcohol would be a deadly mix of two poisons.

Still, I latch on to my glass and sip yet another of the wine's tears.

Aleks looks around the room, taking in the piles of papers and loose sheets littered across the floor. 'This is just like my...' He leaves the words hanging awkwardly, regretting what he was about to say.

'It's OK to talk about your daughters,' I murmur, the alcohol shortening the distance between my thoughts and my mouth. 'Just because mine died, that doesn't mean yours don't have the right to live.'

His eyes crease, as if my grief has pained him for a brief moment. 'It's a bit like that game, "the floor is lava",' he eventually says. 'Do you know it?'

I shake my head.

'My girls used to play it when they were little. The room was exactly like this. They would put sheets of paper, newspapers and magazines all over the floor and jump from one to the other, slipping and sliding around all over the place, obviously.'

'And let me guess, it always ended in a fist fight.'

I chide myself as I take another sip. I'm drinking too much, too quickly.

'Yes, well that's a constant,' he mumbles, almost to himself.

I smile. He talks as much as Ebbe doesn't.

'What are your daughters' names?'

'Iris and Alba.'

'That's beautiful.'

'Birgitta chose them. She's the poet.'

He doesn't ask my daughter's name, and that's a good thing. I hear it enough. I hear it in my mind all the time. Since she died, I've truly understood the words of Cyrano de Bergerac because I've been living them. Her name is 'in my heart like a bell'. Every time I think of her, it's like I can hear that bell ringing – and the memories and feelings resurface. Every single time.

'You're working on the Dalenius case,' he says, gazing fondly at the mess surrounding me.

I nod, looking around in turn at all the papers I've highlighted, annotated and stuck Post-it notes to.

'I'm meeting with Linnius Kero tomorrow,' I say. 'He's an historian. He's published a number of books about Saint Lucia. I don't suppose you fancy coming with me, do you?'

26
Maïa

I'm waiting for Aleksander beside the dock at Rödstuguviken, which is just at the end of my garden, wearing Ebbe's duffel coat with the hood pulled up. The water that kisses the shoreline is frozen, but the bulrushes are still poking through, seeking the sun, swaying in the breeze. A little further away, where the sea is deeper, the sheets of ice are shifting together and drifting apart like the pieces of a puzzle. A puzzle that makes me think of the Dalenius case.

Like I do with every investigation, I'm trying to find the points these murders have in common. I still can't say whether Gustav Hellström was innocent or not, but one thing is beyond any doubt – all the crimes have something to do with Saint Lucia. And so, that's the bone I'm chewing on, as Ebbe would say. I'm gnawing it down to the marrow, because I don't want to leave anything to chance.

I hear the sound of the engine first, then I see the motorboat with Aleksander at the helm. Last night he stayed only as long as it took to finish his glass of Burgundy, then offered to pick me up this morning. He has a boat mooring at the Sticklinge yacht club, six hundred metres from his place and a stone's throw from mine.

'*Hej, hej,*' he says, pulling up to the dock. His smile brings a sparkle to the wrinkles at the corners of his eyes.

I reply with a *Hej* of my own. I'm sure it has a French lilt to it.

He offers me his hand to help me climb aboard. I grab it, purely out of politeness.

The trip to the island of Vaxholm only takes us about twenty minutes. The pale, weak light cast by the already-weary sun is still spectacular. It makes me think of candlelight, conducive to calm, introspection – and love, too.

The chill to the air somehow seems less frigid now – more bracing. It has the heady scent of everything I've forgotten: life, and a certain sense of freedom. I gulp it down like it's a magic potion.

Linnius Kero is waiting for us on the dock, his long, fair, grey-streaked hair sticking out past the earflaps of his hat. I know it's him as soon as I see him. He looks exactly like the photo on his website, just with a few extra wrinkles.

He offers, and I grasp, his bare hand to step down from the boat. His wrist is laden with bracelets that clink together as he guides me ashore.

'*Madame la commissaire Rehn – enchanté*,' he greets me in a melodious French that makes me smile. 'But I imagine you'd prefer to go by Maïa, am I right? Please, call me Linnius,' he adds, with a wink.

'This is Commissioner Storm,' I reply.

'Whose endless legs in running tights stole the show on the television,' Linnius jokes.

Aleksander, who's nearly finished docking the boat, bursts out laughing then hops ashore to shake his hand.

Linnius leads us up a steep flight of steps carved into the rock to a cottage painted the same Falu red as my in-laws' – no, *my* place, I should say now.

Aleksander has to duck under the door frame on the way in.

The living space has a low ceiling, but it's bigger than it looks from outside. I realise we came in through the side door. Dressed with windows looking out to sea and decked out with shelves of books from floor to panelled ceiling, the walls around us are striped with blue and words. A white earthenware stove takes up one corner of the room, and two armchairs separated by a side table sit facing the horizon.

Our host motions to a round table with four chairs and invites us to take a seat. The cottage smells like a traditional Swedish

Christmas: cinnamon, cloves, fresh-baked buns and wood smoke. I can picture my father-in-law now, tending lovingly to the log fire to keep it alive until bedtime. I can still hear the poker scraping at the wood and ashes.

'I'll just be a second,' Linnius says, disappearing through an archway.

He returns shortly after with a tray bearing three blue ceramic cups, a carafe of coffee and a plate of saffron buns.

'Thank you for agreeing to see us,' I say.

'Oh, it's my pleasure, Maïa. Other than the occasional enlightened oddball like me, no one takes an interest in real history these days. They only have eyes for the simplified versions the media and TV channels feed them.

He puts the buns down in the middle of the table.

'As you probably know,' he says, tucking a lock of hair behind his ear, which is pierced with a tiny silver ring, 'these buns are called *lussekatter*. We eat them in December around Saint Lucia's Day, but actually, they have nothing to do with her at all.'

He pours us all coffee.

'Saint Lucia is often associated with things she has no relation to,' Linnius continues. 'In fact, these buns are of German origin, and they were reputed to keep the devil at bay. *Lusse* for Lucifer, disguised as a cat – which is spelled *k-a-t-t* in Swedish. The saffron makes them bright, which deters Lucifer, because he avoids the light. QED.'

He sits down, reaches for the glasses hanging from a string around his neck and perches them on his nose.

'The confusion comes from the Latin word *"lux"*, meaning "light", which is connected both to "Lucia" and "Lucifer". Lucifer actually means "bringer of light". Help yourselves.'

'Light really is a national obsession,' I say, taking a sip of coffee. 'Every bit of Swedish folklore seems to revolve around it. That's hardly surprising for a country steeped in darkness for half the year, I suppose.'

'I've never understood how an Italian saint ended up inspiring one of our deepest-rooted traditions,' Aleksander chimes in, rotating his cup as if it contained a vintage wine.

'Sicilian, actually. She was from Syracuse. But yes, indeed, what the devil is a Sicilian doing in our calendar?' Linnius asks, turning his palms skyward in a very Southern European gesture.

Aleksander smiles. He still hasn't touched a drop of his coffee.

'It's true, it makes no sense, 'Linnius continues. 'Here in Sweden, every tradition has pagan roots, all except for Saint Lucia's Day. And it's because she happened to die at the right time. Let me explain.'

I sink my teeth into a *lussekatt*. The bun tastes divine. It's so fluffy and flavourful.

'Having heard the calling of God, the noble Lucia of Syracuse refused to marry and gave her belongings to the poor. Furious to see his future crumbling before his eyes, her ex-husband-to-be denounced her to the henchmen of the Roman emperor Diocletian, who sentenced her to death. But she survived being burned alive. Even the sword thrust into her body failed to finish her off; that was until a priest came to give her communion. Then, she could depart in peace. That day was 13 December. And,' Linnius raises a finger above his head, 'in the Julian calendar of the time, 13 December was the day we know as 21 December today. In other words, the longest night of the year. The winter solstice. That's how Saint Lucia came to lend her name to the festival when we celebrate the victory of light over darkness. Because from that date on, the days get longer.'

'We have a saying in France that means exactly that: "*À la Sainte-Luce, les jours croissent d'un saut de puce,*" I recite from memory.

'Precisely!' the historian rejoices. 'And then our folklore borrowed something else from a German tradition: for *Christkindel*, girls dress up as the baby Jesus, in white tunics with candles in their hair – but without the red ribbon our Saint Lucia wears at her waist. And so, Saint Lucia's Day was born from a kerfuffle in the calendar and a mish-mash of cultures. And it's not just us in Sweden. People in France celebrate Saint Lucia's Day, too. There are even some of her relics at St Vincent's Basilica in Metz.'

Linnius pours me some more coffee. His hair drapes over his arm like a shawl. He strikes me as quite a handsome man, in all his eccentricity.

'Later on,' he continues, 'Lucia was hailed the patron saint of eye problems. Why? Racked with guilt after breaking off her engagement, she gouged out her own eyes to give them to her fiancé.'

'I thought I remembered something about that!' Aleksander nods with an endearing childlike excitement. 'I have a vague memory of it from school. She came bearing them on a silver platter, didn't she?'

'She did indeed,' Linnius replies, with his mouth full.

'Saint Lucia was therefore a martyr, but also a ... resistance fighter who rose up against an oppressor and died,' I say. 'Actually make that two oppressors. She rebelled against two men: one was the emperor and the other was her future husband.'

'Symbolically, if we're going down this road,' Linnius adds, helping himself to another saffron bun, 'Saint Lucia denounced the barbarity of the Roman Empire and announced the coming of Jesus the Saviour. In other words, she represents the return of the light of day, and also the light in the sense of enlightenment, as in, the end of darkness and of ... obscurantism.'

Aleksander throws me a glance.

'Lucia of Syracuse gave up her eyes,' Linnius continues, 'because even without them, she could see. She knew the Roman Empire was going to fall. She could see the truth.'

I lean back in my chair. A ray of sunlight dances across the table.

Did Daniel and Roland die as martyrs, like Saint Lucia? And Jenny? Is that why they were dressed like her?

If so, for what truth were they sacrificed?

As a pink veil sweeps over the sky, we leave Vaxholm with half a dozen *lussekatter* for the journey home and two copies of one of the books Linnius wrote about the life of Saint Lucia.

My phone vibrates just as I'm starting the boat's engine.

It's my wife, letting me know it will be just me and Iris at home tonight. Alba, our youngest, is sleeping over at a friend's house. And Birgitta is going to be working through the night with the mayor. Sometimes I feel like my wife treats her boss like a child, whose needs keep growing over time. I'm sure Esther takes advantage of her dedication – or perhaps I should say devotion.

I pocket my phone, wondering how long Birgitta will stick it out at the Linds', not that I'd dare ask the question, as it would be selfish of me. That family has more than its fair share of drama to handle, as well as the pressure of being in the public eye. They need help and support.

Maïa is sitting beside me in the cockpit. She's pulled up the hood of her parka. The fur edging spills over her eyes and her hair blows in the wind. She turns and gives me a penetrating stare, as if holding back the urge to ask a burning question.

'What is it?' I ask her, raising my voice above the drone of the engine.

'I'll need access to some of the details of the investigation into the murders of Daniel Brink and Roland Lind,' she says, still looking me in the eye – as deeply as a psychologist gazing into my soul.

'I know.'

She smiles, and the sadness in her eyes evaporates for an instant. 'In that case, can you answer some of my questions?'

'That all depends what you ask me.'

She smiles again, though not as sincerely this time. As if she's still in the grip of grief despite herself.

She sweeps back a lock of hair that's fallen over her face. 'If I were to suggest something, would you be up for it?' she asks.

'Depends what it is,' I reply, raising an eyebrow in surprise.

I ease off the throttle automatically, the same way I turn the radio or the music down when I want to focus on the road. When you're north of fifty, concentration comes at a cost. I know that asking too much of too many senses risks everything going pear-shaped.

'Can we stop the boat?' she asks, staring straight ahead.

'What exactly did you have in mind?' I reply, regretting the words as soon as I've said them as I realise she might misinterpret them as a come-on. I open my mouth again to right that wrong, but she beats me to it.

'Look,' she says, pointing to the bow.

Right in front of our eyes, it looks like a wave of lava has just broken over the sky and set its pink veil ablaze. Wisps of cloud swirl like smoke from the fire in the heavens.

I kill the engine.

Only the lapping of the water against the hull stirs the silence.

On the horizon, bare trees bathe in a golden puddle. It looks like the sun has burst, its contents spraying over all the surrounding islands.

A memory of Iris when she was little drifts into my mind. One summer, during a blood-orange sunset, my daughter asked me to lift her into my arms. She started blowing as hard as she could towards the clouds, to revive the embers and 'keep the sky alive,' she said.

The magic lasts mere minutes. The golden tide ebbs. And the sky turns a pale purple, then blue, then grey once more.

'One last dance before death,' Maïa whispers. 'Thank you. I've never seen anything so beautiful.'

I don't know what to say.

She turns away from the sky and lays her eyes on me.

'In the murders of Daniel Brink and Roland Lind,' she continues, as if we hadn't interrupted our conversation, 'what detail or information springs the most clearly to mind? Don't think about it. Just say the first thing that comes into your head.'

I'm caught off guard. I don't know what I was expecting her to say, but it certainly wasn't this.

For Daniel, it's the Viagra – one of the few details we've kept under wraps. I decide not to say anything to Maïa about that for now.

'For Daniel, it was his empty stomach. For Roland, his relationship with his father.'

'And what aspect that the murders have in common jumps out at you?'

'Um...'

'Don't think. Just let your subconscious decide.'

'Well ... the fact that they were both feeling down and preoccupied before they died,' I say without further hesitation. 'And the time of death, which was the same.'

Maïa nods. 'Could you perhaps ... enlighten me about these points?'

I smile. 'Certainly – though only within the scope of what I'm permitted to say, of course.'

She doesn't return the smile. She's waiting for me to deliver.

'Starting with your first point, Daniel hadn't eaten since lunchtime.'

'When was he last seen?'

'At the end of the afternoon, when he left Vallen after coaching the little kids at football.'

'Maybe he was taken and held captive?'

'There were no injuries on his body to suggest that. No evidence of anything being tied around his wrists, ankles or neck. No residue of any adhesive over his mouth, either.'

'And are you sure there's no evidence of a hypodermic needle between hair follicles, for example, or between the fingers?'

'One hundred percent.'

'Sometimes, when there are two crimes, we tend to look for the similarities subconsciously. And we gloss over key elements.' Maïa digs her hands into her pockets.

'I'll ask Paola, the medical examiner. But I can't imagine her missing anything elementary. The problem is, we don't know what time he disappeared. His girlfriend received a message from him around ten that night, but there's nothing to say for sure that he was the one who sent it.'

'What makes you say that? The way the message was written?'

'No, the fact that it was sent by iMessage, when they always messaged each other on Snapchat.'

'I see...'

'It's possible he was trying to hide his location. He could have turned off geolocation in Snapchat, but that would have been more obvious.'

'He told his girlfriend he was with his dad, and he told his dad he was with his girlfriend. They were supposed to be going to a Halloween party together later, on the island. Which makes me think he was meeting someone in secret.'

'He wasn't necessarily meeting someone. Maybe there was something he had to do.'

'Good point.' Maïa grabs the bag of *lussekatter*, opens it and offers it to me.

I take one of the saffron buns and realise I haven't eaten anything else all day. She helps herself to one, too.

'I presume the two boys didn't know each other,' she goes on. 'You would have mentioned it if they did.'

'They went to the same school, but no, they didn't know each other.'

She lets a mouthful of saffron bun go down, then continues. 'So, to you, the fact that Daniel's stomach was empty means that he was preoccupied, anxious, and possibly stressed about a mystery rendezvous on the night he died. To the point of forgetting to eat?'

'Or losing his appetite, yes.'

She chews and swallows the last bite of her bun. 'And Roland was depressed, too, you were saying?'

'Yes, Daniel and Roland both became depressed a few weeks before they died. Well, "depressed" might not be the right word. They weren't quite themselves. They were feeling down about something. Roland opened up to his boyfriend about it on the day he died. Whatever it was, he said it was something criminal, and if it was true, his mother's career would be over.'

'Ah, so perhaps there was some blackmail involved.'

'Yes, perhaps.'

'Have you been able to ask the mayor about that?'

'I haven't spoken to her since that information came to light, no.'

Maïa nods her head, ever so subtly, again and again.

The sky is nearly black now. I realise we're still just floating out here. With a turn of the key, the engine rasps through the silence.

'How would you answer those questions you first asked me?' I say, as the boat accelerates.

'I would say, the red sash. The elements of the traditional Saint Lucia costume are the crown of candles, the robe and the red sash at the waist,' she says, counting them on her gloved fingers. 'But neither Daniel nor Roland was wearing a sash. If the killer went to the trouble of dressing them in the robe and the crown, why not add the sash, too, or at least leave it in the vicinity of the body?' She pauses and runs her tongue over her lips. 'I don't have the answer to that, but what I do know is that Jenny Dalenius wasn't wearing a red sash either when her body was found.'

28
Maïa

Sophia Akerman has agreed to see me at Ellery Beach House, where we first met more than a month ago.

I sent her a message late last night, asking whether she'd be available today to discuss the case. She replied ten minutes later to say that she'd be spending the day at the hotel spa, and suggested I join her at half past ten, after her first treatment.

Now I'm waiting for her at Coco Beach Club, the casual bar and restaurant downstairs from Palmers, where the Akerman Editions party took place. It still has the same spectacular views over Elfvik bay, but the vibe is more laid back and the music is a touch too loud for my taste. A circular chimney reigns over the immense room filled with dusty-pink sofas and armchairs. The terrace is covered by a blanket of snow. I'm amazed to see a group of brave Vikings emerging from the outdoor pool, which must be heated, judging by the steam rising from the surface.

These courageous swimmers then dash inside to warm up, all wrapped in orange dressing gowns embroidered with the hotel logo. I shiver at the thought of doing that myself.

A moment later, Sophia enters the room wearing one of the same dressing gowns. When she spots me, she waves and comes to join me.

She holds herself like a woman thirty years younger who has never know the pain of an aging body. I wonder how she manages to defy the ravages of time and find myself envying her youthfulness. Her resilience, too.

'Maïa, hello,' she purrs, sliding into her chair with a dancer's grace.

A young waitress wearing the standard uniform – a flared black skirt and white T-shirt with rolled-up sleeves – comes over to greet us with a broad smile.

'Ms Akerman, what can I get for you? And for yourself, madam?'

'Black tea with milk please, Daniella,' Sophia replies.

I order a coffee, and the cheerful Daniella slips away.

Sophia gets straight to the point. 'So, what can I do for you, Maïa?'

'I'd like you to tell me more about your daughter and your grandson to help me get a sense of their relationship and the family dynamic.'

'Of course,' she replies, holding my gaze.

'First of all, who is Gustav's father?'

'Juan Villán, a Chilean man Anna met on holiday. They came back from South America together.'

'Were they married?'

'No,' Sophia replies, lifting her chin indignantly.

My questions are already getting on her nerves. Or striking a nerve. All the more reason to keep pushing.

'Do you know what became of him?'

Our exchange is interrupted by the waitress bringing our drinks.

Sophia pours a tear of milk into her tea. 'No idea. Juan went cold on Anna as soon as he found out she was pregnant. She wanted to keep the baby. He didn't. She tried to change his mind right up until she gave birth, but he took off without ever acknowledging Gustav.'

'What did he do for a living?'

'He was a photographer with no talent. He vanished without a trace and never came back asking for anything, which surprised me.'

'Why was it surprising?'

Sophia dips a spoon into her teacup and stirs a vertical line before returning it to the saucer. 'One word: venality,' she replies, raising the cup to her lips. 'I thought he was motivated by money, but I was wrong. When he took off, he said he was going back home; I'm sure that's what he must have done.'

'Did Anna have any other men in her life?'

Sophia closes her eyes and nods slowly. The armour is coming off. We're talking mother to mother again.

'Too many. Far too many.'

'Did some relationships last more than others? I'm trying to get a sense of whether one of them might have been a father figure for Gustav.'

Sophia smiles. 'Unfortunately not. Or rather, fortunately, I should say, because none of them would have been an example to follow.'

'So, Gustav grew up without a male role model. Unless your husband or your sons stepped in to fill those shoes?'

'My husband had a hard enough time being a father to his own children. His involvement only went as far as passing on the Hellström family name. He had no interest in being a grandfather, either.'

'And Anna wasn't close to her siblings?'

'Anna was always a little ... difficult. She was my youngest. The only girl. And she caused me more grief than my three sons combined. And no, she never got along with them. There's no doubt they used to gang up on her – she complained often enough about that – but the main issue was she was so different from them. Like chalk and cheese. I tried and failed to get them to bond. I suppose I didn't try hard enough. The only person she got along with was her grandfather – my father, Rasmus. They were extremely attached to one another. Overly so, I think. They used to go fishing, walking and golfing together, and they used to read together. My father even dedicated poems to her. Anna was devastated by his death.'

'How old was Anna when he died?'

'Nineteen.' Sophia twirls her cup in the saucer.

I have to resist the urge to place a comforting hand on hers to sponge away some of her pain. I can't relate to her feelings of distance and failure. We only had Alice, and my life was woven together with hers. If it hadn't been, I'm sure I would have seen myself as a bad mother. A failed mother.

'I could do nothing right with Anna,' Sophia continues, looking down at her tea. 'Nothing at all. No matter how I tried to connect with her, nothing worked. I felt I irritated her just by breathing. But everything changed when Gustav was accused of murder. She found herself, so to speak.'

She closes her eyes and shakes her head.

'Saying it like that makes it sound more inhuman than it actually was. What I mean is that Anna found ... well, I suppose you could call it a vocation, a path to follow, a *raison d'être*. She moved mountains to try to prove the innocence of her only son, with the kind of energy and determination I'd never seen in her before. I paid all the legal bills, of course. But she did everything else and, as you know, the whole affair lasted more than twenty years.'

An image of Anna flashes into my mind – a photo of her from Gustav's trial that was printed in the papers when they reported her suicide. A woman who looked much younger than her forty-two years, with all of her mother's watery-blue gaze but none of her strength. The woman in that photo was a world away from the woman who died – with short grey hair, frumpy clothes and a body thickened by time. With every word Sophia says, everything she explains, those photos come to life and Anna takes shape in my mind. A version of her, drawn by her mother. A clear, but brutal portrait.

I cup my lukewarm coffee in my hands.

'I gather from what you're saying that Anna only really took care of her son when he was at risk of being taken away from her.'

Sophia tilts her head to one side and frowns. 'She would

alternate between phases of love for Gustav and complete disinterest.'

'Depending on her romantic ups and downs?'

'Yes, I suppose so. Whenever a man walked out the door, she would latch on to Gustav. Then as soon as another lover came on the scene, she would push him away.'

'Was she ever diagnosed with any kind of bipolar disorder?'

'Are you talking about manic depression?'

'I'm wondering if she had some sort of mood disorder, yes.'

'I don't know. Perhaps.'

Sophia takes another sip of tea. I can tell she's keen to bring this interrogation to an end. Because that's what it is really – even though she's here for a spa day at a beachside resort, not in an interview suite down at the station. Her answers are helping me to get a sense of Gustav, though. Because before we grow into who we are, we begin life as someone's child.

'How did Anna earn a living?'

'I earned it for her. I tried to bring her on board with various projects at Akerman Editions, but she always found a way to weasel her way out of staying: the team didn't like her, the project had no potential, she couldn't see herself doing the job I'd assigned her ... I could go on. She never lasted more than six months in a position. So I ended up paying my daughter to do nothing.'

'And Gustav, what kind of a boy was he?'

'He was everything he could be with a mother like Anna. He had nannies to look after him during his early childhood. Here, it's not like England, where that's quite common. In Sweden, parents find a way to make things work so they can pick up their offspring from school. Materially, Gustav wanted for nothing. I made sure that he and his mother had everything they needed. But he must have been lacking what really mattered: his mother's love – and ours too, I suppose.' Sophia pulls the dressing gown around her chest as if she's feeling cold.

'Did Gustav have any hobbies or passions?'

'He played hockey. He excelled at that, actually.'

'Did he play football, too?' I ask, thinking about Daniel and Roland, even though the chance of there being a connection on that level seems slim.

'Not to my knowledge, no.'

'Did he have a short temper? Was he violent?'

Sophia shrugs her shoulders and wraps her crooked fingers around her teacup. 'I think temperamental would be a better word. Gustav was averse to putting in effort. He never did more than he had to, even when it came to ice hockey. I wouldn't say he was violent, though.'

'Sophia, why was it you wouldn't defend him? Why did you never believe in his innocence?'

'The evidence. It was damning and undeniable. And the fact that no one had ever said no to him. Jenny was the first to resist. To stand up to him. And that was something he just couldn't handle, I figured.'

I give myself a second to breathe and savour my coffee before I ask the most uncomfortable question of all.

'What do you blame yourself for, Sophia?'

A smile stretches her lips, crinkling the corners of her mouth and lifting her cheeks.

'You take a hard line with your questions, Detective,' she replies, glaring daggers at me. 'What I blame myself for, since you ask, is wanting to save our name. I blame myself for sacrificing my grandson and my daughter at the altar of my success. Ultimately, I think I just wanted to rip out that chapter of my story. It was tarnishing our family, our heritage, our legacy. I was angry.' She nods her head. 'My daughter was the one slinging the mud. And it stuck to us all, our ancestors and heirs included.'

'You said you had never crossed paths with the Brinks, but I imagine that won't be the case with the Linds. Do you know Esther and her family at all?'

Sophia sways from side to side in her chair, as a cover of Edith

Piaf's 'La Foule' meanders through the speakers. It's almost like she's dancing.

'I know Esther only very superficially, because she runs my island and our paths have crossed on various occasions in the last few years. But our conversations have always been polite and conventional.'

'What about her husband and their sons?'

'Her sons I don't know at all. Her husband, only by reputation. He's had an impressive career in finance. For a long time he managed acquisitions for Deutsche Bank in London, before returning to Sweden and starting his own business. That's all I really know. I know nothing about their relationship or their family. And I won't risk making any assumptions,' she says, sweeping the air with the back of her hand.

I sip the last few drops of my coffee and can't help but wince. It's gone cold.

'Wait, let me get you another one,' Sophia intervenes.

Before I have time to protest, she raises her arm and motions to the waitress to bring me a fresh cup.

Then turning her attention back to me, she asks, 'Are you making progress with your enquiries, Maïa?'

'Yes. I am.'

'And what's your ... gut feeling?'

The expression brings a smile to my lips. Feelings are the worst thing to bring into an investigation, but here, a feeling is all I have to go on. I don't have any proof for what I'm about to suggest, but I'm certain I'm right. Once again, I admire Sophia's finesse. I admire this woman who draws people like a magnet or strikes fear into them, or perhaps both at the same time.

'My gut feeling is that the murders of Jenny Dalenius, Daniel Brink and Roland Lind are connected. How, I don't know, but I still have plenty of stones left to turn over.'

29
Maïa

It's a glorious morning. Not a breath of wind, and the sun is rising in a pale-blue cloudless sky. Christian has suggested we meet at the Sticklinge golf club to go cross-country skiing. It'll be my first outing of the season. That's one Swedish thing I'm good at, at least: skiing, in all its shapes and forms. It's the best way for me to avoid feeling the biting cold.

After some terrible insomnia, I woke up feeling like I had a hangover. I haven't spoken to Ebbe since I refused to go to Paris and mourn Alice, and I spent the night replaying an idealised version of our marriage in my mind – a quarter of a century, of which nothing but memories remain. No, I should count the time in years, really. Using the century as a unit of measurement is a bit dramatic. I miss Ebbe so much – or maybe it's more our relationship I miss. I wonder how long I'll carry him with me, inside me like this, as if we're both living in my body.

'Come on, Grandma, chop, chop,' Christian teases me.

'Grandma's going to wipe the floor with you, you'll see.'

I step up the pace, revelling in the burning feeling that's spreading through my calves and thighs. The golf course is criss-crossed by ski tracks. We're not the only ones out here. So far, we've crossed paths with a few silver-haired folks and a couple of parents pulling a sled bearing their sleeping offspring bundled up in an insulated cocoon.

'So, are you getting anywhere?' he asks me.

'Oh, you're such a bloody Viking! Give it a rest, will you?'

'Easy there, Grandma. I'm talking about the investigation.' A dog comes bounding over and sits down right in front of us, tongue hanging out, forcing us to stop. It rolls around in the snow with a sniff and a snort, before running to its master, who's calling the dog back with a whistle.

'I'm making progress, but not as much as I'd like,' I reply, picking up the pace again. 'I spent all evening combing social media to get an idea of the victimology for Daniel and Roland.'

'And?'

'And they were two very different boys. Not just in terms of their sexuality, but also their interests.'

'Wouldn't you normally start with what they had in common?'

'They were both the same age. They both lived in Lidingö, but not in the same area. They both went to the Hersby high school. They both played football. But Roland Lind didn't like it, whereas Daniel Brink was mad about the sport. He coached little kids. And, in the last few weeks before they died, they both seemed preoccupied and depressed. There's another thing as well. It's not something they had in common, but something similar they did. Daniel had a secret rendezvous – or rather, he had to go somewhere and kept it a secret. And Roland took off with his parents' boat, more than likely for the same reason.'

'Is that a fact or an assumption?' Christian asks, slowing his stride.

'More a hypothesis. We don't know where those two boys went. To meet their killer, I'd say, but that's an assumption too.'

'Well at least you won't need to do any geographic profiling.'

'I'd need three more victims for that. But yes, a pattern does seem to be emerging. Our killer lives or works on the island. Or has another kind of connection to it. That doesn't exactly shorten the list of suspects, though.'

'Do you think these killings could be linked to the murder of Jenny Dalenius?'

'Yes, I do. All three victims were dressed as Saint Lucia, but all three were missing the red sash. And Daniel's body was found in the same woods as Jenny's.'

'But not in exactly the same place.'

'No, not in the same spot.' Grasping both ski poles in my left hand, I swing my backpack across my chest and pull out my water bottle to take a long, icy drink that sends shivers to my ears.

'And has any of this shed more light on Jenny – our victim zero, if we can call her that?'

'I'm not sure we can,' I reply, slinging the backpack over my shoulders again. 'Her brother still firmly believes that Gustav Hellström was guilty.'

'What does the rest of the family say?'

'Jenny's father is the only one left. He remarried and went to live abroad.'

'Maybe someone out there thinks Hellström wasn't the killer?'

'Maybe, but where do Daniel and Roland fit into the picture? They weren't even born when Jenny died.'

Then it suddenly dawns on me.

'Bloody hell,' I say between my teeth.

'What's wrong?'

'My brain's a pile of mush, that's what's wrong. I'm such a bloody idiot.'

'Stop beating yourself up and tell me what you've obviously just realised.'

'Jenny Dalenius and Gustav Hellström were born in 1983. Esther Lind, Roland's mother – the mayor – grew up in Lidingö, and she was born in 1982. They must have known each other.'

30
Aleks

Esther Lind opens the door and stands there for a few seconds without speaking.

'Sorry, I completely forgot you were coming,' she eventually says, smoothing a hand through her impeccable hair, as if to tame some unruly strands. 'Just let me run upstairs and see Sixten. I'll be back down in a minute.'

'No problem, I can wait.'

I make my own way down the hallway and into the living room, where I find Birgitta sitting on the sofa, laptop on her knees. A second later, Peter barges in, carrying two steaming mugs.

Their greetings of '*hej*' overlap. Birgitta closes her laptop and gets up to give me a quick hug. I notice she isn't wearing the same clothes as yesterday and find myself wondering if she came home to pick up some things or if she keeps a change of clothes here.

'I'll leave you to it,' she whispers.

I resist the urge to take her in my arms and hold her tight. I'm not sure where it's come from, either, because this really isn't the time and neither of us are keen on public displays of affection.

She disappears down the hallway.

'Would you like a coffee, too?' Peter asks me.

'I'd love one, thanks,' I reply, sitting down in Birgitta's place.

'With milk?'

'No, thank you.'

Sounds of a hushed conversation float through from the kitchen before Peter comes back and hands me a mug of my own. Then my mobile rings.

It's Maïa. I decide to let it ring. I'll call her back later.

But then a message from Alvid catches my eye: as we suspected, the only DNA he found on the boat belonged to the Lind family.

I'm about to pocket my phone when a message notification from Maïa flashes up on the screen. I open it, and it takes me a few seconds to grasp what she's suggesting.

The parquet floor creaks, announcing Esther's arrival.

'Where is he?' Peter asks. I assume he's referring to Sixten.

'In our bed.'

'What's he doing?'

'He doesn't want to watch TV. He's on his iPad. Playing Minecraft online.'

Peter nods silently before bringing his coffee to his lips. Esther sits down beside him, but leaves the last mug on the coffee table untouched.

'Esther, you grew up in Lidingö, didn't you?' I ask.

'Yes, why?'

'Did you know Jenny Dalenius?'

She blinks. 'Not intimately, but I knew who she was, yes.'

'You were at the Hersby high school together?'

'Yes.'

'And Gustav Hellström?'

'Yes, he was there too.'

'Did you know him?'

'Yes. Who didn't know the Akermans' grandson?' Esther clasps her hands and places them in her lap.

'Were you at the Saint Lucia's Day concert on the evening Jenny died?'

'Yes, I was in the procession. I was part of Saint Lucia's entourage.'

'And you were also at the party Gustav hosted that night?'

'No, I was a year older than them. I wasn't part of their crowd.'

'Is there anything at all about Jenny, Gustav or that night that you might not have told anyone at the time?'

She shakes her head vigorously. 'No, no, of course not.'

'What about you, Peter?'

'I was studying in London that year. And before that, I didn't live in Lidingö. I grew up in Djursholm.'

'Why all these questions?' Esther asks. 'Do ... do you think Jenny's murder and Roland's are connected?'

'We don't know yet. We're looking into the possibility ... Do either of you know Erik Brink, Daniel's father?'

'You've already asked us that question, and the answer was no.' Esther's losing patience. 'Our paths have never crossed.'

I keep the pressure on, because I don't want to give her a chance to pull herself together. 'How was Roland doing, these past few weeks?'

Esther releases a deep sigh, then crosses her legs and shrugs her shoulders. 'The same as usual.'

'Would you agree, Peter?'

'Yes ... no, nothing was different.'

'Why do you ask?' Esther adds.

'His boyfriend told me he seemed sad and troubled.'

'Really? Did he say why?'

'Apparently, it was something to do with you.'

Esther's eyes widen. 'With me? How so?'

I let the silence linger for a moment, watching her body tense with surprise.

Meanwhile, beside her, Peter sits rubbing his wrinkled forehead with his fingers.

'Roland had found out something serious about you, Esther. Something that could have ended your career.'

Esther's lips begin to quiver. 'What?'

'Do you have any idea what he meant by that?'

She shakes her head. 'No, not a clue.'

'It was something serious enough to warrant a prison sentence, I'm told.'

'Prison? But what ... whatever could he have been talking about? Is that all you know?'

'I was hoping you could enlighten me.'

Esther shakes her head once more, cupping a hand over her mouth. 'I don't understand,' she says, pulling it away again. 'If it was something that serious, Roland would have said something to me. This doesn't make any sense, Aleksander.'

'I'm going to need access to your correspondence and all your messages from the last three months, Esther.'

'Good grief, Aleks, that'll be thousands of emails and letters.'

'Yes, I imagine so.'

'Why? Are you looking for someone who might want to cause me harm? Someone who's threatening me?'

'We're looking for connections. Between Daniel Brink and Roland, and between that family and yours. We're trying to understand what the killer's trying to say – or prove.'

Peter looks at his wife. 'To stop him before he strikes again,' he murmurs.

31
Maïa

The day has come. It's 13 December. Saint Lucia's Day.

The church on the island, a lime-washed building made of stone dating back to the seventeenth century, surrounded by a cemetery of the same vintage, stands at the heart of Lidingö.

I arrived early to save a seat for Christian. I've found a spot for us in the third row from the front – the first one that wasn't reserved – and on the aisle, so we'll have a good view of the procession.

The police, myself included, were expecting islanders and rubberneckers to turn out in their droves for this celebration, which, one way or another, is caught up in two, possibly three murders. Curiosity always gets the better of fear.

We were right: the church is now full to capacity. Not everyone is lucky enough to find a seat. There's a crowd at the back, jammed between the holy-water fonts and the door, standing like a silent choir. Some voices spoke out against the event going ahead, but the mayor's office decided not to give in to terror and to honour the age-old tradition.

Aleksander arrives a few minutes before the festivities begin. The girl with him and his wife must be Alba, their youngest, because I know Iris is in the procession this evening.

Esther Lind is here too, in the front row. Aleksander, Birgitta and Alba sit down just behind her.

I wonder how this woman, this mother, has mustered the strength to come here, and how she's going to be able to sit in that pew and watch her son's classmates celebrate the year that's ending without him. As if his absence hasn't changed everything. As if

Roland isn't dead. As if the world has just kept on turning, stepping on over his body.

Suddenly, there's a clacking sound, followed by a creak as the church doors swing open. The assembly turns to see. A young woman with long, wavy, brown hair appears in the doorway, dressed in a traditional white tunic, tied with a wide, red-satin sash. She's wearing a crown of foliage adorned with five candles and carrying another in a golden candle holder. Her serene face, filled with emotion and pride, flickers in the light of the flame. She's looking for familiar faces in the crowd, likely her parents. Her smile widens when she sees Aleksander, who beams at her in return. But Birgitta, distracted by a discussion with Esther, misses the moment.

Iris Storm is followed by a procession of around twenty teenagers in tunics, all carrying candles of their own. The girls are wearing silver crowns and the boys, tall, pointed, white hats.

There are three sharp knocks, and as the sound of the last echoes around the church walls, the choir finds its voice and the purest of songs fills the church like the faintest of breaths, from the cast-iron floor grilles to the vaulted ceiling.

These voices shake me to the core, as if I'm riding a roller coaster. But something about them galvanises me, too. They're flooding me with feelings I have lost since Alice died. My heart is vibrating to the sound of the song and the shimmers of light from the halos that make everything they touch sparkle – every face, every white tunic, every glimmer of gold, even the green-marble altar.

I close my eyes and feel Christian's warm hand clamping over mine. He gives it a squeeze to tell me he understands, and he's here for me.

The procession advances slowly down the aisle and takes up position in the chancel, around Iris. Aleksander only has eyes for his daughter. The smile on his lips is seemingly eternal. It reminds me of how Ebbe used to look at Alice.

Suddenly, the voices hush and the priest begins to speak, bursting the magic of the moment like a bubble.

My thoughts turn to Jenny Dalenius. What intense joy she must have felt here, in this church, mere hours before her death, singing back the light. What pride, too, having been chosen to embody the tradition.

And then, something terrifying occurs to me: the killer could strike again tonight. The evening of 13 December is an obvious time to celebrate Jenny – or mark her death in a more sinister way. The boys on the island are not the only ones in danger.

As soon as the crowd begins to file out of the church, I lead Christian over to the Storms.

Aleksander smiles when he sees me coming. It takes Birgitta a few seconds to recognise me, but then she beams as generously as she did the first time we met on her doorstep. I force myself to return some semblance of a smile.

'Dr Bergvall,' Aleks says, shaking Christian's hand. 'It's been a while. At least five or six years, no?'

'Really? That long?' Christian sounds surprised.

'Ah, the price of fame,' Aleksander replies, giving him a wink. 'Interpol's a cut above the cop shop in Stockholm, I gather.'

Christian smiles politely.

'This is my wife, Birgitta.'

They exchange a courteous nod.

'Your daughter was fabulous,' Christian says.

'Oh yes,' I add, 'Iris was amazing. What a voice she has!'

Birgitta gives me a look of pride, which quickly fades as she notices something, or someone, behind me.

'I agree, but I'm a bit biased,' Aleksander laughs.

'Please excuse me,' Birgitta says without warning, and walks away.

Aleksander follows his wife with his gaze before turning back to me.

'Do you have a minute?' I ask him, without further ado.

'Yes, of course.'

'I'll wait for you outside,' Christian says to me. 'Commissioner, it was a pleasure,' he adds, before weaving his way through the crowd.

'I wasn't aware you knew Bergvall,' Aleksander says. 'Did you work together at Interpol?'

'No, he's a friend of the family. Listen,' I murmur, in a hurry to share my fears, 'you might think this is a bit of a stretch, but I was thinking, Iris was Saint Lucia this evening and...'

A fleeting smile crosses his face.

Of course, I should have guessed. Aleksander won't leave anything to chance, either. Especially not when it comes to his daughter.

'I know. Don't worry, Iris is not going anywhere tonight. She's staying at home with me.'

32
Aleks

It's half past six in the morning and the sky is as dark as a wall covered in soot.

I barely slept a wink, anxious that I'd get a call announcing the next victim. I don't know how many times I got out of bed to check that Iris was still there, sleeping peacefully, and that no one had snatched her away from me.

Birgitta comes into the bathroom as I'm about to step into the shower.

'Do you have a minute?' she asks me.

She's wearing her turquoise suit and her lips are painted blood red. She's sublime.

Suddenly, I yearn to go back to the time when she would join me in the shower. The time when seeing me naked would fuel her desire for the pleasure of making love between the raindrops, as she used to say.

I turn the tap off and sit on the edge of the bathtub, wincing at the cold enamel against my skin.

Birgitta leans against the sink and tucks a strand of hair behind her ear to keep it from falling across her eyes. She stares at the floor, trying to find her words.

'Do you...' She pauses, stands up straight. 'Do you really think that Roland's death is connected to the murder of Jenny Dalenius?'

'I don't know,' I reply, shaking my head gently.

'Are you planning to tell the media that Esther and Jenny knew each other?'

'No, not at this point.'

She nods, but doesn't say another word. She's still avoiding my gaze, averting her eyes from my naked body.

'What do you have against Esther?' she suddenly asks me.

'Against her? I have nothing against her. What are you talking about?'

'What do you know and what haven't you told us?'

Us. Her choice of word doesn't escape me. But then I think about how I use the same words when I'm talking about the investigation. *Us. We.*

'What do you mean, exactly?'

'That thing Roland is supposed to have told his boyfriend about. The secret that could end Esther's career.'

'I don't know any more than you do, that's why I asked Esther about it. I thought she might have an inkling about what her son had discovered.'

My wife blinks, ever so slowly.

'What's wrong, *min älskling*?'

Her shoulders lift as she releases a silent sigh. 'I have to tell you something,' she says, lowering her gaze.

I wonder what she's about to reveal, and suddenly I feel more naked in front of my wife than I ever have.

'It's about Esther and Peter.'

She pauses, twists her watch strap around her wrist, then flits her eyes briefly over my nudity, before looking away and blinking repeatedly, as if to erase this image of me.

I wrap a towel around my waist, then sit back down on the edge of the bathtub.

She doesn't protest.

'They have a somewhat ... unconventional arrangement,' she says. 'It's very honest, but out of the ordinary.' She opens her mouth, closes it again, stands up straight. 'Esther and Peter ... they practise free love.'

Now it's my turn to tense up. I don't know what I was expecting, but it wasn't this.

'You mean, they each ... do their own thing in bed with other people?'

'More or less, yes. Well, it's mostly Peter,' she continues, gazing into the void. 'But with Esther's consent.'

'So he's not faithful, but she is?'

'Well, the notion of fidelity doesn't extend to their sex life. They're a happy couple, but they're not ... sexually exclusive.'

'So they raise their family together, but they don't sleep together? Or maybe they do from time to time, but obviously not the way they should, because otherwise they wouldn't go looking elsewhere.'

Birgitta opens her mouth again, then clamps it shut.

'And what about Esther, does she have any designated lovers?'

'Neither of them have "designated lovers", as you put it, Aleks.'

I wonder why she hasn't said anything about this before now. Why she hasn't shared this secret with me. We would have talked about it. We would have pretended not to judge them. But we still would have. And would have laughed about it.

'Why did you keep this from me?' The question slips out in spite of myself.

Birgitta bites her lip, smudging the red lipstick. 'Because it's private. It's not my life, it's theirs.'

'Still, you were in the loop.'

'Yes, because I'm supposed to be a buffer for them, Aleks. If I'm not in the loop, how can I fend off the attacks?'

She's still looking at me without seeing me. I'd almost rather she left.

'You do understand that we're going to have to do some digging around this,' I say.

'Yes, I know.'

'And you know what a devastating effect it could have on Esther's career, if the press gets wind of it.'

'Not necessarily.'

I sneer. 'Not necessarily? How very optimistic of you.'

'Plenty of couples lead lives like this without talking about "free love", Aleks.'

'Alright, I see what you're saying. Not everyone who opens their relationship opens it the same way. And I don't suppose they shout about it from the rooftops, either. But far be it from me to tell you how to do your job ... So anyway, all that to say, you were wondering if Roland had found out about their little arrangement, were you?'

My wife nods and purses her lips.

'Birgitta, there's nothing illegal about this situation. Some might find it immoral – myself included – but it's not against the law. So, you think that Roland might have seen Esther with her lover, whoever was flavour of the month, is that it? Maybe a lover who wasn't of legal age?'

'I don't know, Aleks,' she says, shaking her head, staring at her flesh-coloured tights. 'I just thought ... I didn't want you hearing about it from someone other than me.'

I nod. No words of thanks come to me. My phone starts ringing. It's on the edge of the sink, just behind her.

'I'll leave you to it,' she says, casting me a glance.

She turns to leave, then changes her mind and comes back towards me. She gives me a chaste peck on the lips and walks out of the bathroom.

I pick up the phone.

'We have a third one,' Alvid announces on the other end of the line.

33
Aleks

At five o'clock this morning, in the north-west suburbs of Stockholm, two medical interns were heading home after their shift in the emergency department at Karolinska Hospital, when, walking through the Solna churchyard, they noticed a person in a white coat lying on the ground on one of the paths. They hurried to help, but it turned out to be a dead body lying there, dressed in a Saint Lucia tunic, skull caved in and topped with a crown of candles.

It's already past eight by the time I get to the station.

The stench of death clings to me as I walk into the incident room. I'm desperate to wash it off, to wipe away the horror, but I haven't had the chance.

My team greets me with a solemn silence that feels like a punch in the gut. Or maybe it's the lack of sleep and the brutal awakening that's making me sick to my stomach. Some are sitting in their chairs, others leaning against their desks, iPads or notebooks in hand. Siv's standing at the far end of the open-plan space, by the corridor that leads to the interview suites. This is a first: she never usually joins in our investigation briefings. But nothing in this case surprises me anymore.

'Right,' I say, putting my cup of coffee on my desk. 'This time, we didn't have to look very far to ID the victim. He was found with his rucksack on his back and his work badge around his neck. We're looking at Mikkel Martinsson, forty-four years old, cardiac surgeon at Karolinska.'

'Bloody hell, forty-four?' says Jasmine, one of the detectives, stretching out the vowels in a thick *Skåne* accent that betrays her roots in the south of the country.

I give her a weary nod. 'Before you ask, the two interns who found him were on shift from six in the evening to four-thirty in the morning, without a break. They were busy treating the crash victims from the pile-up on the E20, so they're not in the frame at all.'

I take a sip of coffee and continue.

'Mikkel Martinsson was single and had no children. He lived in Stockholm, near Odenplan, less than twenty minutes' walk from Karolinska Hospital, where he worked. His colleagues told me he came to work on foot every day, whatever the weather. Last night, he saw his last patient at eight-thirty, before discussing a number of cases with the group of interns he was supervising. He left the premises at two minutes past ten, as confirmed by the CCTV at the entrance to the cardiology unit and the system that scanned his badge. He should have headed south from the hospital if he was going home. But instead, his body was found to the north-west, which suggests he may have been meeting someone.'

'Are we sure we're not dealing with a copycat? Because going from killing teenage boys to a man three times their age is a bit of a stretch,' Jon, another detective, says, scratching at the beanie on his bald head.

'Forensics are analysing the tunic and the crown as we speak. But I can tell you that the tunic was slit all the way down the back, like it was for Daniel and Roland, and that's not a detail we've shared with the public. Paola's already elbows deep in the autopsy. We'll know more about the murder weapon and time of death as the day goes on.'

'Has his phone been found?' Jasmine asks.

'No, just like with the others, there's no sign of the victim's phone.'

'What's the obsession? Doesn't the killer know that practically everything is in the cloud?'

'Like you say, *practically* everything, but not everyone has enough cloud storage to back everything up. And it's easier to keep track of some things, like private conversations or chat history, if you store them locally on the device.'

Jasmine nods and crosses her thin forearms tattooed with philosophy by Dante, Bob Dylan and Eleanor Roosevelt.

'So, we're going to start by searching our victims' virtual lives,' I say. 'Browsing history, emails, whatever else is in the cloud. I've also asked the mayor to give us access to her public correspondence from the last three months. That's going to be a lot to sift through.'

In the corner of my eye, I notice Siv leaving the room, phone pressed to her ear.

'I can take care of pulling footage from surveillance cameras,' Jon suggests.

'Perfect. There are quite a few near the hospital and in the churchyard. Maybe we'll get lucky.'

'Jasmine, you go to Martinsson's place. Karina's there already. I'll see you there a bit later.'

'What about social media?' she asks, wrapping her thick scarf around her neck.

'I'll take care of that.'

I pick up my coffee, then put it down again.

'I know this isn't what you all want to hear, but we're going to take everything apart. It's going to be painstaking work – a mammoth task – but that's the only thing we can do at this point. We have to go back to the drawing board. Forget whatever theories we had, forget that our first two victims shared a similar profile, and focus on finding the connection between all three of them. Because there has to be a connection.'

34
Aleks

Mikkel Martinsson's place turns out to be the penthouse suite on the fourth floor of an apartment building in the Vasastan area, north of the city centre.

Ignoring the tiredness in my legs, I bypass the lift and take the stairs – out of habit and sheer athletic masochism.

The only door to the fourth floor has no handle and requires a key to open it. I knock a few times, and Jasmine comes to let me in. She stands to one side as I walk past her, then shuts the door behind us.

I can see a uniform, with their back to me, kneeling in front of the cupboards of an open-plan kitchen with a huge, white marble work surface, topped only by a Nespresso machine and a kettle.

'*Hej*, Commissioner!' the sergeant calls. I know him, I just can't remember his name.

I give him a wave in return.

'Karina's not here?' I ask Jasmine.

'Er ... no, she wasn't feeling well. She went home. Hassan came to take her place.'

'Alright. Just let me know next time, OK?'

'Yes, of course. Sorry.'

The apartment, long and fairly narrow, is set up like a loft: no walls, just furniture, shelving units and bookcases to separate the living spaces. Even the bathroom, at the south end, if my bearings are right, is completely open. The walk-in shower is separated from the bedroom only by a low partition of glass blocks.

Jasmine winces. 'From his bed, he can watch whoever he brings home taking a shower. Thank God the toilet has a door,' she adds, pointing to the only private space inside the apartment, which faces the shower. 'I could never live in a place like this.'

'Don't worry, you couldn't afford to anyway,' Hassan says jokingly, closing a cupboard door. 'Look at this view, boss,' he adds, pointing to a series of floor-to-ceiling windows.

In spite of the grey sky and low cloud, they seem to flood the apartment with light, as well as offering a breathtaking view over the rooftops and a tree-lined square below.

'With or without the view, it's still a voyeur's apartment,' Jasmine replies.

I let my eyes wander over the string of living spaces and the deep sofa oriented towards the Stockholm skyline – not the TV, the way most people would set it up.

'What have you found?'

'Hassan has been going through the kitchen. I've been focusing on the bedroom and the walk-in wardrobe.'

'No, I mean, have you found anything to confirm that he was a voyeur? Or is that a judgement you've made?'

Jasmine lowers her eyes and slowly hunches her shoulders.

'That wasn't a reproach, Jasmine, and it wasn't a trap, either. It was a genuine question. When I look at this apartment, I see a pleasant, generously proportioned, light-filled space. So what jumps out at you when you look around it?'

'I just think it's … weird … the open shower. It makes me feel uncomfortable.'

'Anything else?'

She shakes her head and her ponytail sways lazily across her back. 'No, nothing in particular. I just … It's just a feeling, that's all. I didn't find anything out of the ordinary. Nothing kinky, nothing bizarre. Mikkel Martinsson was a connoisseur of cheese, charcuterie and cigars, judging by the contents of his fridge. Not exactly the best example for a heart specialist to set, if you ask me. Anyway…'

'And his computer?'

'It was on the table in the lounge. I put it in an evidence bag. I bagged the charger, too. That was plugged in under the desk. Do you want to see those now?'

'No, I'm going to have a look at the lounge and then the office area.'

'That's on the other side of the kitchen, behind the bookcase. But it's all pretty minimalist – there's not much to see.'

'OK, thanks.'

I walk through the loft and stand in front of the glass bookcase, which must have been custom-made to marry with the sloping ceiling. It contains hundreds of books, most of which seem to be about cardiology and cardiac surgery. The rest are an eclectic mix of old encyclopaedias, cookbooks, novels and nonfiction in various languages. Nothing unusual.

I move around to the other side of the bookcase and find a desk accompanied by a storage unit with two drawers. The desk is a simple surface made from the same frosted glass as the bookcase. On it, there's a jar of pens, a few copies of *Båtliv*, the boating magazine Birgitta subscribes to, a copy of the *Financial Times* dated last weekend, a ramekin filled with peanuts and raisins, and a mug containing dregs of coffee.

I look around me and call out to whoever's listening, 'Does anyone have a pair of gloves?'

'Wait a sec, I'll get you some,' Jasmine replies.

She comes out of the bathroom and walks over to the entryway to fetch a pair of latex gloves. She hands them to me before returning to the other end of the apartment.

I pull the gloves on and open the top drawer of the unit. It's filled with hanging file folders containing various bills. The second drawer is no different to the first. I remove all the folders and place them on the desk, to go into evidence bags later.

The desk sits against a wall, which is bare – like all the others in the apartment – and illuminated only by two sconces.

Jasmine and Hassan are heading into the bathroom as I enter the lounge. I sit down on the sofa. In front of me is a coffee table made of dark wood streaked with a lighter grain, which looks to be about a metre and a half square. On it are two hardcover books and another bowl of peanuts and raisins.

To my right is a long sideboard made from the same wood as the coffee table. On the surface is a leather tray containing several bottles of alcohol – whisky, port, rum and a Japanese gin I'd be more than happy to sample – as well as a pile of three hardcover books from the same collection as those on the coffee table and a lamp with a white marble base and grey fabric shade.

Looking around, I realise there's nothing ornamental in this home. No photos, no paintings, no candles or candle holders. Nothing besides these books, which, judging by their titles, seem to be more surface than substance. The titles on the spines of those on the coffee table are *A Dog's Life* and *A Cat's Life*, while those on the sideboard are *Life*, *My Planet* and *Sunny Days*.

I lean forwards and reach for the top one, *A Dog's Life*, hoping the content is more about life and less about dogs. As I slide it towards me, I realise it's not actually a book – it's a box. I open it and find a binder with black pages, all of which are empty: a photo album. *A Cat's Life* reveals the same thing. I get up to fetch the box titled *Life* from the sideboard. The album inside this one reveals a white envelope, around ten centimetres by five, affixed to the centre of one of the card pages by four photo corners.

Jasmine comes over to join me. 'What is it?' she asks.

'No idea.'

I detach the envelope. On the page behind it, I see that something has been handwritten in white marker:

Geetha – 2 June 22

Long – shoulder

Amber

The flap of the envelope is not sealed.

I open it.

It contains two small, rectangular pouches made of translucent paper.

'Oh, shit,' Jasmine whispers, seeing a dark mass of something inside.

Gently, I pinch the edges of one of the pouches together. It opens like a mouth. A mouth full of black hairs.

V

Today, I heard something so surreal I had to wonder if it was someone's idea of a joke.

'To minimise the risk of assault: one, avoid wearing heels you can't run in. Two, place a pair of men's shoes outside your door. Three, never wear your hair in a ponytail – it's too easy to grab. Four, put a sign or a sticker at your front door that says Beware of the Dog, even if you don't have one. Five, always carry pepper spray. Six, wear trousers that are difficult to take off.'

As we both know, the vast majority of rape victims – seventy-seven percent, apparently – know their attacker. So, the rapist already knows the victim doesn't have a dog and doesn't have a man in her life – or if she does, he doesn't live with her or he gets home late at night. And what the hell are trousers that are difficult to take off, anyway? What are we supposed to wear? A chastity belt?

I understand that it's about finding solutions, but aren't we approaching the problem the wrong way? Ultimately, who should change the way they behave? The victim or the attacker?

35
Maïa

It's eight in the evening.

I'm at home.

My glass of red wine, an Amarone with a garnet robe, is on the floor beside the cushion I'm sitting on, in the midst of an archipelago of paper-stack islands.

Aleksander is sitting on the sofa facing me. He's telling me about Mikkel Martinsson, the third victim, and what he's discovered. The wine is dancing in his glass, stretching its legs with every twirl, as Aleks gives me the lowdown. It strikes me how good it feels to be here, working with him.

'How many did you find?' I ask him.

'Forty-seven, in all. Forty-seven envelopes. Forty-seven women's names.'

'Each containing several strands of hair from their heads, and some pubic hair?'

'Sometimes just the strands.'

'And always the same information?'

'Yes – systematically: first name, date, hair length and fragrance. At first, I thought the last thing was a colour, but as I opened more envelopes I realised it must be the perfume they were wearing.'

I lean to one side to reach my glass. 'Trichophilia,' I say, taking a quick sip. 'Also known as a hair fetish. I'm sure there must be a word for sexual obsession with pubic hair, too...'

'Indeed there is,' Aleksander replies, suppressing a smile. 'The staff at the station had a field day with this stuff. An attraction to pubic hair is called pubisphi ... no, pubephilia. And get this, the fetishes we tend to hear about most – feet, animals, excrement, you get the picture – are not even the half of it.' He places his empty glass on the floor. 'There are people who get turned on by sunlight, bees and wasps – jeez, good luck with those – or by watching someone fall down the stairs.'

That makes me burst out laughing. The release does me good. It feels like a ray of sunlight, but not in a fetishy way, I should add.

I get up to fetch the bottle from the coffee table, which I've pushed against the wall to make space in the living room.

'Are the autopsy results in yet?' I ask, refilling our glasses, ignoring the insufferable inner voice that's telling me to stop relying on my crutch – my baby bottle, more like.

Aleks nods. 'According to Paola, time of death was no later than midnight. Martinsson left the hospital at two minutes past ten.'

'The same time as the first two victims.'

'Same murder weapon, too?'

'Precisely the same. With an escalation of violence, however: Martinsson took three blows to the head, with a greater degree of force.'

'There must have been CCTV around the hospital, I imagine.'

'Yes, but all the footage shows Martinsson walking alone towards the churchyard. The only cameras in the churchyard are by the church itself, quite a long from the actual scene. So that's a dead end – no pun intended.'

I smile. 'Are you focusing on one aspect in particular, or are you just digging as best you can?'

Aleksander takes a sip of wine before he replies.

'We're digging as best we can. Martinsson's death has completely messed up the patterns we were building of the victims.'

I nod.

He elaborates: 'We've gone from two teenagers, basically the same age, who went to the same high school, lived in Lidingö and played football at the same club, to an adult surgeon in the city who had a hair fetish.'

He certainly has a way of summarising a situation, I think with a smile.

'Do you see any common threads, no matter how tenuous they might seem?'

Aleksander frowns. 'Martinsson had a boating magazine in his apartment, and Roland Lind's family owned a boat. Martinsson had a big purple birthmark on his forearm and Daniel also had a small one on his chest. None of them had children.'

I tilt my head to one side and roll my eyes.

'Well, you did say, no matter how thin a thread,' he says, with a sheepish smile. 'To be honest, no, I really don't see any common threads.'

'How tall was Mikkel Martinsson and what did he weigh?'

'One metre and eighty-eight centimetres, and eighty-five kilos.'

'So, about twenty kilos heavier than Daniel and Roland, which could explain the excessive violence – if the killer was worried about being able to overpower the victim.'

'Perhaps, yes. That hadn't occurred to me. There's nothing to say the killer couldn't be a woman, you know.'

'True, nothing rules that out. People tend to be less suspicious of a woman, too. They generally see men as more of a threat. So it would have been easier for a woman to approach Daniel and Roland.'

I uncross my legs and stretch them out in front of me. I smile to myself at the sight of my hideous moth-eaten wool socks and think how quickly Aleks and I have reached a level of comfort in our working relationship.

'Perhaps Brink and Lind were patients of Martinsson's?' I suggest.

'Good thinking. I'll ask the parents ... What are your thoughts about Martinsson? And that catalogue of women, does it suggest anything to you?'

'The most fascinating thing for me is that his collection was hidden in a box disguised as a book in plain sight in his living room. When he had people over, or brought someone home, he must have got a kick out of knowing his conquests, or his prey – or snippets of them, at least – were right there for them to see, if only they looked. Have you drawn up a list of the names to check against his colleagues? If you ask me, given how many hours a week he spent there, the hospital must have been his hunting ground.'

My gaze lands on the two boxes of archives Aleksander brought over, which are sitting side by side on the coffee table. Archives from the Jenny Dalenius case. I wasn't expecting him to share so generously with me. My colleagues are usually much more territorial. And yet, there's nothing like a pair of fresh eyes on a case to spot new connections. The Interpol flag will always fly over my career, and that's what Aleks will fall back on if he has to justify his initiative with his superiors, whom I very much doubt are in the loop about me. If I'm right, and they're not, I'll appreciate his willingness to bring me on board all the more.

'So, what do you make of all this?' he asks me, holding his glass to his lips.

'I think the killer has a story to tell. There are too many differences between the victims for them to have been chosen at random. In other words, he – or she – had an axe to grind, specifically with Daniel, Roland and Mikkel.'

I pause to contemplate Aleksander and his combed-back hair, like Ebbe's.

'The fact that Mikkel Martinsson was killed on the thirteenth of December – not only Saint Lucia's Day, but also the same day Jenny was killed, makes him the main victim, or at least the most significant. So, if I were leading the investigation, then he, and his place, are where I would focus the search for answers.'

36
Maïa

It was late by the time Aleksander left, and I didn't get to sleep until the early hours. It's always like this when I get involved in a case. I have a hard time disconnecting from the flow of ideas that forge paths, build bridges and spark connections in my mind. I play with the pieces of the puzzle, assembling parts that don't slot together at first glance into what Christian calls a *Kama Sutra* of the mind, to make sure I leave no lead unfollowed and avoid falling into the trap of twisting facts to fit the theory, or theories, I've constructed.

Before he said goodnight, Aleksander suggested that I work on Mikkel Martinsson's profile. I didn't have the heart to tell him I was already planning to do that. Not just because Martinsson was killed on the same night as Jenny, and with a great degree of violence, but also, to be perfectly honest, because I'm intrigued by his peculiar proclivity.

When I wake up, shortly after seven, I make myself comfortable on the sofa, cup of coffee within reach, and set about scouring the web in search of insights about the latest victim. I doubt that the surgeon was the type to share anything online, but I figure some people out there must have an opinion about his life – and death. That's the beauty of social media: people love hiding behind their keyboards and taking advantage of the megaphone effect. Every 'like' is worth oh-so much love.

Aleksander has brought me up to speed with the basics: Martinsson spent his early childhood in the west of Sweden, before moving to Stockholm with his family at the age of twelve, where he continued his education. He never had any ties to

Lidingö, and he was four years older than Gustav and Jenny, anyway. His home paints an accurate picture of the man he was: other than the noble materials he selected to furnish the place – more for comfort and durability than to flaunt his social status, in my opinion – the apartment contains nothing superfluous. Mikkel Martinsson only possessed what he used: the books he read, the plates and cutlery he ate with, the clothes he wore. He wasn't miserly or frugal, but he had a minimalist concept of luxury. His clothes were designer; he bought his charcuterie from Köttkompaniet, an artisan butcher in central Stockholm; and his cheese came from Androuet, a French *fromagerie* in the upscale Östermalm area. No, Mikkel Martinsson wasn't stingy. He was selective. And he led a rich life behind closed doors, a life of fantasy, or rather, fantasising, that revolved around one – no, two things: women's head hair and pubic hair. And if he could afford to leave his most treasured collection – his trichophilia souvenirs – barely hidden in fake books in the middle of his living room, it was likely because he rarely received guests. The absence of a table and chairs has reinforced my intuition. Even his kitchen only had one bar stool. If he brought women home, it wasn't to have dinner with them or to leaf through books.

Martinsson must have taken genuine pleasure from knowing that anyone who set foot in his home would unwittingly be just one spark of curiosity away from discovering his eroticised keepsakes – the trophies not unlike those some serial killers take from their victims to give to their wife or their child. Mementoes that are hidden in plain sight.

Who were these women whose hair ended up in his collection? Patients? Perhaps, but they would have to be patients he'd slept with. I can't picture him going around with a pair of scissors and cutting their hair in the middle of a consultation, or when they were on the operating table – not that he would even have been alone with them during surgery. The image is so absurd, it makes me smile.

I get up from the sofa, make myself another cup of coffee and sit back down again.

Mikkel Martinsson was not active on social media. He only had Facebook, and his last post, related to a cardiology conference in Ottawa, was in 2019. However, there's now an outpouring of messages on his profile page. People have been expressing their condolences, posting photos of themselves with Martinsson, who was, let it be said, a very handsome man.

I start reading the messages, most of which have more emojis than words.

Then suddenly, something catches my eye: an angry-face emoji under a comment praising Martinsson's life.

I click on the comment in question and unroll the thread, selecting the translation option.

You're all hypocrites! someone named Maria Lannister has posted.

A series of reprimands and insults follow – users protesting without really asking Maria Lannister what she's talking about.

Then she adds:

Everyone knows what Martinsson was up to and everyone just keeps their mouth shut. You make me sick.

Elisabeth Von Ahn, the manager of Karolinska Hospital, is waiting for me in a meeting room on the fifth floor of the building. She's accompanied by a man who's a head shorter than her.

Both are wearing black suits and white shirts, and both get up to greet me, although they remain standing behind their chairs at the end of the long conference table.

'Hello, Commissioner,' the manager says, giving me a nod. 'I've asked Dr Torsten Vikman, the head of our Cardiology Department, to join us. He's known Mikkel since he was an intern. Please, do sit down.'

Dr Vikman gives me a forced smile.

They take their seats again, and I sit down across the table from the manager. With their hands joined in prayer on the table, they're almost the mirror image of each other. An uncomfortable silence sets in, and I know I've come knocking at the right door.

'Can you tell me about Mikkel?' I ask, looking at them both in turn. 'Did you know him personally?'

'Torsten?' Elisabeth Von Ahn says, turning to her colleague.

Vikman quickly adjusts his tie and clears his throat. 'Yes, I knew Mikkel well,' he begins. His eyelids are batting so quickly, it looks like his eyes are closed. I wait for a few seconds to go by, but he adds nothing.

'How long had you known him?'

'About twenty years.'

'Did you ever see him outside the hospital?'

'Er ... not really, no.'

'Meaning?'

Torsten sits up straight, then fidgets as if his chair is suddenly uncomfortable. 'We must have played golf once or twice and gone to a few dinners together, but he wasn't part of my circle of friends.'

'And what kind of person was he?'

The doctor's mouth twists into a clownish grimace.

'Was he friendly?' I suggest. 'Personable or ... somewhat reserved?'

'He was ... friendly, yes, and very personable.'

'What kind of doctor was he?'

'He was an excellent doctor.'

'What did his patients think of him?'

He shrugs, as if he doesn't know what to say. 'They were ... satisfied.'

'No complaints about professional misconduct?'

'None whatsoever,' Elisabeth Von Ahn chimes in now, shaking her head.

'What about his relationships with colleagues? Was he well liked?'

'His relationships were excellent,' Vikman replies, sitting tall. 'He was on very good terms with his colleagues.'

'And what about his students? This is a teaching hospital, isn't it? How were things on that front?'

'Good. Very good.'

I lean back in my chair and smile at them both, one after the other. 'Ms Von Ahn, Dr Vikman, I'm not here to recruit Mikkel Martinsson. I'm here to find out who might have hated him enough to bash his head in with a hammer. So, I would greatly appreciate it if you would kindly stop feeding me this sugar-coated and presumably untruthful script, because it's highly unlikely that he never put even a single foot wrong over the course of a twenty-year career.'

Elisabeth Von Ahn releases a discreet sigh and places her palms flat on the table. 'Listen,' she says, staring at her hands as if she's studying all the rings on her fingers, 'Mikkel really was an excellent doctor. He was dedicated and he loved his job. He never counted his hours, he would always stay at the hospital if a patient or his colleagues needed him, and he loved teaching cardiology.'

'But?'

'But his love of innuendo was a bit much,' she mutters.

'What do you mean by that?'

'He liked to play with words and their connotations. Lots of doctors get a kick out of that kind of thing.'

'I know what "innuendo" is. I'd like you to explain what you mean by "a bit much".'

The hospital manager opens her palms to the sky and holds the position for a few seconds. 'He used to make jokes ... with sexual connotations, like a lot of doctors do. But only in jest.'

'Could you give me some examples?'

She turns to Torsten, who's frozen to the spot, eyes glued to his lap, where his hands are almost certainly clasped.

'He would often make remarks about the physical appearance of his colleagues,' she continues. 'Or certain ... gestures.'

'Like?'

'He stroked the hair of one of the women he worked with...' She lowers her eyes. 'And sniffed it. He told her she smelled like ... like sex. But it was just a harmless comment. The intern in question laughed it off.'

I stay silent, trying to find the right words to reply, because the first ones that come to mind are laden with anger – so much anger.

'I know it's hard to wrap your head around, Detective,' she continues, 'but our jobs mean we walk a fine line between life and death so often, we need humour to lighten the atmosphere, so the stress and the pressure of all the responsibility doesn't take its toll. Surely you can see that?'

'I can see that very well, but the kind of humour you seem to think is harmless is not only an abuse of power, but also blatant sexual harassment. And I'm sure you know that sexual harassment is a crime. That's why you've been beating around the bush since I walked in the door. So, I suppose there have been complaints about him.'

'There was one accusation of rape, but the accuser dropped the case.'

The silence that follows is suffocating, as if all the air has been sucked out of the room.

'I find it terribly unfair, Detective,' Von Ahn continues, 'to drag the reputation of Dr Martinsson, and that of our teaching hospital, through the mud for a matter of revenge.'

'Revenge?'

'When Mikkel was cherry-picking interns to work on his team, Anita Vasic didn't make the cut. Right after that – the very next day, in fact – she came to me to accuse him of rape.'

'Do you know what happened to her?'

'She still works here at the hospital, in Cardiology. She's on Dr Vikman's team.'

Elisabeth Von Ahn looks me straight in the eye. She tips her chin at me, lending herself an air of defiance. But I think she's really trying to give credibility to her story.

'If Dr Martinsson did rape her, do you really think she would have carried on working in the same department as him?'

38
Aleks

I knock on the door. Two short, sharp raps.

A young woman in blue scrubs with long, brown hair and a centre parting opens up.

'Anita Vasic?'

'Yes?'

I smile. 'I'm Commissioner Storm. Your colleagues told me I'd find you in the break room. Could I trouble you for a few minutes of your time?'

Her eyes glaze over with apprehension for a second, but she nods and invites me in, without releasing me from her gaze.

The small, windowless room has only a harsh overhead light. It's equipped with a kitchenette, a table and four chairs.

Anita stays standing, arms folded across her chest.

'I'd like to talk to you about Mikkel Martinsson,' I say.

'Yes, I gathered that.' She unfolds her arms and sits down.

I take a seat across the table from her. 'I've just spoken with Elisabeth Von Ahn. She told me about your accusation of rape against Dr Martinsson.'

Anita nods and bites her lip.

'If you'd rather talk to one of my female colleagues, we can certainly arrange that.'

'No, I don't mind. But thank you.'

'Is here alright for you?'

'Yes, it's fine.'

'Can you tell me what happened?'

'Do you want the official version, or what actually happened?' she asks, giving me a smile that takes nothing away from the look in her eyes.

'I'd like to know both versions, but yours is the one that matters.'

She places her hands on the table and starts to fidget with an empty sugar packet that's lying next to a paper cup.

'It was back in June, when I was on shift. I loved working with him. I felt like I learned more with him than with any of the other doctors. He would never lose patience when he was explaining procedures. He always took time for everything – with patients and with us, his students.'

Anita pauses to sweep some stray sugar granules from the table with the back of her hand.

'Later, I realised that he wasn't generous, and he wasn't a teacher. He just liked being the centre of attention. He liked having a captive audience that would hang on his every word. And I misinterpreted his approach. He put us in uncomfortable situations, but it wasn't to make us tougher. That wasn't why he did it at all.'

She puts her elbows on the table and cups her face in her hands. 'It was right after we checked on a patient who'd just had a triple bypass. He let me do the talking, and as we left the room, he congratulated me on my presentation and how I explained things in simple terms to the patient. I followed him into his office.' She nods her head slowly. 'It was at the end of the shift, in the early hours of the morning, and the only reason I followed him was to continue our conversation,' she explains. 'He shut the door behind me. And then he kissed me. It was such an incredibly gentle kiss. Tender. Almost romantic. I kissed him back. He was stroking my hair. Then he wound it around his hand like a piece of rope. And he yanked it. So hard it made my neck crack.'

The door to the break room opens and a man comes in, mug in hand. He's wearing the same blue scrubs as Anita.

'*Hej*,' he says to both of us.

We return the greeting.

He fills his mug with coffee and leaves the room.

Anita stops fidgeting and lets her hands fall into her lap. She stays silent for a few long seconds, and I wonder if she's reliving that moment or just standing outside the gates of memory.

'He pulled my trousers down with one hand,' she suddenly says. 'Then he pulled his own down, too. Without letting go of my hair.' She stares at her hands. 'I don't know why I didn't scream. Why I didn't try to push him away. I don't know.' She shakes her head. 'I still don't understand.' She releases a deep sigh.

Her fingers find the sugar packet again, which is now in the shape of a snail's shell, and start unrolling it like one of those noisemakers people blow into at birthday parties.

'You can imagine what the other version was. The official version: I wasn't chosen to stay on his team, so I cried rape to discredit him. I'm sure that's exactly why he didn't choose me: he knew that if I accused him of anything, he would have the perfect explanation – she's lying to discredit me because I didn't choose her. I have to admit, it was a genius move.'

'Why did you withdraw the accusation?'

She lifts her gaze towards me. The look in her eyes is cold, determined and fearless. 'Because I realised I would never win. An intern versus an attending – a prestigious one, too ... that would have been a foregone conclusion. So, I asked myself what I wanted to salvage from all this. And my place was right here, in this cardiology unit, at Karolinska. This was where I'd dreamed of working.'

She's speaking slowly, not rushing her explanation at all.

'Anyway, it was only a question of time. I knew that he would end up falling. That others would speak out. I knew that we would be stronger together. Because a man like him never has just one victim.'

IV

Something's occurred to me: it's not just the rape itself that crushes you. It's all the afters too. The infinity of afters that will never happen because of the hurt. The hurt that stops you from walking, laughing, loving, trusting the way you did before. Everything gets rewritten around that moment.

There will never be as many words.

There won't be as many chapters.

The horizon of possibilities narrows as you no longer recognise the body another has ravaged. Ultimately, rape is a form of colonialism, don't you think? And rapists are invaders who occupy, dominate, exploit a territory that doesn't belong to them: the body and the life of another person. They reshape the borders, the learning, the culture and the language of that territory, and impose their own. They belittle, they domineer, and they inflict pain.

And they leave nothing unscathed.

39
Maïa

I haven't seen the afternoon go by.

I ran some errands at the end of the morning, made myself a sandwich and a coffee, then returned to zigzag my way through the pieces of the puzzle on my living-room floor.

I take a long drink of water, then put the bottle down between two photos of Jenny. She's lying on the frozen ground in the woods at Abborrparken, dressed in her tunic. A crown of candles sits over half her face. Like a fallen star on a bed of moss and broken twigs, her blonde hair twinkles with frost.

Traces of alcohol and wax, as well as Gustav Hellström's DNA, were found on her tunic and underwear. Her parka was found several metres away, along with her backpack and tights.

The staging of Daniel's, Roland's and Mikkel's bodies is strikingly similar to this scene. Male copies of the same crime.

But I can understand Aleksander's reluctance to establish a direct link between these murders and Jenny's. At the time, even though the media didn't show any images of the scene, some photos did end up circulating online, so anyone could have imitated the composition and details.

Although Mikkel Martinsson's murder has led us to stray from our initial theories, from a clear victim profile to another than makes no sense, I have a strange feeling that we're getting somewhere. Perhaps it's because there's new information about the killer to be gleaned from Mikkel's death, we just can't see or understand it yet.

Saint Lucia represents the return of the light in the sense of knowledge, Linnius Kero told us, because even without her eyes, she could see and know. What did Daniel, Roland and Mikkel know? In the name of what truth were they sacrificed? Were they somehow all connected to Jenny's murder? If so, how? Mikkel lived in Stockholm with no ties to the island. And neither Daniel nor Roland were born at the time Jenny died. Should we be looking for a connection between their parents? Erik Brink, Daniel's father, only moved to Lidingö with his family when his son was born – to be closer to his business, the office-supply shop he still owns and operates. In 1999, Peter Lind was studying overseas and didn't know his wife yet. That leaves Esther Lind, now a public figure, who knew Jenny but didn't socialise with her. Maybe there's something to dig up there.

Another possibility is that Daniel, Roland and Mikkel were being punished for the rapes and murders of other victims the same age as Jenny – crimes for which they would now never go on trial. That's plausible for Mikkel, I feel, but less so for Daniel and Roland.

Either way, the question remains the same: what's the connection between the victims? What do they have in common?

I yearn to talk to Ebbe about it but have to settle for interior monologues. Christian would tell me to stop trying to be in control. He would say that life has treated me harshly enough this year; I shouldn't be imposing emotional limits on myself as well. I know that, of course. But I still feel that if I don't restrain myself, my husband will forever be my crutch.

I look at the photos of Jenny her parents shared with the Ministry of Justice for the trial. Some, taken the summer before her death, show her in a bathing suit standing on a dock, arm in arm with Gustav and her best friend, Sarah Wahlgren. Jenny's damp hair clings to her bare shoulders, overlapping with Sarah's darker locks.

There's a knock on the door. A tap of my phone screen tells me it's seven in the evening. It can only be Aleksander. He said he was going to come by in the early evening.

As he steps through the doorway, he gives me an elusive smile. His mouth widens to a grin when he sees the carpet of papers on the living-room floor.

'Do you really work better like this, rather than sticking things up on the wall? I wouldn't be able to read a single bloody word without my old-man glasses.'

'You're not the only one,' I say, pulling my reading glasses out of my pocket to show him. 'I have more of a surface to work with on the floor than I would on a bulletin board. How did it go at the hospital? No, wait – tell me what Brink and the Linds told you first. Did they know Mikkel Martinsson or not?'

'No, his name and photo meant nothing to them,' Aleksander replies, tiptoeing a path to the sofa.

'Did their sons ever see a cardiologist? They could have had an appointment without remembering the doctor's name.'

'Good point, but that's not the case. And none of them have ever needed to see a cardiologist, either. Erik Brink and the Linds, I mean. The same goes for their youngest son Sixten.'

'Damn it.' I move a cushion out of the way and sit down beside him. 'What did they tell you about Martinsson when you went to Karolinska?'

Aleksander tells me about his interview with the manager and the cardiologist. I raise my eyebrows at the stance they seemed to take about Martinsson, and they go even higher when I hear about the accusation against him. Then Aleks details his conversation with the accuser – or the victim, I'd rather say, Anita Vasic. I shake my head to myself.

Not all men are rapists, but all rapists are men. There really is something rotten in the kingdom of testosterone.

'Anita didn't say his name a single time,' he continues. 'She talked to me about him for nearly half an hour, and not once did she name him.'

I think about this woman, deciding to stay there and work alongside her rapist, refusing to give in, refusing to let him take everything from her. And I can understand her. She chose to cling to the life raft she'd built with her own sweat and sacrifice: her career.

'So,' Aleksander continues, 'now we're wondering how he got that hair from those forty-seven women. Whether he raped them, too.'

'You know, there's a lab in the States that has used paleogenetics to develop a technique for building a complete DNA profile from degraded hair samples – hairs without roots, for instance. It's a recent development, from 2019.'

'Yes, I've heard about that.'

'That company, Astrea, is making a fortune from genetic genealogy, but they also work on cold cases. With the scale this investigation is taking, maybe you can get the powers that be to fork out for some tests?'

'Maybe.'

'Was there any hair of Anita's in that collection of his?'

'Yes, there was quite a lot.'

'Were you able to ask her if she's the one behind that pseudonym, the one that sounds like something out of *Game of Thrones*?'

'The person who pointed the finger at Martinsson on Facebook, you mean?'

'Yes, Maria Lannister. She still hasn't replied to the private messages I sent.'

'I only got that info as I was leaving the hospital. I did go back, but Anita Vasic was with a patient. I'm waiting for her to call me back. I can't see her being the type to accuse Martinsson on Facebook, though.'

'Oh, I'm so sorry,' I say, springing to my feet. 'I haven't offered you anything to drink, have I? Gin or red wine?'

'Gin.'

'Tonic?'

He nods, and I head into the kitchen.

It occurs to me, as I open the fridge for the bottle of Schweppes, that its contents are the same as when I was a student. I should really try and start cooking again.

Returning to the living room with two glasses, I hand one to Aleksander and take a sip from my own as I sit down again.

'I've contacted Sarah Wahlgren, Jenny's best friend,' I tell him. 'She lives on the west coast, in Falkenberg. Did you know she's a renowned artist now?'

'No, I didn't.'

'She's a painter and a sculptor, and she's had exhibitions all around the world. She's working on a collection for a gallery in Japan at the moment, but she has no plans to come to Stockholm before January, so I'm going to pay her a visit the day after tomorrow.'

'Good plan.'

'She was the closest person to Jenny and Gustav, and she was at the party that night.'

Aleksander takes a sip of his gin and tonic. 'You really don't like beer in this house, do you?'

I shake my head. 'I'm not a fan, myself. Except for Guinness.'

'Ah, well, all is not lost.'

'If Ebbe were here, you'd have plenty to choose from, I'm sure.'

He takes another sip, runs his tongue over his lips and looks at me. 'How do you cope with his absence and ... the void?' he asks me.

I smile, because I can imagine Ebbe laughing at the question.

'I'm sorry,' he says. 'That was insensitive of me. Don't feel like you have to answer that, Maïa.'

'No, it's alright. I like talking about Ebbe.'

That's not a lie. I'm still smiling, actually. Nothing warms my heart as much as the memories of the man I love.

'I imagine him,' I say. 'I imagine his presence. I imagine him answering me. I create a sort of ... mirage with the memories of our years together. And when the mirage evaporates, I chide myself for playing that game.'

I cast my eyes around all four corners of the room.

'Everything is imbued with his presence. He's everywhere around me, so I'm always waiting for … I don't know … a word, a sound, the slightest caress from him. I find myself sniffing the air for the scent of him. But memories are fickle: as soon as you really look, they vanish in a puff of smoke. Work has been helping, though. Since I started chipping away at this case, I've needed less … less of Ebbe. Since the first anniversary of my daughter's death, too. I can't begin to tell you how much I dreaded that moment, so much, Aleks. Shocker, I know.'

It feels like the gin is burning my throat. Or maybe I'm getting a lump in there because I'm talking about the death of my husband.

'Ebbe was in the car with Alice. But he didn't die on impact. Not like her. He was in a coma for weeks before he succumbed to his injuries. All that time, I really, truly believed a miracle would happen. Well, I've lost my daughter, but at least I'll have Ebbe, I thought. I hardly left his bedside the whole time. I would come home to have a shower, change my clothes and go right back again. But he died. During those two hours in the day when I wasn't by his side. I was so angry that he'd left me, you can't imagine. And then I understood. I understood that he had to go, too. He was in the car with Alice. He couldn't keep on living since he couldn't save his daughter. He was never going to make it. If I think about it, he spared me the suffering of seeing him decline. But here is where I'm closest to him.' I laugh. 'Good grief, just listen to me. Anyone would think I was talking about God.'

'Maybe he's yours?'

'I don't believe in God,' I say with a smile.

I inhale sharply, and now my whole chest feels like it's burning.

'You know, at first I was only coming to Lidingö to scatter his ashes – and that's something I still haven't found the courage to do. But when I started planning this trip, I realised I really wanted to be here, in Sticklinge, in the red house, as my daughter liked to call it.'

'It isn't too hard to be here without them?'

'No, on the contrary. Now I understand that the people we love are no different to problems: wherever you go, they follow you.'

40
Maïa

Cautiously, I walk up the three icy steps of Sophia Akerman's porch and ring the doorbell. It takes a minute for her to answer the door. She's dressed in a white down jacket, an angora hat and après-ski boots. This morning, she once more oozes a princely elegance that makes her seem almost unreal. Sophia is a symbol of far more than a woman. Suddenly, I wonder what it is about her that fascinates me. Perhaps it's the way she rules over her solitude and her grief with a certain ... detachment? I don't know.

'Hello, Maïa. Gustav's things are in the pool house. I'm sorry, I haven't had time to get some salt put down.'

She descends the frozen steps with greater agility and grace than me. Together, we walk across the garden, fresh snow criss-crossed by deer tracks, to a miniature version of the main house.

Sophia takes a key out of her pocket and unlocks the door. The building is more like a cottage than a pool house, with a large living room, kitchenette, bedroom, mezzanine and bathroom.

We take our boots off, and I follow Sophia through to the bedroom. The wooden floor feels cold beneath my feet.

A cardboard moving box sealed with brown tape sits in front of a wardrobe.

Sophia sits down on the bed. 'How long has it been since you asked me about his things, Maïa?'

'Just over a month, I think.'

She nods silently.

'If you hadn't said something, I don't think I'd have ever got around to it. When I think about prison, I think of deprivation. I know that sounds silly and a bit simplistic, but it is what it is.'

She sighs, and her forehead wrinkles. 'The prison sent Gustav's things to Anna's house, but only after she died. The package was held at the post office for three official weeks before being returned to the sender. It then took several more months for them to send it to me at the publishing house, and then it was buried among boxes of books.'

She takes a long, unflinching look at the box, with all its stickers and marker scribbles.

'I haven't opened it. And I've kept it out here so I won't be tempted to. It would be like rummaging around in a funeral urn. What are you supposed to do with the debris of a life someone wanted to end?'

As she asks the question, she stares out of the window at the sea view.

There's something haunting about the image of a hand plunging into ashes. I can almost feel the sand of bones slipping between my fingers. I try to shake the sickening sensation from my mind.

'It was the same with Anna,' Sophia adds. 'A company took care of clearing out her apartment and selling it. I didn't keep a thing besides what she had on her bookshelves. All the memories I need are in here,' she says, tapping a finger to her temple.

She gets up and hands me the key.

'I'll leave you to it, Maïa. Feel free to take anything that might be useful. I'll be in Stockholm today. My driver will be here in half an hour. You can leave the key in the door when you go.'

'Perfect. Thank you, Sophia.'

The door swishes closed behind her. I sit down in front of the box and scratch at a corner of the tape until I can peel it away. Then I empty the contents onto the floor. It's mostly books. A few crime novels, some science fiction, a collection of poetry by Rasmus Akerman, Sophia's father. There's a Discman, too, along with some Pink Floyd, Guns N' Roses, Ulf Lundell and Roxette CDs. And two A5-size notebooks, each with around a hundred pages.

I glance at my phone. I only have about an hour before I need to drive to the prison in Kumla, about two hundred kilometres away. I asked Aleks if he had any objection to me going there to build more of a profile of Gustav. He had nothing against the idea, so Sophia arranged for me to meet the warden.

I open the first notebook. The first page begins like a diary, on 3 October 2021. In a few lines for each day, the entries that follow provide a more or less detailed description of Gustav's days behind bars: what he ate, what he read, what physical activity he did, as well as various altercations, and also visits from Anna. At first, the entries are like lists, sometimes with just a few words. Then, as the pages go on, words stretch into sentences, then paragraphs.

I keep hold of the notebooks and put everything else back in the box. The fact that there's no correspondence in there doesn't escape me. Prisoners at Kumla have no internet access, so mail and visiting hours are their options for communicating with loved ones. Did Anna write letters to Gustav? If so, why didn't Gustav keep them?

I make myself comfortable in the living room and open the first notebook again. I'm looking for one date in particular: 13 December 2021. There's no entry for that day. The diary skips from 9 December to 16 December.

9/12/2021
Mum came to see me today. She was stressed. Borderline unpleasant. She talked to me about Grandma, but I stopped listening at some point. I was thinking about the thirteenth coming up in a few days' time. About that fucking painting of Saint Lucia I can't stand to look at anymore. And about Jenny.

16/12/2021
I told Linda I don't want to write anymore.
She told me to open this book anyway and write the date.
I don't see the point, but whatever.

In the following days, up to 8 January, Gustav only wrote the dates, one below another. I leaf quickly through the rest of the diary, which ends on 19 December 2022. I go back a few pages. All he wrote on 13 December was the date. The entry for the next day reads as follows:

> *14/12/2022*
> *Linda's gone to light a candle for Jenny, and another for her family, at the church in Lidingö.*

A glance at the time tells me I have to leave. I only have a minute to flip through the second notebook quickly. It starts on 20 December 2022 with Gustav writing about the ice-hockey season. The entries become thinner and thinner, until 13 March 2023, the last one, ten weeks before his death by suicide.

I slip the notebooks into my bag and walk out of the pool house, leaving the key in the door as Sophia asked. Then I get behind the wheel.

41
Maïa

The traffic is light, so it only takes me a little more than two and a half hours to drive to the prison in Kumla, which is west of Stockholm, in the centre of the country.

The prison governor, Matteus Rosander, has a snowy-white beard and a thick mane that spills down the back of his neck. He invites me into his office, where the only window looks out over an immense field. The nearest house must be at least two kilometres away. I have to remind myself that we're at the nerve centre of the largest prison in the country.

'I've spoken with all our guards and group leaders,' he says, pouring us each a coffee. 'Milk? Sugar?' He peers at me over his round-rimmed glasses.

'Black is fine, thank you.'

'And I've drawn up a list of the inmates and staff Gustav interacted with.'

'Thank you. I appreciate you taking the time to gather that information.'

'You're very welcome,' he replies, handing me my cup. 'The Akerman Foundation made a substantial donation that paid for the renovation of our library and funds our group workshops. It's the least I can do for Sophia.'

Rosander sits down at his desk and balances his cup on his prominent belly for a second, like I used to enjoy doing when I was pregnant with Alice.

'I imagine that with the hundreds of inmates you have here, you can't keep track of them all individually, but did you know Gustav Hellström well?'

'As you say, we have more than five hundred inmates here. Only a rare few do I really know. I see those who are in isolation or who take part in the workshops more often, however. I've even been known to participate in those myself. It was in those circumstances that I met Gustav – one autumn, I think ... it must have been in 2021. Yes, that's right. It was after Covid that he started the writing workshop.'

'What type of man was he?'

'Ah!' Rosander exclaims, opening his mouth wide. 'Like the others: dispirited. Prison is a cruel ecosystem, and for someone like Hellström, from the upper crust, it was fatal. You know the saying, the bigger they are, the harder they fall? The same goes for the upper classes. And when they pick themselves up again and adapt to the prison system, they blend into the background. No one really knew who the new Gustav was, not even himself.'

'I found some notebooks in his belongings – a diary of sorts – in which he mentions someone named Linda.'

Matteus nods and his beard brushes against his chest.

'Linda Holgersson, yes. She was the one who led the writing workshops. She wasn't a professor of literature or a Swedish teacher. She was a writer, because she wrote books, but that wasn't her career. It wasn't how she made a living. Like most writers, I suppose. Now, philosophers – I don't know how they make a living from twiddling their thumbs all day and thinking about it. If you want my opinion, philosophy is like curling: nobody gives two hoots about it because they have no idea what it's all about ... I do apologise – all that is to say that Linda's a psychologist – a doctor, even. Dr Linda Holgersson.'

'Oh, really?'

'Yes, she stepped in to replace another group leader who went on maternity leave. Gustav had been in her workshops but only took part half-heartedly – mostly to score points for good behaviour, I think. But with Linda, he really got into the spirit of things. The guards noticed a difference in him, too. Once a week, they would work together for three or four hours, depending on the project.'

'Was it you who decided to hire a psychologist for this type of workshop?'

He laughs, smoothing the ends of a moustache that makes me think of the one sported by Marcel Pagnol's Uncle Jules in the film *My Father's Glory* – a true masterpiece of facial hair.

'Not at all. It was Linda who reached out to me. But I have to admit, her techniques were tremendously successful for our inmates.' He sighs and leans back in his chair, which tips backwards with him. 'Linda stopped working with us this past summer, and I haven't found anyone to replace her yet.'

'Do you know what became of Gustav's work?'

'Wasn't it in with his belongings?'

I shake my head. 'All I found was one completed notebook, and the beginnings of another one.'

'Ah, then I've no idea. Linda should be able to tell you more. I'll give you her details.'

'Thank you.'

I take a long sip of coffee, then I ask the question I've been saving for last, knowing I'll be walking on eggshells:

'Regarding Gustav's suicide, was that surprising to you at all, given that he only had a few months to go before he was released?'

Rosander's head sways from side to side. His lips and moustache twist into a dubious pout. But he doesn't take offence.

'Yes and no. Gustav spent his entire adult life here. When Saltvik opened in 2009, he could have been transferred there. It would have been further for his mother to drive, but the prison was brand new and much more comfortable – attractive, even, for lack of a better word. But he preferred to stay put. I think the idea of changing environments was stressful for him.' He plants his elbows on his desk. 'I get a lot of flak about reintegration. I'm supposed to prepare inmates here for that, yada yada yada. But how are they supposed to fit back into a society that wants nothing to do with them?'

I think back to what Gustav wrote in his notebook about Linda lighting candles in church for Jenny and her family, and I wonder what really went on between them. Was there more to their relationship than met the eye?

'You said that Linda Holgersson resigned this past summer. Gustav died by suicide at the end of May. Is it possible that she might have developed a personal relationship with him?'

'Not that anyone noticed, at least. But he wouldn't have been the first inmate to develop feelings for a group leader, and she wouldn't have been the first to fall for a criminal, either. But some people wondered if it might have been the very opposite.'

'What do you mean?'

His head sways from side to side again. 'Tongues have been wagging a bit since Linda left. It could just be gossip or rumours. There might not be any truth to it. These are just things people have heard in the corridors and told me.'

'What have they been saying?'

'That maybe she drove Gustav to suicide.'

Esther said there would be thousands of pages of correspondence to go through, and she wasn't wrong. I reach for another letter in the pile, whistling the way my daughters do when they're asked to unload the dishwasher or set the table.

I've just texted Birgitta to let her know not to expect me home for dinner, because I have to work even later than I thought. She already knows that my evenings and weekends won't be my own until this case is closed.

Now I reach for another envelope.

I had no idea that so many people still wrote letters by hand to threaten or criticise their elected representatives. I wonder where they find the time and energy to go to battle over the width of a path or the kinds of flowers that are planted on roundabouts.

My phone beeps several times in a row.

The first message is from Iris, letting me know that she and her sister have arrived at my parents' place in Skärhamn. Birgitta and I will be joining them to spend Christmas there, just over a week from now. The second message, from Alba, contains a photo of her, Iris and my father pulling funny faces. The third is from my mother. She too wants to reassure me that they're all safe and sound, and she's sent me a photo of Fanny with her tongue hanging out beside four mugs of hot chocolate topped with whipped cream and marshmallows to prove it. I suppose the girls aren't growing up that quickly, after all.

The last message is from Calle, one of the parents who coaches the junior team with me. No one else is available to coach the kids this afternoon and he's wondering if I can take care of it. I haven't been to a single training session since the second murder, and I can't bring myself to say no, even though I'll need to leave here just before three this afternoon so I can pick up my football gear from home first. I'll come back to the station straight after training to make up the time.

I text Calle back to let him know he can count on me. Then, just as I'm starting to read another letter, there's a knock at my open door.

I look up.

Jasmine is standing in the doorway, and Karina is by her side.

'Excuse me, Inspector?'

'Yes, Jasmine?'

'Can we speak with you in private?' she asks.

I nod, and can't help but notice that Karina can barely tear her gaze away from the floor.

'Is everything alright? Please, take a seat.'

'Thank you,' Jasmine replies, closing the door behind them.

Karina still hasn't said a word.

'What's wrong?' I say. Something about the situation makes me think of my daughters, coming to own up to something.

'So ... I haven't been entirely honest with you, Inspector,' Karina murmurs, lifting her gaze timidly. She's wringing her hands nervously. 'I know ... well, *knew* Mikkel Martinsson.'

'Meaning?'

Jasmine gives me an embarrassed glance. Karina still won't look me in the eye.

'I think I'm one of those forty-seven women,' she says, toying nervously with the ends of a blonde lock.

I close my eyes and pinch the bridge of my nose.

'That's why you didn't go with Jasmine to search his place.'

I open my eyes again and see her nodding.

'Well, at least we can't be accused of planting evidence. Jas, did you know about this?'

'I knew Karina wasn't actually sick when she didn't turn up, but

I wasn't aware she knew Martinsson. As soon as she told me, I insisted she come and tell you.'

'And when was that?'

'Just now, about half an hour ago.'

'Right ... Karina, I'm going to need you to tell me what happened, OK? But we're going to do this by the book, in an interview suite,' I say, getting up. 'We can't afford to mess this up.'

I'm tired. Tired of this case that seems like it's never going to end.

'Would you like Jasmine to stay with us?' I ask her.

'Yes, if you don't mind, Inspector.'

'No, not at all.'

We go into the first available room and sit down at the rectangular table, Karine and Jasmine side by side, across from me.

I reach for the built-in audio console and start the recording, stating the time and the date – 16 December 2023 – for the record.

'Commissioner Aleksander Storm, in the presence of Sergeants Karina Granqvist and Jasmine Haddad. Karina, you came to see me a few minutes ago to tell me you knew Mikkel Martinsson.'

'That's correct, Commissioner.'

'Could you please explain the nature of your relationship?'

She nods, then remembers to say 'yes' for the sake of the recording. She looks down at her hands in her lap and starts talking.

'I met Mikkel Martinsson in May this year, when I took my dad to Karolinska Hospital for a cardiology appointment. My dad's family doctor had referred him to Martinsson for shortness of breath and fainting. At the end of the appointment, Dr Martinsson asked for my email address to keep me informed.'

Karina pauses to clear her throat before she continues.

'That very evening, I received a message from him, saying this was highly inappropriate, but would I be willing to have a drink with him. He left it up to me to choose when and where. My wish was his command, is what he wrote. I thought that was...' she shrugs '...very gallant and charming of him, so I agreed. We met up a few days later, at a restaurant and bar in the city centre I often go to. It was a...' she closes her eyes for a second '...a very nice evening. He was witty, he was intelligent, and he was cultured. I felt like I'd hit the jackpot.' She scrunches her eyelids. 'When the bar closed around eleven, he suggested we finish our conversation at his place "in all good conscience". I remember those were his exact words because I made a joke about how old-fashioned an expression it was. I felt confident. I trusted him. He was older than me. He was respectable. He wasn't a stranger. I didn't see any harm in it.' Her lips stretch into a sad smile. 'When we got to his place, he poured two glasses for us. Two glasses of white wine. We sat down on the sofa and carried on talking. Then he just leaned in towards me. Slowly. As if to check that I would let him kiss me. And I ... I did. I let him kiss me.'

Karina pauses, moistens her lips. She gazes further into the void.

'He started stroking my hair...' Her body tenses as if a shiver has just run through her. 'And then, he moaned with pleasure and grabbed my hair in his fist. His kiss became more ... I felt like I was choking. He forced me onto my back, pulling me down by my hair, as if my body was on the end of a piece of string. Then he straddled me and...'

She stops to catch her breath.

Like I always do at times like this, I think about my own daughters.

'I ... it's not like I wasn't strong enough to push him away. I could have pushed him away and walked out the door. But I didn't. I was ... paralysed.' Her lips are quivering.

'Did you report him for rape?'

'No. I knew firsthand what the police would say: I went to his place voluntarily after a date. The door to his apartment wasn't locked and I'm a police officer, so I know how to defend myself. So no, I didn't say anything about it. Not until he died.'

'Who did you talk to?'

'My brother.'

I nod. 'Do you know someone called Maria Lannister?'

Karina pales. 'That's ... that's the name my brother uses on Facebook. He's not ... well, I mean ... he could have ... but it's just a joke, that name on his profile. He's married. They have a child. Why do you ask?'

I reach for my phone and show her the screenshot Maïa texted me.

'Here's what he wrote on Martinsson's Facebook page: "Everyone knows what Martinsson was up to and everyone just keeps their mouth shut. You make me sick." Who is "everyone"? Who is he referring to?'

'That's what I wanted to tell you about, really ... not just what happened to me. I went online and found some forums for women like me – women who've been raped. These forums geolocate users, so I soon found two women who had been assaulted by Martinsson. They shared their real identities with me. We messaged back and forth a lot. But when I saw them posting their condolences on his page, it shocked me. That was when I talked to my brother about it. It didn't occur to me until later that they might have been afraid.'

'Afraid of what?'

'They might have been worried about being accused of his murder. I was on patrol with Jas when it happened, so I'm out of the frame. But maybe they didn't have an alibi.'

'What about your brother? Do you know where he was on the night Mikkel Martinsson was killed?'

Katrina runs her tongue over her chapped lips. I suspect she's suddenly realising what her brother's involvement could mean.

'Leopold was at home with his wife and their baby son, who was born last week.'

I leave the station two hours later.

Leopold Granqvist's wife has confirmed his alibi for the night of 13 December: her husband didn't leave their house, in Bromma, west of Stockholm, all night. His phone wasn't detected anywhere other than his home, but I've still dispatched two officers to check with the neighbours and corroborate his claims. Obviously, he could have left home without his mobile, but that's a lot of what-ifs for a thirty-three-year-old man who's just become a father and doesn't have so much as a parking ticket to his name.

I park in the street outside our house while I run inside to get my football gear as quickly as possible.

I head straight down to the basement to grab the training cones, along with a couple of balls for any kids who forget to bring their own. Then I dash up the basement stairs to get my gym bag from the cupboard by the front door.

As I cross the living room, I freeze at the bottom of the stairs. I can hear sounds coming from the floor above.

The kinds of sounds that normally belong only to Birgitta and me.

Suddenly, my whole body seems to implode. And I feel something that ties my stomach and my heart in knots – the death of the entire life story I thought I'd been writing up until now.

43
Maïa

The taxi drops me off in front of 48 Upplandsgatan, in Stockholm's Vasastan neighbourhood, at 8.30 pm precisely. Christian would get a kick out of my punctuality.

Here, at the heart of the capital, winter is not as magical as it is on the island. Piles of grey snow peppered with gravel line the gutters. The pavements that haven't been cleared are sheets of ice topped by a layer of fresh snow – skating rinks in disguise, just waiting for unsuspecting pedestrians to step on them.

Dr Linda Holgersson, the psychologist who led writing workshops for the inmates at Kumla, lives on the top floor of this building, which to my Parisian eyes, seems inspired by the Haussmann style of my former city.

I contacted her as I left the prison, explaining that Gustav's grandmother has asked me to re-examine the Jenny Dalenius murder case. She suggested we meet after she had seen her last client of the day. I'm going to Falkenberg tomorrow morning to meet Sarah Wahlgren, Jenny's best friend, and I'd prefer to see Linda while everything is fresh in my mind.

Linga Holgersson opens the door wearing a woolly hat.

'Oh, hell,' she says with a laugh when she catches her reflection in the hallway mirror. 'I completely forgot I still had this on my head!'

She whips it off to reveal a short, dark haircut and a large forehead, smooth and bronzed.

'Did you drive or take a taxi?' she asks, leading me through to the kitchen – a generous room with mouldings on the ceiling and three windows looking over the street below.

'I took a taxi.'

'Ah, well, in that case, perhaps I can twist your French arm and have you sample a glass of Californian wine? It's truly sublime.'

I smile. When it comes to wine and gastronomy, the whole world considers the French palate so refined as to be a frame of reference. Far be it from me to contradict that.

'I assure you, I have nothing against the New World.'

I join Linda at the kitchen island, where she's uncorking a bottle of red. On the dark butcher-block work surface, there are half a dozen blue-and-white salad bowls brimming with fruit and vegetables, making this Scandinavian apartment look like something out of a Mediterranean summer.

'They called this one "The Pessimist",' she says, glancing at the label on the bottle. 'But I promise you, with a wine like this, no one stays that way for long.'

I laugh.

Her smile lifts her high cheekbones, rosy as they are from the cold.

'What was it that led you, as a psychologist, to teach writing in a prison?' I ask her, right off the bat.

'A client of mine,' she replies, plucking two stemmed glasses from a cupboard with pale-blue doors. 'She was a soldier in the Swedish elite special forces.'

Linda fills our glasses and slides mine across the island to me. The wine's violet-red robe is reminiscent of a Muscat.

'She was raped while she was serving overseas,' she says, plunging her long, straight nose into the glass. 'As I was helping her to get over her trauma, I realised the problem was a societal one. Our culture conveys representations of rape that don't line up with reality at all.'

'How so?' I ask, sliding myself onto a bar stool.

'Well, we tend to think that rapists are all strangers, perverts and creeps, whereas in more than three-quarters of cases, the victims knew their attacker. Also – and this is the most damaging popular belief – we tend to assume that rape victims will scream, shout and try to defend themselves. But guess what? Three-quarters of them are paralysed by fear. Literally. That's not just a figure of speech. Their body goes rigid and doesn't move. Their hands might go numb. They might feel drowsy or even pass out. That reaction is not something they choose. Not at all,' she says, shaking her head. 'And if that's how they react during the assault, it doesn't mean they're giving consent.' She wags her right index finger to say no, and the wine dances in her glass. 'That reaction has been programmed into our brains by millions of years of evolution,' she adds, stressing every word. 'Since a time when the predators we feared the most weren't humans – like they are nowadays – but animals. We would freeze, we would play dead so that the predator would lose interest in us and leave us alive. All that to say, when neither fight nor flight is possible, the amygdala – that's the part of our brains that deals with fear – takes control and sends an order for the body to stop moving.'

After a quick sip of wine, she continues.

'In fact, it's as if the nervous system short-circuits and cuts off the spinal cord, because to stay alive when we're face to face with a predator, we have no choice but to freeze. Without this mechanism, the body could succumb to a fatal dose of hormones – cortisol and adrenaline, in this case. Neuroscience has proven what we psychologists have been saying for decades: just because a victim doesn't defend herself, it doesn't mean she consents to what she experiences as an assault. I helped my client to understand that when she was raped, she wasn't fighting another soldier in enemy territory. Her brain didn't access or activate her combat training. No, she reacted the way she always had to stop a man's unwanted advances: she asked him politely to stop. Then, when he went ahead away and did what he felt he was entitled to do, her nervous system took over and she was paralysed by fear.'

My eyes grow wide.

'The big problem is that not enough people are aware of, or

understand, this state of shock and paralysis,' she continues, as if she can read my mind. 'The way the traditional mindset goes, if a rape victim doesn't defend herself, it means that she's consented. For a long time, our laws were founded on that premise. The reform in 2018 brought about a necessary and crucial change, by establishing that sex without consent is rape, even in the absence of threat or force. Giving consent no longer means not saying no – it means saying yes. That's a giant leap for victims. The real work, now, is to integrate the change into society. And even here, in Sweden, we have a long way to go.'

She leans against the counter and gives me, the police officer, a sad smile. Because I represent these laws. And because I, too, at some point, must have judged women who didn't defend themselves. Women who didn't say no, but who didn't say yes either. I hope I haven't. I hope I've never fallen into that trap. I hate the idea of doing the sisterhood a disservice by perpetuating the myths and preconceptions that women are somehow to blame, even if they're the victims.

'That case made me realise that mentalities have to change,' she continues. 'We have to promote a culture of consent. Information and education are the key to getting the message across that if someone doesn't clearly say yes, they mean no. One way we can make a difference is to educate men in prison. Men who are serving time for rape or sexual assault. Then we can hope they won't do it again when they get out.'

She swirls the wine in her glass, then looks up and smiles at me with her brown eyes.

'Go on, have a taste,' she says. 'I need to know what a woman from France thinks of this wine.'

There it is, the famous French barometer. I smile and take a first sip to fill my tongue and palate with flavour.

'The woman from France approves,' I say with a nod.

'Ah!' She nods her head too, with a broad smile on her lips.

Then her gaze falls into her wine.

'It's nice for me to be able to talk about Gustav,' she says, watching the burgundy tears stream down the inside of the glass.

I wait for a few seconds to go by, but she doesn't elaborate.

'I found two of his notebooks with his belongings,' I say, allowing myself another sip, crossing my fingers that Dr Holgersson won't clam up on me.

'Journalling can be very powerful,' she replies. 'It might not seem like much, but writing things down in a journal can help people learn about themselves, reflect on their aspirations and explore their identity – and that can go further than what they write down on paper. Introspection leads to self-reflection. It helps people take their first steps towards wellness.'

'What else did you do in your workshops?'

'I had the participants work on traumatic events in books and stories and films, without them necessarily realising the depth of the subject matter. I asked them to write about the "tipping point" – the moment when everything changed for whichever fictitious character we were discussing. Then, they each came to see me individually and we talked about the text they wrote. We did that in the "goldfish bowl", a room with glass walls inside the library. It was through those one-on-one sessions that I really got to know Gustav.'

'What did you observe during those sessions?'

'He had a morbid fear of what would come after. After his life behind bars. I think his family name – and the privilege that came with it – weighed heavily when he was thinking about what he might face.'

'Did he ever mention someone named Mikkel Martinsson?'

'That's the cardiologist who was killed, isn't it?'

I nod.

'I don't have any recollection of that, no.'

'Did he talk to you about Jenny at all? And the night of the murder?'

'Oh, it took him a long time to open up to me about that. In the beginning, he kept saying, over and over again, that he was innocent. Like he'd learned the words by heart but they didn't mean anything anymore. Then he told me, maybe six months after we started, that he often thought about Jenny with her crown of candles and her white Saint Lucia tunic, the way she was when he saw her for the last time.' She grips the stem of her glass. 'Two months before he died, he was consumed by a never-ending sadness. Then, a week before he ended his life, he told me he had discovered something he couldn't fathom, and he just couldn't wrap his head around it.'

'What was it?'

Linda shrugs. 'I don't know. He never told me.'

'Do you think it might have been something to do with Jenny's death?'

'I don't know.'

She takes a deep breath, as if filling her lungs with fresh air, then lowers her eyes.

'But I knew he was going to kill himself.'

She pauses.

Well, that's one question I won't have to ask her.

'He told you that?'

She shrugs her shoulders again. 'In a way, I think he did. And I think he had a right to end it all, if that was what he wanted. The burden he was carrying had grown heavier – much heavier. Whatever he found out, he couldn't live with it.'

III

Today, I went to see a therapist. A psychologist who specialises in treating PTSD. She works with rape victims – survivors, she said.

What she said was liberating for me. She didn't talk to me about grief, or rebuilding. She talked to me about fear. She explained that paralysis triggered by fear – tonic immobility, she called it – happens to sharks, deer, mice and rabbits. It happens to pilots, too, in air emergencies. Would anyone ever ask them if they froze at thirty thousand feet because they really wanted the plane to crash?

So, I am not crazy. I am not weak. I am just like those animals: the fruit of evolution.

The therapist encouraged me to write things down.

I told her I'd prefer to talk. And she replied: 'Even if what you write looks like tiny islands of words separated by oceans of silence, keep going.'

44
Aleks

After the forests, and their evergreens that seem to cling to one another to survive the cold, come the fields, seas of white spiked with bare trees. Soon, we'll be driving along Lake Vättern, a body of water that splits Sweden down the middle and ends in the town of Jönköping on the southern shore.

Maïa is sitting in the passenger seat.

Last night, I messaged her to ask if she would mind if I joined her on her trip to Falkenberg. I offered to drive. I know the route like the back of my hand, because I drive it several times a year when I visit my parents.

Maïa's telling me about her visits to Matteus Rosander, the prison governor at Kumla, And to Dr Linda Holgersson, the psychologist who specialises in treating PTSD.

'She admitted that she knew Gustav was going to kill himself.'

'And she told you, just like that?' I ask, turning to her for a second.

Maïa nods. 'It was insanely arrogant of her,' she continues. 'Or excessively honest. But strictly speaking, she isn't risking anything. First of all, it's my word against hers. And legally, there's nothing I could do about it. Here in Sweden, I'm just an ordinary citizen. She could also claim that client confidentiality was more important than any necessity to alert the prison staff.'

Maïa pauses and stares at the road for a moment. I don't know where the conversation has taken her, but for a few seconds, she's somewhere else.

'I think,' she says all of a sudden, 'that, all those considerations aside, Linda Holgersson believes deeply in the freedom to decide your own death. And when you think about it, that was the only freedom Gustav had.'

She leans forwards, rummages through the bag at her feet and pulls out a stick of lip balm.

'Oh, and you know what?' she says, before bringing it to her lips. 'It didn't occur to me straight away, but she only lives a few minutes away from Mikkel Martinsson's place on Dalagatan. Two streets east. Because I don't know Stockholm that well, I only realised when I was walking around, looking for a taxi home. Apparently Gustav never mentioned Martinsson's name to her though. To be fair, I didn't ask her if she knew the cardiologist, but she knew he was dead. She could have seen that in the news, of course.'

Maïa coats her lips with balm and keeps the stick in her hand.

'It completely slipped my mind last night,' I tell her, 'but we've identified Maria Lannister.'

She looks at me in surprise. 'Ah. Do tell...'

I fill her in about Karina's revelations, as well as her brother's reaction.

'I don't see what connection that could have to Jenny,' Maïa says. 'I can't make sense of it all.'

'Maybe there *is* no sense to it.'

Maïa nods her head in silence.

Vättern appears on our right and, just like every time I drive by here, I'm struck by the beauty of this lake, which looks like it's about to spill over the road. It's the halfway mark on the journey to my parents' place in Skärhamn. My daughters always used to look forward to reaching this point, when they were younger and had a habit of asking if we were we nearly there yet. To be fair, it is about a six-hour drive from Stockholm.

I blink, and remember the sound of Birgitta's voice. Her moans of pleasure.

I only stayed for a moment yesterday, at the bottom of our stairs, listening to her make love, before I did something that still surprises me: I turned around and left. Without a word, carrying only my training bag, the cones and the footballs. As if I was the guilty party who should be running away.

When I finished training, I saw a message from her. She said she'd be back late, too.

I stopped in at home and went upstairs, feeling a weight on my chest that made it hard for me to breathe. In our room, the bed was made. I threw a few things into a bag. I didn't want to see or feel her naked body next to me that night. So, I got a room at the Arena Hotel and texted her to say that I was going to see a witness on the west coast. *OK*, she replied, adding her usual *Luv U*, which made me feel sick to my stomach. Maybe she took advantage of the opportunity to bring her lover back to our place. *Our home*. How could she have cheated on me in our home?

'Is everything alright, Aleks?' Maïa asks, suddenly staring at me.

Her questions snaps me out of my waking nightmare. I struggle to find the right words. I hesitate to share those that do come to mind, then acquiesce.

'No … it's … Things are complicated at home. With Birgitta.'

She nods her head slowly. 'I understand. Do you think it's something you can repair?'

The frankness of her question is disarming. And my answer is brutally honest.

'No. Birgitta has met someone.'

Maïa places a hand on my forearm. She doesn't say the words that usually come with a gesture like that, dripping with compassion.

'I'm here if you need to talk,' she simply murmurs. 'Or if you need to say nothing at all. I'm very good at sharing silence.'

She smiles and pulls her hand away.

'Are your daughters alright?' she asks, without taking her eyes off me.

I nod, unable to say another syllable.

'Well, that's all that really matters, Aleks.'

45
Maïa

Built at the end of a bay facing the Kattegat, a strait connecting the North Sea to the Baltic, Sarah Wahlgren's home sits on a stretch of rocky land edged by a narrow, pebbled beach. With its sky-blue façade, wood trim and white fence, complete with a tinkling bell on the gate, it looks like a doll's house.

Sarah's waiting for us on the porch, dressed in a long, beige woollen dress and a wide, brown leather belt. Her blonde or grey hair, I can't quite tell, is cut short, military style.

'Hello, do come in.' She motions to us with her right arm. 'The wind today is unbearable. If it didn't do such a wonderful job of shaping nature, I'd keep it locked up in a box.'

She ushers us inside, shutting the door on a gust that moans like it's trapped and can't get in – or out.

'Commissioner Storm, is that right?' she asks Aleksander as we take off our shoes.

'It is.'

'You worked on the case back then, Maïa tells me. But I don't remember you at all.'

'That's right. We didn't meet, though. I was a sergeant then, working under Commissioner Bodin, who took a wry pleasure in burying me in all the paperwork.' He smiles unenthusiastically.

We follow Sarah through the entryway to a living room where the walls are studded with French windows, each with the same vintage handles as those at my in-laws' house in Sticklinge. She invites us to sit beside her on a long, Baroque-style sofa with ornate legs. In front of us, on a round, olive-wood coffee table, Sarah has laid out a plate of traditional Christmas ginger biscuits, a pitcher of milk and a large stainless-steel coffee pot, which I might have mistaken for a carafe were it not for the chunky black lid.

'Coffee?' she asks.

'Yes, please,' we both say, and she serves us each a cup.

Aleksander's staring at the floor, as if he needs to take a moment to bottle his sadness and keep it from overflowing.

When he looks up, I see that he can't help but notice the bronze, life-size chair sculpture under a window to our right. Impossible flowers seem to bloom from what would be the wood and straw of its seat; stalks of every nature – water lilies, roses, tulips, amaryllis and hydrangeas – climb skyward from the chair as if it were their bed.

'That chair is simply magnificent. It's just like a garden,' I say, struggling to find the words to capture its beauty.

'I created that piece to honour the memory of my grandmother,' Sarah explains. 'She was more than a hundred when she died this year, and she always said that old age was a privilege afforded to those who leave an empty chair at their table for strangers.'

I don't know what it is about this chair that captivates me so much. 'Happiness comes from other people,' I murmur.

'I'm not sure I'd say happiness. But perhaps a certain kind of wisdom that soothes the heart. Either way, I'm still trying to find it,' Sarah says, bringing her cup to her lips.

Then she turns to face us, with her back against the arm of the sofa.

'I haven't been following the news about the Saint Lucia murders at all,' she says, without further ado. 'You mentioned what's been happening when we spoke on the phone, Maïa, but I have no interest in knowing whatever's turning the world upside down. I don't have a TV. And I have a team of people to manage my website and social media. I refuse to even dip a toe into that cesspool of hate.' She cups a palm to her face as if to shield her eyes. 'My neighbours, who live in the yellow farmhouse on the bay just south of here, usually keep me informed about anything that's really, truly necessary to know. That's what happened when they found the first victim, when the press compared that murder to Jenny's. The neighbours came here to let me know.'

'How long had you known Jenny?' I ask her.

'Since our first year of primary school in Sticklinge. We had a pretty easy-going friendship because I didn't want her place and she wasn't after mine, either.'

'What do you mean, her place and yours?' Aleksander asks, taking a sip of coffee.

'Jenny loved to sing. She loved to be front and centre, but she wasn't arrogant about it. Her aura put her there, simple as that. In the place where she belonged. I was always more into filming, painting and sculpting, even back then.'

She tilts her head. A mask of grief suddenly stretches over her face.

'We shared the same zest for life, but mine was always directed more inwardly. We also shared the same sense of humour and dedication to school. We were both so conscientious.'

'Was she well liked by her classmates and teachers?' Aleksander asks.

'Very much so.'

'No conflicts with friends?' I ask.

'None at all. With Wilma, her twin sister, though, things were unbearable. It didn't dawn on me until much later, but for her, it must have been horrible to live with a carbon copy of herself yet feel like she was just a cheap imitation.'

'What happened between the two of them?'

'It was more what didn't happen: they barely talked to one another. They basically ignored each other.'

'Was it always like that?'

Sarah shakes her head. 'No, it started in high school.'

'Do you know why?'

'It was the oldest story in the world...'

'Wilma was in love with Gustav?' I ask.

Sarah nods. 'But it was an unspoken love.'

'Between the twins, you mean?'

'Not just them. Jenny never said anything to me about it. I didn't ask, and Wilma never mentioned it, either.'

'Did Gustav know how Wilma felt?'

'No, I don't think so. He only ever had eyes for Jenny, anyway.'

'Did you ever see him behave violently towards Jenny?'

'Once. Jenny wanted to break up with him. She didn't say anything to him, but I think he must have sensed it. He had been drinking. I saw him yank her by the arm.'

'Why did Jenny want to break up with him?' Aleksander asks.

Sarah lets out a deep sigh and turns her palms upwards. 'She wasn't really in love with him. But his love for her was...' she bites her lip '...intrusive, shall we say. At sixteen, that voracious kind of love was too much. She couldn't do anything without him. Even girl things, you know. He would always tag along.'

I remember the photo of the three teens at the beach.

'As I understand, they weren't together anymore when the party took place.'

'No, they weren't.'

'Why go, then?' I reiterate the question I asked Lukas, Jenny's brother.

'The party was for everyone in our year. It was impossible not to go. Plus, Jenny was Saint Lucia. And we all wanted to have a bit of fun.'

'And what happened?'

Sarah falls silent for a moment, clasping the cup in her hands.

'Sorry,' she suddenly says, rubbing a hand over her crew-cut hair.

'It's alright, Sarah, take all the time you need.'

'No, I ... I was just thinking about the last time I saw her. It's a happy memory, because she was smiling.'

I know only too well how that final moment can haunt

someone, eating away at them, if it was confrontational, violent or simply painful. Thank goodness my last words to Alice and Ebbe were spoken with love.

Sarah smiles, as if to echo my memory. 'Gustav was holding her hand. They were going upstairs, to where the bedrooms were. She gave me a knowing look and a sly smile, which made me laugh.'

'Had they got back together, then?'

Sarah curls her lips and her left shoulder twitches. 'I don't think so. They were just going to have a shag. I suppose they got a bit carried away by the spirit of the evening. Gustav dreamed about getting back together with her, but I don't think Jenny would have stayed with him. She wasn't a huge fan of Gustav's mum, anyway. Anna was ... bizarre. Always taking things too far. She didn't mean any harm, but she didn't always behave like a parent should. She was even eyeing up some of the guys in our year.'

Sarah closes her eyes for a second.

'I never thought anyone would ever lay a hand on Jenny.'

'You just said "anyone"', Aleksander chimes in. 'Does that mean you don't believe Gustav was guilty?'

'Oh, don't get me wrong, Gustav was guilty alright. I saw him run after Jenny when she left the party.'

'She left without you?' I'm surprised to hear that.

'We ... I was with some friends of Gustav's. I didn't see her leave, but I was there when Gustav called after her from the window. That's what I explained at the trial: I heard the front door slam, then Gustav, who was with us, went to the window to see who it was. He must have seen Jenny, because he shouted her name. Then he ran out of the room and we heard the door slam a second time.'

She exhales, closes her eyes and smooths the skin on her forehead.

Aleksander gives me a glance. It's time for us to go.

'I put a box together for you,' Sarah says as we're standing up. 'With some memories of mine and Jenny's. Some photos, some things we wrote. And I put the VHS tape in there, too. The one I filmed at the start of the party.'

'Wait – there's a video of the party?' I look at Aleks, who seems just as surprised as I am.

'Did you give the tape to the police?' he asks her.

Sarah furrows her brow. 'No.' She shrugs and wipes a hand across her forehead. 'To be honest, the thought didn't even cross my mind. Gustav was arrested almost immediately. And I only filmed the beginning of the party, anyway. At least as far as I remember; I've never been able to watch that video. Just the thought of seeing Jenny in her white tunic ... She looked like an angel.'

The image makes her stop, as if her friend was suddenly right in front of her. As if those words had somehow made her reappear.

'That's exactly what it was like, you know,' she adds. 'It was like someone had killed an angel.'

46
Aleks

The Strandbad Hotel, where Maïa has booked rooms for us, is right on the sand at Skrea Strand, the most popular beach in Falkenberg. The façade looking out on the sea is dotted with windows offering glimpses of breaking waves, stretches of jetty or corners of sand – sometimes all at once. And at times like now, here in my room, you can hear the roaring of the sea enraged by the wind.

We didn't have lunch, so Maïa's suggested we dine 'Swedish style' – in other words, around five o'clock.

When we got here, I had a quick shower before calling my daughters and my parents. 'Oh, we're all doing wonderfully here, love,' my mum said with her usual cheeriness that many mistake for sarcasm. 'Are you going to pop in?' Skärhamn is only two hours away from here, but I can't take the time away. The investigation has to keep moving, and I can't drag Maïa along with me, just to give my girls a hug. Still, I know it would do me the world of good.

I shake my head, as if that simple movement could oust the fears that fill my mind when I think about the girls, not to mention the terrifying feeling that keeps haunting me: the feeling that the story of my life, as I knew it, is over. It has ended with a brutal full stop. One I never saw coming.

I can't stop questioning the past. How can I know what was true and what wasn't in Birgitta's words, in her smiles? How many times has she slipped into bed beside me, wishing she was somewhere else? Where is she right now? Is she going to spend the night with him?

I can't imagine how I'm going to break the news to the girls.

There's no easy way to say it. I don't know how I'm going to shape a life for the three of us, either.

What is clear in my mind is that there's no room for me to forgive, reconcile and rebuild. Birgitta has changed. The woman I thought I knew would never have brought her lover home, and especially not into our bed. To be fair, I don't know where they did it. Against a wall? In the office we share? In the bathroom? After years of having sex in silence to avoid waking the girls, I thought we'd forgotten how to enjoy ourselves, how to enjoy each other, out loud. Clearly, she hasn't forgotten. Or maybe he's reminded her.

I close my eyes. The soundtrack of that moment floods my mind: the pleasure and the abandonment in Birgitta's voice as I stood at the bottom of the stairs.

What was she missing? What didn't I give her that she went to find elsewhere? Was it love at first sight, or is this just a fling? Did she get fed up of touching and tasting the same skin, kissing the same lips, feeling the same caresses, taking the same person inside her? Am I somehow guilty of always taking the same path to pleasure with her? Have we been stuck in a fucking rut, so to speak, and I've been blind to it?

I let out a long breath and realise something: not once have I asked myself about her lover's identity. I don't actually give a shit who it is. It doesn't matter. The one thing that does is that Birgitta's having it away with someone who isn't me.

I get up, leave the room and go down to the hotel restaurant.

Maïa's already at the table. She's nibbling a breadstick, head turned towards the waves crashing onto the sand and the jetty.

'You must be starving,' I say, as I take the seat facing hers.

'I certainly am, but most of all, I'm incurably early. I can never get anywhere right on time. It's a terrible habit,' she says, raising her eyebrows before reaching for a piece of focaccia. I laugh, straightening the cutlery at the side of my plate.

Maïa's looking at me, but it's not like she's examining me. Her gaze feels more like an embrace than an intrusion.

'Do you want to drink something?' she asks me.

I nod.

I order a Falcon, and Maïa, a glass of red. A Barbaresco I absolutely must taste, she assures me.

The waiter, a tall waif of a young man, brings our drinks, and we order two daily specials – *biff Rydberg*, which is a posh version of *pyttipanna*, the classic Swedish hash fried with leftover potatoes, beef and onions. What started out as a dish for the people was gentrified in the nineteenth century when the chef at Stockholm's swanky Hotel Rydberg crafted a noble variation for his distinguished clientele, with bigger, more tender chunks of meat and by separating the various components on the plate. Who knew that my girls were actually being choice when they insisted on separating their peas from their rice when they were younger?

'What do you think about what Sarah Wahlgren told us?' Maïa asks, lifting the Barbaresco to her lips. 'Oh, wait a second,' she adds, offering me her glass. 'Have a taste before you start on your beer.'

I take the wine from her and wet my lips, and immediately think about the bottle of Chianti that Birgitta and I shared on Saint Lucia's Day when we got home from the concert at the church.

'Very nice,' I reply half-heartedly, without having really savoured the sip. 'In fact, you asked questions that the police should have asked at the time,' I continue, handing her glass back. 'It's like we settled for picking up what was lying around instead of actually digging. That was the first I'd heard of any rivalry between Jenny and her twin sister. Sarah Wahlgren told you more today than she ever told us.'

'That's because back then she was sixteen years old, Aleks. She was a teenager who'd just lost her best friend, her confidante for the past ten years. And in the most horrific of ways, no less.'

'Fair enough, but I'm sure you would have been able to get her to talk. Traumatised or not, she would have told you everything she revealed this afternoon. You have this ... I don't quite know how to put it ... You have a way of putting people at ease, or rather, you hold space for them to share their story. Not to give a witness statement, but to tell you what really happened.'

'You were there with me. We asked her the right questions, that's all.'

'It has nothing to do with the job. It's something that comes from within you. Like an aura. Most people listen to answer. You listen to hear.' I take a sip of my cold beer, and it makes me yearn for summer. 'You're one of those people who keep an empty seat at their table, to invite strangers for dinner.'

She gives me a smile.

The waiter brings our food to the table and hopes we enjoy our meal.

'Do you remember,' Maïa asks, after a bite of *biff Rydberg*, 'when Sarah said she would never have believed that anyone would lay a hand on Jenny and you asked her why she said "anyone" if she thought Gustav was guilty?'

My mouth is full, but I nod my head a few times.

'Did you notice she said a similar thing about the murder, just before we left?'

'Yes, she said: "It was like someone had killed an angel." Don't you think that's just an expression, though? A turn of phrase?'

'There was another time like that, too. I can't remember when, or what, it was exactly. Maybe one time she said "we" instead of "I", or something. It just seemed a bit off to me. So no, I don't think it was a turn of phrase. It was too stilted. And too strange, for a woman who believes Gustav was guilty.'

She takes another bite or two, then carries on.

'Now, what I really want is to watch that video.'

'First, we have to find something to play it on. I didn't think about that when we left Sarah Wahlgren's place. Maybe she had a VCR lying around somewhere. Seems like she lives the way I wish I could – pretending it's still the 1990s.'

'They have a VCR here, in the children's play area. Owe, at the reception desk, told me the place is empty after five o'clock, so we'll be able to watch the cassette in peace. As for your nineties nostalgia, just think about the fact you wouldn't be able to track your kids with their iPhones.'

'Oh crap, that's true.'

'See, it's not that bad, really – influencers making a fortune filming themselves eating or making their bellies shake.'

I laugh. 'You've got to be kidding me.'

'No, I swear. There really is a guy who does that. He's a genius. He films himself going about his day, then *pow!* at the end of the video, you see him making his belly rolls roll. And *boom!* he gets millions of views.'

We laugh, and the weight that's crushing my chest feels a bit lighter. As the conversation flows and the beer goes down, the distance grows between me and my wife. When we've finished our meals, Maïa orders a cheese plate and asks the waiter for some *pepparkakor* and bread to go with it. I'm happy with a coffee.

'You see, the rumours are all true,' she says, topping a ginger crisp with a slice of blue, 'the French really are cheese addicts. But it's not our fault. Cheese has casein in it, and casein releases opioids during digestion. And opioids are addictive.'

'All I see is that you're eating cheese with *pepparkakor* for some strange reason.'

'Oh, the ginger with the blue – any kind of blue – is simply divine. But seeing the face you're pulling, I doubt you feel like trying it.'

'No, thanks,' I reply. 'My espresso is all I need.'

Five minutes later, we leave the table. First I head up to my room to fetch the VHS tape, then we go down to the children's play area in the basement. It's a vast room with a stage, a dress-up chest full of costumes, a big box overflowing with dishevelled dolls and bashed-up toy cars, and huge foam blocks piled on top of one another.

The TV, VCR and DVD player are in a quiet corner of the room behind a dividing wall. I insert the video cassette into the player and sit down beside Maïa on a vinyl play mat, remote control in hand.

The film starts playing automatically.

It begins with a close-up of something white, before fading out to reveal first a part of a Saint Lucia tunic, followed by some blonde hair, then that same hair cascading down a back, and finally the crown of candles on top. The young woman wearing it turns to face the camera. It's Jenny. Music is blasting in the background. The camera zooms in on her face. Jenny winks, then the camera pans out again. She's standing outside the front door of a house. She opens the door, and the volume goes through the roof as the camera captures the sight and sound of dozens of teenagers inside. Guided by Jenny, who is shot from behind, the camera weaves its way through the crowd as everyone it pictures gives it a wink, pulls a face or sticks their tongue out, not one of them without a glass or cigarette in hand.

Suddenly, I freeze.

'Holy shit!' Maïa cries. 'There,' she says, pointing to the screen. 'Go back a second.'

She saw it, too.

I rewind the tape and press pause.

The silence that follows stretches for seconds.

'Holy shit,' she says again, but this time it's more of a whisper.

47
Maïa

It's almost eight in the evening by the time we knock at Sarah Wahlgren's again. She opens the door wearing black latex gloves and a navy-blue smock with dark stains on it.

'What's happened?' she asks, inviting us in. 'You said it was urgent?'

'We're so sorry to intrude for the second time today, Sarah,' Aleksander says. 'We need to know if you recognise someone.'

'Alright. That's fine, of course.'

'It's a person who appears in the video you filmed at Gustav's party,' I add.

Aleksander unlocks his phone and shows her a photo of the video screen.

Sarah takes off her gloves and suddenly, her eyes widen. She freezes, then takes two steps back, bumping into the hallway table, making the legs screech over the stone floor.

In one swift, joint movement, Aleksander and I spring forwards before she falls, me catching her by the arm and him, by her waist.

'Sarah, are you alright?' I ask.

Her head bobs up and down quickly. She seems short of breath.

'Let's sit down, shall we?'

She nods, more slowly this time, staring into the void like she's disconnected from her body.

I walk her through to the living room.

The sound of cupboard doors opening and closing floats through from the kitchen. A few moments later, Aleksander appears with a glass of water and hands it to her. She looks up, thanks him and takes a sip.

Aleksander sits down beside me.

'Thank you, I'll be OK,' she says, giving us a smile that suggests the exact opposite.

'Do you know that man?' Aleks asks her.

'Yes. Mike. I don't know his last name.'

'Can you tell us how you know him?'

She runs a hand over the bristles of her hair, all the way from her forehead to the nape of her neck.

'He was a friend of Gustav's. From ice hockey.'

'When did you first meet him?'

Her lips start to quiver. 'That night,' she whispers.

I place a gentle hand between her shoulder blades. She turns to me and gives me a brave smile. A smile that oozes so much pain, I have to resist the urge to wrap my arms around her.

'What happened that night, Sarah?' I ask her.

'I don't understand,' she says, rubbing her forehead. 'He was there ... on the video I shot that night? I don't remember...'

'His face is only there for a second. What is clear to see, however, is the birthmark on his forearm.'

She runs another hand through her crew-cut hair. 'Can ... can you tell me why you're interested in that man? Do you know his full name?' She looks at us both in turn.

'His name is Mikkel Martinsson,' Aleksander replies.

In the video, with his chubby face and shoulder-length hair, there's only a vague resemblance to the man he had become twenty-four years later.

Sarah doesn't react to the name. She just shakes her head in silence.

'He was killed the same way as the first two victims,' Aleks explains.

She inhales deeply as she processes the news.

'Do you mean he was dressed in the tunic and had the crown of candles on his head, like the others?' she asks.

'Yes, and he was killed on Saint Lucia's Day – well, that night,' Aleks adds.

Sarah clamps a hand over her mouth.

'What happened that night, Sarah?' I ask her again.

She blinks her eyes a few times.

'We were raped.'

'You were, and Jenny was?'

She gets up from the sofa and goes over to the bronze chair and its flowers. She stands beside it and stares out of the window, over the dark waters of the bay.

'I don't want to give evidence officially. Never.'

I look to Aleksander. The answer is his to give. Here, in Sweden, I can't guarantee anything.

'I understand,' he says.

'I don't have the ... the strength to confront those men. To get through a trial.'

'No one will ask you to, Sarah.'

'Alright,' she murmurs.

The moon casts a ray of light on the sea. The shorebreak rumbles like thunder.

'Jenny went upstairs with Gustav,' Sarah begins, speaking clearly. 'They were holding hands and she was smiling. I was chatting with Mike ... sorry, Mikkel, in the hallway by the front door, but we kept getting pushed back and forth by people coming and going, and lots of people were starting to leave. So we went into the TV room for some peace and quiet. I could tell he liked me. He was older than me, twenty, he said, and I was ... I suppose I was flattered that he was interested in me. The look in his eye was ... no one had ever looked at me that way before. At that moment in time, it was as if I was all that existed for him. As if the universe started and ended with me. Then Wilma, Jenny's sister, burst in with two boys I had never seen before, but ... but Mikkel knew them. Wilma told me that she'd been looking for me and that we should be getting home. Jenny would probably be spending the night there, she said, and we'd better leave now.'

Sarah's voice begins to waver and choke with tears. She allows herself a second before she goes on.

'She obviously wanted to get rid of the two guys who were with her. But I wanted to stick around with the twenty-year-old man who only had eyes for me. So, Wilma and those two sat down on the sofa with him and me, and the five of us kept on drinking and joking around. While we were talking, he started stroking my hair.' She brings a hand to her head. 'All the way from the roots to the ends. Then, after a while, he leaned in and kissed me and I was...' She turns her gaze to the window again, as if she wants to disappear into the dark waters beyond, illuminated only by a sliver of the moon. 'I was completely ... absorbed by that kiss.'

She falls silent.

'Now,' she goes on, 'I can verbalise what happened. It was as if time had stood still. When he pulled away, I heard Wilma asking the two guys to stop. They had pushed her onto her back on the sofa and pulled her tunic up to the top of her thighs. They were leaning over her and touching her. Everywhere. I was going to get up from the sofa we were on to help her, but then I felt this pain in my head that stopped me from moving. With the alcohol I'd drunk, it took me a second to realise that it was Mike, pulling me by the hair. He grabbed my hair with both fists, pushed me onto my back and started to rape me, still holding me by the hair like he was pulling on reins. And he never let go.'

She heaves a long sigh.

'After a time,' Sarah continues, 'a time that seemed like it was never going to end, even though I still don't know how long it actually lasted, Gustav came into the room. He apologised – I think he said something like "sorry for barging in" – probably thinking he was interrupting something intimate. Mike ... Mikkel replied: "No, stay, Gus. The more the merrier..." I still remember the look on Gustav's face. He was afraid. Then one of the other two guys said: "When they say no, it just means they want it more."'

Sarah pauses, and the echo of those words brings my whole body out in goosebumps. *When they say no, it just means they want it more.*

'Mikkel asked him if two at once was too much for him to handle. He taunted him. He said maybe he only got into Jenny's pants because of his grandma's money. "Come on, whip it out and show us what you've got!" he called out at him. Gustav went red with shame and anger. He came over to Wilma and started touching her breasts ... and then something happened that I couldn't see, and none of the guys could see, either, because they had their backs to the door. Wilma told me later what it was. Jenny had opened the door a crack and seen what they were doing to us. When she noticed her, Wilma shook her head to tell her to get out of there. So they wouldn't rape her, too. Jenny took to her heels and fled. We heard the front door slam, like I told you this afternoon, and Gustav rushed over to the window. He called out to her and ran after her. The front door slammed again – and that's when they stopped. All three of them. He ... Mikkel, pulled his pants and trousers up and kissed my hair a few times, right here,' she says, pointing to the crown of her head. 'Then he vanished with the other two. The door slammed again, and Wilma and I heard a car drive off.'

Sarah folds her arms and cups her elbows in her palms.

'I cut my hair the next summer, when Wilma killed herself. I've never let it grow since.'

I had assumed it was cancer and chemo that had made her lose her hair, but it was Martinsson who made her sick forever. I look at her shaved head and think how much pain and suffering just one man can inflict.

'Wilma tried to save her sister by signalling for her to leave, but she always felt like she had sent her to her death. That's why we never said anything. We didn't want to end up like Jenny.'

II

The hardest thing is pretending. Pretending that I'm alright. Because I can't tell them my story.

So ... you had been drinking?

What were you wearing?

Did you say no?

Did you push him away?

Did you scream?

I can't tell them I did none of those things.

Anyway, if you survived, it can't be that bad, can it?

Do you have any injuries to show for it?

No, sorry, nothing you can see. Not everything that's broken is visible.

However, now some parts of me are missing. Essential parts of me, replaced by what you left behind when you grafted yourself onto me.

48
Aleks

We left the Strandbad Hotel in Falkenberg just after six this morning, to get back to Stockholm by lunchtime.

Based on what Sarah told us last night, our killer went after one of the Saint Lucia's Day rapists: Mikkel Martinsson. But who were the two others? And are their lives in danger now, too? Evidently, seeing what happened to Martinsson. But where do Daniel Brink and Roland Lind fit into the picture?

There are three ways we could try to track down the men who raped Wilma Dalenius, Jenny's sister. The first is to put a name to every male face that appears in the video. However, according to Sarah, quite a lot of the people there weren't in their year or didn't go to their high school. So, it would be difficult to identify them all – plus, not everyone there would have been filmed. The second is to age every male face in the video, which would take a considerable amount of time. And the third, which we're about to make a start on, is to explore leads at the Stockholm Wildcats, the ice-hockey club where Gustav played – and where, according to Sarah, he got to know Mikkel Martinsson and perhaps the two other rapists.

Last night, when we got back from Sarah Wahlgren's, I contacted the Stockholm Wildcats club to let them know that as part of our enquiries into the death Mikkel Martinsson, I would be paying them a visit around lunchtime today to check their lists of members.

Someone named Robert Keuter replied to my email around midnight to say he would be there to greet us.

The Stockholm Wildcats arena is located not far from

Stockholm University, in Norra Djurgården, just across the bridge from Lidingö.

As we pull into the car park, I call the number Robert gave me. A minute later, a man in a gilet and a cap with the club's logo on it comes jogging out of the building towards us, belly wobbling under his white T-shirt.

'*Hej hej!*' he calls, shaking our hands with a clammy but firm grip and gracing us with a smile that curls the ends of his grey moustache. 'Follow me. I'll take you up to the conference room. We've got everything you'll need up there.'

He opens a fire door to our left, and we follow him up two flights of steps, then down a corridor to the room in question. Its double doors are wide open and, even before we go in, we can see the huge glass wall at one end, which looks over the ice. The arena is all decked out in Stockholm Wildcat colours. The logo – a lion with an orange mane and gaping jaws containing the letters S and W – takes pride of place at centre ice.

'Please take a seat,' Robert says to us. 'I'll make us some coffee.'

We each pull out a chair and sit at the conference table.

'When the press started talking about young Hellström again, it really hit me how old I was getting,' Robert says, slotting a capsule into the machine. 'It's been more than thirty years – thirty-two, to be precise – since I started training the little kids, and nearly ten since I started lending a hand on the administration side of things, which came about because Lars, our office manager, got run over by a golf cart. I know it sounds funny, but he was just as bashed-up as if he'd been hit by a car. Long story short, I was only supposed to help out while he was out of action, and look where that got me! All that to say, when I got your email, that name, Martinsson, rang a bell. He's the cardiologist at Karolinska who was murdered. I saw it on the news. My God, these killings.' He shakes his head. 'I don't know how you sleep at night.'

He serves us each an espresso and returns to the machine to make himself one.

'I never trained Martinsson. He joined the juniors directly, so I didn't know him personally. "Mike" was his nickname on the team. Now Hellström, on the other hand, I did train him.'

Robert sits down across the table from us and adds milk and sugar to his coffee with the twirl of a spoon.

'Oh, that kid – what a waste,' he says, shaking his head. 'And I'm not just talking about the terrible thing he did, that girl he killed. Such a waste of talent, too. He was naturally gifted at hockey, but he just didn't give a shit. He didn't know how to push himself. As soon as he got outside his comfort zone, as soon as it wasn't ... exciting to skate hard, whenever it felt like work to him, you know, when we were doing drills, things like that, he just lost interest. He just started shooting his mouth off instead. Basically, he was a shit-stirrer. He was the proof that hard work, dedication and perseverance make all the difference. Talent alone is not enough. I say that often enough to the kids I train. If only he'd invested himself in the game, maybe his demons would have let him be.'

'Do you remember who he used to hang out with?' I ask, taking a sip of my coffee.

For a few seconds, Robert's gaze drifts over the empty ice. He pulls up his cap to scratch his forehead, then gives his head a shake.

'I'm sorry, I don't remember. All I can picture is him, with his skates and his stick, when we were training and playing the game.'

Robert gets up from the table. 'All the yearbooks are here,' he says, pointing to the wall and a set of shelves lined with orange spines. 'You'll find the photos of every team for a given year, organised by age group and gender. The first team a boy plays on has his birth year. For example, for the boys who were born in 1983, their team would be P83-1 if they were on the first team – that's the strongest – and so on. Right, I'll leave you to it,' he says, tipping back the dregs of his coffee. 'Good luck. We redecorated in here a couple of years ago and the idiot who unpacked all the boxes afterwards didn't think to put everything back in order.'

'We're only looking for Gustav's team, so it shouldn't take us too long.'

'Oh, right. But which team do you mean? Which year are you talking about?'

'What, your players change teams every year?'

'Not every year, no. It depends on their development. They change depending on the level they're playing at. And from sixteen onwards, the really good players can play with the adults. In other words, you can't always use the year of birth for reference, because a kid born in 1983 could end up playing with others who were born in 1980 or 1981, you see.'

I nod slowly, as the scale of the task we're facing begins to sink in.

'And none of this has been digitised?' I ask, scrabbling at one last scrap of hope.

'Only since 2009. But here, you've got everything, all the way back to the end of the eighties, I think.'

Maïa bites her lip to restrain a smile.

'Anyway, just give me a call if you need anything,' Robert says, holding up his mobile. 'And feel free to make yourselves more coffee. There are clean cups in the cupboard under the machine.'

'Thank you, Robert,' I say, sorely tempted to ask him to stay and give us a hand.

'It's the least I could do,' he says, and leaves the room.

'I can't give you a literal translation,' I say to Maïa, who's already getting up, 'but I can give you a quick summary.'

'I think I caught the gist of what he was saying. Basically, we're going to be living off kebabs in this room for at least the next two meals.'

'And because I'm such a gentleman, I'm buying.'

'How generous of you.' She smiles and turns around to pluck the first yearbook from the far left of the top shelf.

'Robert has a lilting accent I can't quite place,' she says, bringing the book back to the table and sitting down again. 'I like the way he articulated, without melting too many words together. So, even though I missed a lot of that, I think I grasped that Gustav could have been on the P83-2 team one year, then P83-1 the next. I'm guessing that "P" stands for *pojkar*, the boys, and "F" is for *flickor*, the girls. And when we get to the adults, it'll be "M" for *män*, and what's the word for women, again?'

'*Kvinnor*.'

'Ah yes, of course. So we can set aside all the *flickor* and *kvinnor*,' she goes on, giving a French twist to the pronunciation.

'The way you just said that sounded like you were talking about boxes of breakfast cereal for kids,' I laugh.

'Just wait until I get you to pronounce "Nuits-Saint-Georges". That'll soon wipe the smile off your face. Right, how do you want to do this?'

'Now you're just trying to be polite, because I get the sense you already have a system up your sleeve.'

'True. That was just a technique of mine...'

'...to give me the illusion that I'm the one in charge.'

'Damn it, you know all the tricks.'

'When you're a man like me in Sweden, Maïa, you've got years and years of gender parity under your belt.'

'And you think this is what parity looks like?'

'Parity is getting your balls crushed and not being able to say "ouch".'

Maïa bursts out laughing. 'You deserved to be emasculated, Storm. Anyway, here's how we're going to play it. Let's focus on 1998 and 1999, and on boys who were born in 1983, obviously. But we'll also keep an eye out for those born in 1979, 1980, 1981 and 1982, because Martinsson was that bit older.'

Nearly three hours later, we still haven't been out to get a kebab and we've just had our third coffee.

We've found the books with Martinsson in them, but we're still looking for Gustav.

'Right, I think it's time for me to be a gentleman,' I say, pulling on my parka and patting my pockets for my wallet.

'No jalapeño for me, please,' Maïa says, turning yet another page. 'Unless you want to make me look like a tomato.'

'Do you mean literally, or just as red as one?'

'Both,' she chuckles.

Finally, I find my wallet buried in my inside pocket. I'm about to leave when Maïa cries out.

'Bloody hell, there it is!' She's tapping her index finger on an open page. I retrace my steps and peer over her shoulder.

'Look!' she says, still tapping her finger on the name.

Then she turns and looks up at me, and smiles.

'There it is. We have our connection.'

49
Aleks

I dropped Maïa off at her place, then I went home to leave my bag and have a bite to eat before heading back to the station, where I have a suspect to interview.

As soon as I open the front door, it makes me feel like I'm nuzzling the nape of Birgitta's neck. Her scent is lingering in the hallway, as if she's just come and gone. This time, I check to see if her coat and handbag are hanging in the cupboard, but there's nothing there.

Not wanting to find myself in the same situation as I did two days ago and catch her *in flagrante* again, I texted her early this morning to say I'd be stopping in at home sometime after lunch.

I make myself two open-faced sandwiches with *tunnbröd* – flatbread with butter, cheese and peppers – and a coffee, and I look out on the snow-covered garden as I eat. Any thoughts my wife floats into, I shoo away. But she is everywhere, in every object that sits in this house, in every memory created within these walls.

I'm sweeping a few crumbs off the corner of the kitchen counter where I ate, when I hear the front door opening and the clacking of Birgitta's heels.

The pit in my stomach instantly gapes open.

'Aleks!' she calls from the entryway.

The chain of her handbag clinks as she puts it down on the glass console table by the door. I hear the rustling as she takes her coat off, the swishing of the cupboard door and the soft sound of her stockinged feet walking towards me.

'Aleks? Where are you? How did things go?' As she says those last few words, she pokes her head into the kitchen. 'Ah, there you are,' she says with a smile. 'I saw the car in the driveway. So, what did you find out?'

I take one look at her and wonder how life can change so completely from one day to the next, from one hour to another. How you can leave the house in the morning and kiss the wife you love goodbye, then come home that evening to a stranger.

I cast my eyes over Birgitta and realise that everything that used to be my temple is now my tomb. I can't stand the sight of her anymore.

Her smile withers, her body tenses.

'I want to you to leave,' I say, not thinking about these words that sound so right.

These words that feel so good to say.

'I want you to leave,' I repeat, as if I need to taste the words again to be sure that's what I want to say.

'What?' She blinks, and a nervous smile freezes her lips.

I give her a moment. To let my words sink in. So she knows that I know, and that it's time to stop lying to me.

'I was here when you were getting your rocks off, on Saturday afternoon.'

Her mouth gapes. She pales as a combination of shock and horror slaps her in the face.

'You have one week to clear out your stuff. And to talk to the girls. You can find yourself somewhere else to sleep, too, because staying here is out of the question.'

A tear trickles down her cheek. Her lips are quivering. 'Aleks, please...'

'I don't care who you were with, or why. For God's sake, Birgitta, you fucked someone else here. *Here*.' I bang my fist on the counter.

A long silence follows. A silence that breaks my heart, but sets me free.

Before she can take a step towards me, I stride across the kitchen and brush past her in the doorway. Then I put on my coat and my shoes, and walk away from what used to be our home.

50
Aleks

'Monday, the eighteenth of December, 4.42 pm,' I say, glancing at my watch. 'Commissioner Aleksander Storm. This is an interview with Erik Brink.' Then I state, for the benefit of the recording, that Erik Brink has chosen not to have a lawyer present.

Erik Brink closes then reopens his eyes. The word 'interview' seems so innocuous, but there's always something unsettling about being questioned by the police.

'Commissioner, your colleagues who came to bundle me into the back of a police car made me close up shop. Two hours before the end of my work day.'

'Erik, do you confirm that you have waived the right to have legal representation?'

'Yeah, it's alright, I don't want a lawyer. Your colleagues said this was urgent. They said it was about Daniel. What's going on? Have you found out who killed my son?'

'Did you know Gustav Hellström, Erik?'

His eyes widen in surprise. 'Gustav ... Hellström?' he repeats, shaking his head. 'Er ... yes, I heard his name on the news ... after Daniel died.'

'You didn't know him personally?'

'Personally? No,' he replies, twisting his mouth into an undecipherable pout.

'Alright. You've also told us you didn't know Mikkel Martinsson either. Are you still sure about that?'

'Yes, why? What does all this have to do with Daniel?'

'I'm getting to that. Can you tell me where you were on the thirteenth of December 1999?'

Erik sneers, crosses his arms and leans back in his chair. 'Is this a joke? How do you expect me to remember what I was doing in 1999?'

'The thirteenth of December 1999 was a memorable evening, Erik, and everyone who was there remembers it in great detail.'

'Listen, I don't understand a bloody word of what you're saying, or what the hell you want from me. So you'd better hurry up and tell me why I'm here, and get this over and done with, because I don't have anyone paying me a salary, alright? When my shop is closed, I don't make any money. I know it's hard for a civil servant like you to grasp that idea, but that's the way it is.'

'Very well then, Erik. In that case, I'll get straight to the point. It seems to me that you knew Gustav Hellström quite a bit better than you claim.'

'Oh, really?'

'You were on the same ice-hockey team. That's what the records of the Stockholm Wildcats told us. Team P83-1. For three years in a row, no less, so you must remember.'

'Maybe. But I don't recall the names of everyone I ever played with on the team.'

'I remember who was on my team when I played.'

'Well, you've got a bloody good memory, then. Because I'm sorry, but there's no way I could tell you who I knocked a puck around with twenty-five years ago.'

'So, you know it was twenty-five years ago.'

'Well yes, I stopped playing after that.'

'After what?'

He gets up from his chair. 'Listen, Commissioner, I don't mean to be impolite, but if you don't have any news to share with me about Daniel's murder, I don't see what the heck I'm doing here. I have to go back and open up the shop.'

'Alright, I'll be a bit more specific then, Erik. Let me explain. Please sit down again.'

Erik Brink huffs and puffs, then does as he's told, but not without slapping his palms on his thighs.

'On the thirteenth of December 1999, Gustav Hellström had a party at his house in Lidingö. At that party, Sarah Wahlgren was raped by Mikkel Martinsson, and Wilma Dalenius was gang-raped by two other individuals. Wilma was the twin sister of Jenny Dalenius, who was found dead later that night. As you know, Gustav Hellström was arrested and went to prison for her murder. And he died by suicide in May this year. Wilma also died by suicide, a few months after her sister's death. It so happens that Wilma and Sarah were both wearing their Saint Lucia tunics when they were raped, and Jenny was still wearing hers when she was killed. Does that not ring any bells about what your son was wearing when we found his body? Is the reason you're here getting a bit clearer now, Erik?'

51
Aleks

I decide to give myself a minute before I step into the interview room. I unscrew the lid of my water bottle and take a long swig that's far too cold and turns my throat to ice.

Straight after Erik Brink's interview, I went to see Siv, then I phoned Maïa. We'd hit the nail on the head. *She'd* hit the nail on the head.

We only did half the work we should have, all those years ago, during the first investigation. We failed two victims and let three rapists roam free. But now, suddenly, we have an opportunity to address the error of our ways. At long last, we can hitch the missing carriages to the train and drive it towards the light at the end of the tunnel. We can never know everyone's truth about what happened on the night of 13 December 1999, but we can at least piece the whole story together. Erik Brink has just given me his version. Now I have to corroborate and substantiate his claims.

Siv pokes her head around the door to the incident room, which is adjacent to the interview suite. 'Aleks, are you good to go?'

I nod and open the door.

A woman with dark hair – that's all I can see of her, her locks are so long and flowing – is leaning over and whispering something into Peter Lind's ear. She stops and sits up in her chair when she sees me come in. I sit down and put my water bottle on the table.

'Monday, the eighteenth of December 2023, 7.07 pm. Commissioner Aleksander Storm. This is a video-recorded interview with Peter Lind, in the presence of his lawyer, Barbro

Sundvik.' Then I get straight to the point: 'Peter, did you know Mikkel Martinsson?'

'Not personally, no.'

'And did you know Gustav Hellström?'

'Yes.'

'Could you please explain the nature of your connection?'

'Strictly speaking, I've never had a connection to Gustav Hellström, but my wife knew him, and the media and the police have mentioned his name in connection with the death of our son.' He hangs his head, and his lips start to move as if he's chewing on something.

'Where were you, Peter, in 1999?'

'I already told you, I was studying in London that year,' he replies with a sigh, as if this interview has already gone on long enough for him.

'What about the thirteenth of December 1999, specifically?'

'Probably in London, too.'

'Probably?'

'Yes, probably. How do you expect me to remember what I was doing on a particular night, more than twenty years ago?'

'That's funny. Erik Brink just gave me the exact same answer.'

Peter drills his eyes into me, trying to gauge what I know and what I'm assuming.

His lawyer leans towards him and whispers something in his ear again. Peter whispers something back to her, and their exchange lasts for another minute or so before they both sit up again.

'Peter, if I were to ask you the same question I asked you the day after Roland died, that is, why you argued with him the night before, would you still tell me that it was about football?'

'What else do you want me say? That it was because he was gay?'

'Only you know the answer to that, Peter, but I sincerely doubt that you blew up at him because of his lack of enthusiasm and commitment to football training.'

Peter is sitting completely still. His face is a closed book.

'Do you know what your son and Daniel Brink – Erik Brink's son – had in common, other than the fact that they were both targeted by the same killer? They were both preoccupied, sad, depressed, even, in the weeks leading up to their deaths.'

Peter lowers his eyes and automatically touches the bezel of his watch.

'Our theory, since the beginning of this investigation has been that Daniel and Roland had both arranged to meet someone on the night they died. And I think that person was supposed to bring them, on that very same night, the proof of whatever terrible thing that person had discovered. That shocking secret, so shameful it could ruin your wife's career. So what did Esther do, Peter? Was she the one who silenced Daniel and Roland to protect everything she'd worked so hard for?'

'Are you out of your mind? Esther would never do such a thing!'

'Are you really sure of that, Peter?'

'Never! Esther would never sacrifice our son to protect herself.'

'So, you're the one who sacrificed him, then—'

'Just shut up!' Peter bangs his fist on the table.

The clang from his metal watch strap echoes around the room. His lawyer places a hand on his forearm.

'Commissioner, I will not tolerate any unfounded accusations against my client.'

'What I think,' I go on, ignoring her warning and looking Peter straight in the eye, 'is that Roland confronted you about something on the night he died. Something he had found out recently. Something that would mean "prison for sure", as he said to his boyfriend. I think, before he took the boat that night, if that is indeed what happened, your son talked to you about what he had found out. And that's the reason he's dead.'

Peter shakes his head. His mouth starts wobbling. 'No, that's not why he died,' he says, in a haughty voice. 'It can't be ... not that.'

'What happened on the night of the thirteenth of December 1999, Peter, that could end Esther's career?'

Peter hunches his shoulders around her ears and starts to cry. 'There's no way that could be the reason. No way!'

'What happened at Gustav Hellström's party, Peter, on the thirteenth of December 1999?'

Barbro Sundvik whispers something lawyer-like in his ear. He shakes his head and sniffles. She lets out a subtle sigh.

'What happened to the Dalenius twins, Peter?'

His eyes are glued to his fingers, which he's constantly pinching and rubbing.

Then, suddenly, he takes a deep breath and starts talking.

'I met Mike – Mikkel Martinsson – at a party I went to in Djursholm, where I was living the summer I finished high school. Mike was ... I don't know, a bit crazy. Extreme. But popular, in the sense that it was ... cool, I suppose, to be seen with him. And he was a real magnet for girls. When I came back to Sweden, in between university terms abroad, we would always hang out. The year before that, he introduced me to Gustav and Erik – Erik Brink. The three of them were in the same ice-hockey club, and Gustav, who was a really strong player, sometimes came in as a sub if one of the guys on Mike's ... Mikkel's team was injured. Gustav's mum wasn't around much, so I went over to his place a few times to watch ice hockey and football on TV, and to have a smoke, that kind of thing.'

Peter wipes his nose with the back of his hand.

'That year, I came back to Sweden after exams, a few days before Saint Lucia's Day. Gustav was throwing a party on the thirteenth. He was crazy about that Jenny Dalenius girl, and I reckon, even though he never said it, the whole reason for the party was to win her back. Martinsson was always teasing him. He used to tease us, too, because we weren't exactly ... outgoing when it came to girls. Martinsson said if we didn't do something about it, he'd just have to assume we were gay. And that night, well ... we had to win a bet. Mikkel said he bet we couldn't find a girl who was game for ... for sleeping with both of us.'

He runs his tongue over his dry, cracked lips. He's staring at his interlaced fingers on the table. A silence sets in, and Peter seems to lose his train of thought.

Time for me to give him a nudge.

'And you picked Wilma, is that it, Peter? Wilma, Jenny's twin sister?'

He nods. 'Wilma didn't ... She didn't really say no ... she—'

'Commissioner,' his lawyer cuts in, 'I'd like a moment to confer with my client before this interview goes any further.'

'Peter,' I insist, overruling Sundvik. 'I think it would be in your interest, as well as the interest of the investigation into Roland's murder, for you not to stop here. Erik Brink has already confessed to everything. Holding anything back now would reflect badly on you.'

'Peter,' his lawyer counters.

He turns his head, but doesn't look at her. Then he blinks and turns back to me.

'Wilma killed herself the year after. That was when I realised what we'd done. When I admitted to myself that we'd raped her.'

His lawyer leans back in her chair and rubs the wrinkles of concern on her forehead with her fingertips.

'What happened at the party, after Gustav left?'

Peter takes a deep breath as if he's preparing to answer the question, but it takes him a few seconds to reply.

'We left, too.'

'Who do you mean, *we*?'

'Mikkel, Erik and me.'

'On foot?'

'No, we drove. Mikkel had a car.'

'Even after all the alcohol you'd drunk?'

'Mikkel was driving. He didn't drink any alcohol.'

'And where did you go?'

'Mikkel dropped us off in Stockholm city centre and I caught a train home to my parents' in Djursholm. Erik went home too, I assume.'

'When you left Gustav's house, did you see anyone else, either inside the house or outside?'

Peter shakes his head. 'I can't remember ... I don't know ... Gustav went after Jenny, I do remember that. They must have had an argument, I suppose. But that was the last time I saw him: in that room, that night.'

'Did you see Martinsson or Brink again afterwards?'

'No.'

'Not even to decide if you were going to tell anyone what happened, or get your stories straight?'

'No, never. I never saw them again. Not once.'

52
Aleks

As I leave the interview suite, I switch my phone back on and see that Maïa's tried to reach me a few times. Her last message was from a quarter of an hour ago:

Call me back as soon as you can. Sophia Akerman wants to see us. It's urgent.

I grab my parka and check my other messages as I leave my office. I take the stairs and am just about to walk out of the station when Esther's voice stops me in my tracks.

'Aleksander?'

I turn around.

I hadn't seen her, sitting in the reception area.

She gets up and stands in front of me. 'Can you tell me what's happening?' she asks me, with no preamble.

'We're questioning your husband in connection with the murder of your son, Esther, and that of Jenny Dalenius.'

She bares her teeth with rage. 'Don't you dare tell me you're going to drag my whole career, our whole life, through the mud to defend that Dalenius slut? Do you have any idea what they were like, those twins? Girls who charmed the pants off people and then cast them aside like dirty tissues. Both of them. Jenny more than Wilma, for sure. Even at their age they were already like last week's flowers – nothing left to offer. And they didn't even realise it.'

'It doesn't matter what they were like. Wilma was raped. Your husband raped her, Esther.'

She shakes her head and sneers. 'Did you not hear a word of what I just said to you? You want to tear our life apart for what –

some kind of pseudo-justice? That's exactly what I'm fighting for, Aleks! To stand up for women who really need defending, not those who drop their pants and sleep their way to the top, then scream blue murder as soon as they trip and hurt themselves.'

'No means no, Esther, even for those who say yes most of the time. Their "no" is just as valid as everyone else's. You must know that it's not always possible to express that clearly. But believe me, all I'm trying to do here is arrest whoever killed three people, your son included.'

'Have you heard yourself? What you're trying to do is destroy me.'

'What are you talking about? I'm searching for your son's killer, Esther, for fuck's sake.'

'Really? You're seriously telling me that dragging my husband down to the police station like a common criminal isn't an act of vengeance? You're really going to pretend that this has nothing to do with my relationship with Birgitta?'

I'm about to open my mouth and reply, when the nuance in those words slaps me in the face.

I look at Esther, who's right in front of me, perched on her heels, reeking of self-importance and arrogance, and I think back to all those evenings Birgitta had to work late. The nights, too. All the attention she was paying her boss. *Esther, Esther, Esther.* And, no pun intended, I suddenly feel like the biggest dick in the world.

53
Maïa

I've discovered something. Could you come over to my place this evening, Maïa? The police should be here too. Can I leave it up to you to get in touch with Commissioner Storm? Thank you.

Sophia sent me this message around seven this evening, and I tried to contact Aleks straight away, even though I knew he'd probably still be mid-interview. He called me back from his car to bring me up to speed with the latest developments and let me know he was already on his way.

I should have listened to my inner voice, I tell myself as Aleks gives me the lowdown on the other end of the line. I should have followed my intuition when it told me the killer must be hitting where it hurts the most – people's children. No doubt about it, these killings were motivated by vengeance. The killer wanted to deprive Erik Brink and Peter Lind of the very essence of their lives. Martinsson had no children. He lived by himself, and for no one but himself. For that reason, the killer hit him the hardest – literally. His murder is by far the most significant of the three, as I thought. Unlike the two others, Martinsson was a veritable predator. And based on what Brink and Lind have now said, he was the instigator of the events that night.

'The killer wanted to take everything from those who took everything from him – or her,' I say out loud.

'That's right. Which means, as you seem to be suggesting, the killer could be a woman.'

'Or several women,' I reply, turning up the heat. 'I called Sarah Wahlgren to ask for her alibis on the nights of the murders.'

'How did she react?'

'Very calmly. She had me wait a minute while she checked her diary, then said it looked like she was in Falkenberg every time. She only actually remembers the night of the thirteenth of December, because she was at home painting.'

'We could start by triangulating her phone, and also check with whoever she's in regular contact with—' He breaks off and I hear him suck in air through his teeth. 'Bloody hell, I'll never buy the girls one of those de-specced microcars teens can drive without a licence. A kid just shot out in front of me onto a sheet of ice and only just managed to keep it on the road. Those things are coffins on wheels, I tell you. Anyway, where was I? Oh, yes. We still don't know what really happened to Jenny.'

He's right. There are still so many unanswered questions about Jenny. What happened to her after she left Gustav's house? Did Gustav really kill her? Were Martinsson, Brink and Lind mixed up in her murder? Could Wilma have killed her sister in a rage to punish her for running away, only then to take her own life, tormented by remorse? Or was it someone else?

A wall of light suddenly flashes into the car like sheet lightning.

'Is that you flashing your lights at me, Storm?'

'Ah, so it is you in front of me, then.'

I laugh.

'We're nearly there. I'll follow your lead,' he says, before hanging up.

I disconnect the call too and keep driving for a hundred metres or so, with Aleks right behind me. Then we turn into the driveway that leads to Sophia's house.

54
Maïa

The young woman who greeted me the first time I was here gives us the same shy smile.

She takes our coats, waits for us to remove our shoes and invites us to follow her. She leads us across the hall and up the stairs, then turns right on the landing and guides us to the double sliding doors of a spacious study lined with bookcases.

We find Sophia at the far end of the room, sitting on a red sofa in the bay of a window, with two generous beige armchairs facing it. Her posture is prim and proper, her ankles crossed. She's leafing through a book in her lap. Beside her, there is a row of what must be fifteen cardboard boxes, only four of which are open.

She greets us with a nod. Her face is pale and tense.

'Ms Akerman,' Aleksander says.

'Good evening, Sophia,' I add.

'Officers, thank you for coming so quickly,' she replies, inviting us with a gesture to sit down facing her.

'What have you found, Sophia?' I ask her.

She looks me straight in the eye and smiles, but her face doesn't light up. On the contrary, sadness seems to deepen the furrows of concern.

'I feel a little ... ashamed of myself, Maïa. I've been allowing my feelings to dictate my actions, and I've been using my age as an excuse for doing so. But growing old should never be an excuse. I was Gustav's grandmother. I realise now I should have taken care of his belongings personally. So, I had them brought up here, to my study.'

Sophia pauses as the housekeeper comes into the room and sets a tray with cups, a French press, a pitcher of milk and a sugar bowl on the table. She pours the coffee, then takes her leave.

'Please help yourselves.' Sophia gestures to the tray. 'In the box of Gustav's belongings,' she continues, 'I found the book Anna gave him for his eighteenth birthday. She took it to the prison for him. It was his favourite poetry collection, a book of my father's called *Scars of Silence*. He gave Anna a limited edition as a present the last Christmas before he died.'

Sophia reaches forwards for her cup of coffee.

'Anyway, I thought it was high time I started looking through the boxes from my daughter's apartment. I came across this numbered copy in the fourth one. It was illustrated by a friend of my father's. I opened it to read the dedication and found a photo of Anna with her grandfather, as well as an envelope addressed to my daughter. It didn't look like my father's writing, so I opened it.'

Sophia returns her cup to the tray, then extracts a thin envelope from the book in her lap. She holds it out for me to take.

'Could you please put the envelope and its contents on the table, Sophia?' I ask her. 'To avoid getting our prints on it.'

She shakes her head. 'Yes, of course, I should have thought of that.'

She does as I ask and unfolds two sheets of paper, which she sets on the table in front of us. Both sheets are A5 format, and both have been torn from a notebook.

'It's a letter from Gustav to his mother,' Sophia says, picking up her phone from the sofa beside her. 'I'll read you the English translation, Maïa. Commissioner Storm, I'll let you read the original.'

25 May 2023
Mum,
I have so much to say to you. So much. But even if every word could tell a story, it still wouldn't be enough.
*   You've never loved me as much as you have since I was*

accused of the worst. And I've never felt you so close to me, so caring, so protective of me as I have since the world locked me up with the other monsters. You have been my rock, Mum. Thank you for having faith in me. Without that, without you, I would never have found the strength to survive here.

But to be fair, Mum, I can't keep living a lie. I can't keep lying to you anymore. I've spent more than twenty years doing that, and I'm sorry. So terribly sorry. I liked being the person you talked about wherever you went, the one you stood up for, the one you told people about. I liked being in his skin, the suit you stitched together with every word.

But now I know, I truly know, that you'll love me in spite of this. In spite of my lie, in spite of my suicide. I'm not leaving you, Mum. I'm freeing you. I'm freeing you from the weight of defending me and fighting for me.

Jenny was the love of my life, but she saw something she shouldn't have.

Jenny came back to me that night. She was all mine again. She fell asleep in my arms. She was so tired. Of course she was, with the emotion of leading the Saint Lucia procession, being our queen, drinking at the party, and us getting back together. Our wonderful reunion.

I left her to sleep and went downstairs to find the guys. Martinsson, Brink and Lind. By the time I got down there, almost everyone had gone home. I found the three of them in the TV room. Martinsson was with Sarah. Erik and Peter were with Wilma. I should have realised that what I walked in on, what I saw, was rape. But all I heard was Martinsson teasing me about two girls at once being too much for me to handle. He said the only reason Jenny went out with me was because of Grandma's money. Then he said: 'Come on, whip it out and show us what you've got!' I wanted to prove him wrong. So, I went over to Wilma, because she was basically a copy of Jenny, and I started touching her.

I don't know how long it was, maybe two or three minutes later, I heard the front door slam. I went to the window and saw Jenny running away. She didn't even put her coat on, she was just dragging it behind her. I called after her. She looked back at me, but she kept running.

She must have seen me touching Wilma. She saw the monster that Martinsson had drawn out of me.

I felt so angry and so scared, Mum. I was angry at myself and scared that Jenny would never want anything to do with me again. I went outside to run after her.

I caught up with her in the woods. In Abborrparken, on the shortcut she always used to take to get home. She called me a monster and a rapist. She said she never wanted me to come near her again. She said she would go around telling everyone who I really was. I tried to tell her it wasn't what it looked like. It wasn't really me. I would never have slept with her sister.

I told her she was meant to be with me. She laughed in my face. She said there was no way she'd ever let me touch her again. I tried to reason with her, make her see sense. I tried to remind her of what she loved about me, what brought us together, but she put up a fight. She scratched me and pushed me away, as if I really was the monster she said I was. I just wanted her to shut up. And I acted without thinking.

I can't leave this place, Mum. I can't get out of prison and lie to people. Not even just to make you happy. I can't leave this place and own up to the errors of my ways, and inflict that shame on you.

I want you to know that I'm saying goodbye with my heart full of your love. The love that's carried me through every day and guided me towards the light. I want you to know that I'm going in peace, because I've paid my dues to Jenny and her family. Take care of yourself, Mum.

Love you forever,
Gus

Sophia puts her phone down and clasps her hands over her father's book.

I need a minute to process Gustav's words.

'I'm sorry, Sophia,' I say, resisting the urge to wrap my arms around her.

She smiles at me. 'At least I know I have nothing to reproach myself for.'

We take the letter with us when we leave to have it examined and checked for fingerprints.

Without a word, we get into my car. I start the engine and crank the heater. Then, we share a necessary silence. A silence which, if spent in solitude, would be filled with infinite sadness. Together, we can carry it differently.

I try to imagine what it must have been like for a mother to spend her life fighting for her only son's innocence, only to learn from a stroke of his pen that he was guilty all along. Guilty of a heinous crime. How does a mother come to terms with the fact that the child she raised was a murderer – and a rapist, to boot? What a colossal shock it must have been for that woman. She must have felt so deceived, so uprooted. Abandoned all over again. As if there were a pattern repeating itself in Anna's life: first her parents, then her son's father, and now her son. She didn't give herself time to move past the denial phase. Or perhaps her own suicide was a way to reflect her son's and keep the shameful secret. To smear Lukas Dalenius, Jenny and Wilma's brother, one of the people who campaigned the hardest against Gustav – by hitting him where it hurt the most: in the classroom with his students. To punish him, too, for throwing her faults in her face. For handing her a mirror tainted by the kind of regret we use to paint another portrait of ourselves.

If only she had been a present mother. If only she had cared better for Gustav when he was a child. If only men hadn't taken that all-consuming place in her life. If only she had been there the night of her son's party, on 13 December 1999, none of this would have happened.

Aleksander puts a hand on mine, then gets out of my car and into his own, and drives off a few seconds later.

At that moment an image comes rushing back to me. Something that shouldn't have been on that envelope. The envelope containing a letter that shouldn't have made it into Sophia's hands – at least not the way it did.

I pick up my phone straight away and call Aleks. 'Stop. I need to see the envelope again.'

'OK,' he simply replies.

I see him reverse and then park in front of me. He gets out of his car and into mine again.

I switch on the overhead light.

Sophia gave us a freezer bag to put the envelope in. I turn it towards the light and say, 'Look at the postmark, Aleks. Look at what it says.'

55
Maïa

Dr Linda Holgersson opens the door.

She gives us a fleeting smile, then steps aside to let us in.

'I wasn't expecting to receive such a ... late visit,' the psychologist says, pulling her dressing gown tighter around her chest. 'What's happened?' she asks, without inviting us any further than the entryway.

'We've found the last letter Gustav wrote to his mother,' Aleksander says. 'Did you know that he'd written it?'

'Yes.'

'Was that how you knew he was going to die by suicide?'

'No, not at all. He could just as easily have been writing to his mother about starting a new life, of sorts, when he got out. It was more the way he talked about things that made me think he'd decided to die. He had found a certain kind of ... peace with himself.'

'Do you know what was in the letter?'

She shakes her head. 'No.'

Aleksander holds her gaze. 'Are you trying to tell me that after everything you shared, Gustav Hellström didn't tell you what he wrote in that letter?'

'That's exactly what I'm telling you, Commissioner.'

'And did you have any suspicions about what it contained, Linda?' I follow on.

'Yes, I had my suspicions.'

Aleksander gives her a short, exasperated smile.

Linda is like a woman of the law: she chooses her words wisely. Supposing is not the same as knowing. It strikes me that she would make an excellent witness in court, so long as she was on our side.

'It's interesting,' she says, almost to herself. 'What Anna did. Hers was a case of total denial. She couldn't accept her son's decision. It was too much for her. She let the anger drag her down.'

'What was the nature of your relationship with Gustav, Linda?' Aleksander asks.

She gives him an amused look. 'It's crazy how everything, for men, is connected to sex.'

Aleksander's about to object, but she's a step ahead of him.

'Not that I'm directing that criticism at you in particular, Commissioner. It's simply the male emotional construct. It's the way we've shaped you. Us women, you men, society in general. Your phallus is so visible, everything has to revolve around it. On that point, I'm with Freud.'

She adjusts the flaps of her dressing gown.

'I was captivated by Gustav's case, because I could sense an immense conflict in him, though I never got to the bottom of it. When he decided to die by suicide, I understood that, for all of his twenty-something years behind bars, he had tried to conform to the image of himself that his mother had defended in the media. He wore himself down doing that. And he did what he did to set himself free.'

I can see the sadness in her smile.

'You asked me about the nature of our relationship, Commissioner. I consider myself his saviour.'

'He killed himself and you think you saved him?' Linda is clearly testing Aleksander's limits.

'Yes. He understood that he couldn't face the world and carry the weight of a twenty-odd-year lie. He couldn't deny the terrible damage his actions had caused. If he had been released, Gustav would probably have fallen into a severe depression and may well have started raping women again. At least that way he would have had control over something in his life.'

'So, do you think he raped Jenny, then?' I ask her.

'Gustav talked a lot about the last time they slept together. I'm sure he's eroticised the memory and the years have softened the details, but I do think what they did at his house was an act of love. I also think he went on to assault her in the woods.'

'You're the one who sent the letter to Anna, aren't you?'

She looks at me in surprise.

It was postmarked Vasastan, the area where she lives. The letter couldn't have been sent from the prison, because it would have been read. And the authorities would have been alerted to its contents.

'Yes.'

I wait for her to elaborate, but she falls silent.

'I suppose Gustav wanted his mother to know he was guilty,' I say. 'He wanted her to have that information so that she, and she alone, could decide what she wanted to do with it. Obviously, she decided to take the truth to her grave.'

'No, not really,' Linda replies. 'Otherwise, she would have destroyed that letter. Where did you find it, if you don't mind me asking?'

'In a book written by Rasmus, her grandfather.'

Linda smiles. 'Rasmus Akerman. Gustav's great-grandfather. Anna's beloved grandfather. And his *Scars of Silence*. "There is as much of us in your sighs, / As of you and your light in my silence."'

She pauses.

'Have you ever heard of Stanislavski's "Magic If" theory?'

'No,' I reply.

Aleksander shakes his head, too.

'He was a Russian actor whose techniques formed the foundations of the Actors Studio methods used by many Hollywood stars. The "Magic If" is one of those techniques. It all boils down to asking yourself "what if": for example, what if I were in that character's shoes, what would I do? I often use it with my patients to unlock the doors of their psyche. Based on what Gustav told me, I think Anna Hellström's whole life was built on a single "if". If Sophia had loved her daughter the way she was,

Anna would have been a far better mother to her son. She would have been protective, nurturing – and present.'

'That's quite the burden to bear, as a parent, don't you think?' Aleksander says. 'Such determinism connected to our actions, the mistakes we make, whether we're present or not.'

'That's why I never had children, Commissioner.' She smiles with her eternal serenity.

She pulls her dressing gown tighter around her chest once more, and looks at us both in turn. 'You still haven't asked me the real question, have you? The one that brought you here at this indecent hour.'

Aleks smiles. 'Who else did Gustav write to, Linda? Or, perhaps I should put it this way, who else did you send a letter from Gustav to, Dr Holgersson?'

56
Aleks

Twenty-four hours later

I settle in to the interview suite with a curious sense of satisfaction and weariness. It's like I'm about to finish a book I started twenty-four years ago.

The door opens to reveal a dark-haired woman in a beige suit and black heels, followed by an athletic-looking man in his early thirties with pale-green eyes: Lukas Dalenius, Jenny and Wilma's brother, the primary-school teacher Maïa went to see in his classroom in Sticklinge at the beginning of the investigation. The only time I saw him before now was at his parents' house, when Jenny died. Back then, he was a nine-year-old boy, curled up in the arms of his mother, who had no strength left to hug him.

As if on autopilot, I state the date and time, the names of those in attendance – making a mess of the lawyer's, who corrects me – and make it clear that the interview will be video recorded, all the while mentally preparing myself to use the Magic If. What if Sarah and Wilma had gone to the police? What if, twenty-four years ago, I had arrested Martinsson, Brink and Lind? What if our justice system, in all its progress, hadn't persisted in demonising rape victims to such an extent? And what if I hadn't crossed paths with Maïa? Where would I be in solving this case?

I sigh as subtly as possible, then set about writing this final chapter.

'Lukas, did you receive a letter from Gustav Hellström shortly after his suicide?'

'Yes,' he replies, holding me in his hypnotic green gaze.

'What did that letter say?'

'It said that...' He clears his throat, then continues: 'It said that he had killed Jenny. That he had raped and murdered her. It said that my other sister, Wilma, had also been gang-raped that night by Erik Brink and Peter Lind. And that her friend Sarah had been raped, too, by Mikkel Martinsson.'

'Did you already know that Wilma and Sarah had been raped that night?'

'No.'

'Who else did you tell about that letter?'

His gaze falls to the table. He shakes his head. 'No one.'

'Did you try and find out if what Hellström wrote was true?'

'Of course I did. I reached out to Sarah. I phoned her. But I didn't mention the letter. I just asked her if it was true. About her being raped and Wilma being gang-raped. She ... confirmed the facts, but she didn't want to say any more about it.'

Sarah neglected to tell us that Lukas had contacted her. Was she trying to protect her friends' little brother? The sole survivor of the family. The last collateral victim. Without a doubt.

'Had you stayed in touch with Sarah since Jenny's death?'

'Yes. She was the only person who bothered checking how I was doing when I was with a foster family, in Västervik.'

'Did she show you the video from Gustav's party?'

Lukas doesn't answer. He plants his elbows on the table and scratches his chapped lips with a fingernail.

'We found an email inbox on your computer belonging to a certain JenWild13. Who is that?'

He moistens his lips. 'It's me. That's an account I use.'

'Why would you pose as a woman?'

'JenWild is an apocope formed by the first names of my sisters and the D of our family name. The number 13 is a reference to the date of Jenny's death.'

'That pseudonym must have made it easier for you to approach the victims, if they, like me, thought it was a woman's name, don't you think?'

Lukas squirms in his chair as if he's trying to find a comfortable position.

'In that account, we found emails that were sent to Daniel Brink and Roland Lind encouraging them to connect with you on Snapchat. Who did you contact first?'

'Daniel Brink.'

'What did you tell him?'

Lukas holds me in his piercing stare, but not in an aggressive way. 'I told him that his dad had raped a sixteen-year-old girl, who went on to kill herself. I told him I didn't want money. I wasn't asking for anything in exchange. I just wanted him to listen to me, because he needed to know who his father really was. And then I...' He tilts his head. 'I asked him if he was there when his mum died, and if he was sure she had a stroke. I suggested that maybe she had found out the truth about Erik, too.'

'How did you know the details of Mrs Brink's death?'

'It was all in Daniel's school records. His mother's death had considerably affected his studies. As a teacher in the Lidingö school district, I had access to that information.'

'But Daniel's mother did die of a stroke.'

'Whatever. Either way, I planted a seed of doubt in Daniel's mind,' Lukas replies, pressing his thumb into the time-worn edge of the table.

'And what did you do after that?'

'I drip-fed information to him and asked him to check if it was true. The fact that his dad used to play ice hockey with Gustav. Jenny's murder. Gustav's suicide in prison. Wilma's suicide, too.'

'How did the two of you communicate?'

'By Snapchat.'

'And then what happened?'

'As I had hoped, he ended up asking to meet me so I could show him the proof.'

Lukas closes his eyes.

'He was surprised to see me. He was expecting a woman. I told him it was my sister who his dad had raped. Then I said I'd show him the evidence and he could do with it what he wanted.'

'How did you kill him?'

'I opened my backpack and pulled out the hammer. For a couple of seconds, he didn't react. He didn't understand that it was for him. I hit him with it. On the head. Then I laid him down on the ground and dressed him the same way as my sisters. So that Erik would get the message. The tunic they were wearing. The crown that fell out of Jenny's backpack, which Gustav put on her head, at an angle, as if he was trying to hide the part of her skull he had just bashed in. But not the red sash. Wilma used hers to hang herself in the garage.'

His lawyer lowers her eyes.

'What did you do with their personal belongings and their phones?'

'They're in a locker in my classroom.'

I think back to the iMessage Daniel's girlfriend was surprised to receive after ten that night.

'Did you use Daniel's phone to message Thea, his girlfriend?'

Lukas shakes his head.

So, Thea was right. Daniel didn't want her to be able to track his location.

'And how did you approach Roland?'

Lukas takes a long breath in through his nose.

'Roland was much easier to convince. He had seen his dad with other women. He thought his dad was homophobic, too. And because he was gay, he obviously wasn't happy about that. My revelations tied in with what he already thought: his dad was a pig, and now he was going to wreck his wife's career, too. I met him on his family's boat, which he had tied up at Tahiti beach, not far from Rödstuguviken bay.'

He pauses, blinks, then continues.

'Then I cut the boat loose, and it drifted, with his body on board, over to Djursholm. Which was a bit of poetic justice, really, since Peter grew up there. Do you have any water?'

'We'll have some brought in for you,' I reply, knowing that Siv is in the control room. 'And what happened with Martinsson, Lukas?'

His mouth twists in disgust. A dark cloud of anger looms over his face.

'At the RVSA, the rape victim support association I'm a member of, there were two women who'd had a run-in with him. I knew their names. He had raped one of them in her home. So, I pretended that what he did had been caught on a nanny cam and told him that the woman wanted a million kronor, or else she'd put the video on social media. I arranged to meet him in the Solna churchyard, not far from the hospital, to show him the video. Mikkel Martinsson was a monster. A perverted monster. A menace to women since his first wet dream. And the police would never have stopped him. Our justice system doesn't deliver justice. I'm sure that's no surprise to you, Commissioner. Most of the time, it finds ways to apologise to those who should be the ones doing the apologising. It's only been five years, here in our country, since we took the onus off the victims – the survivors, I should say – to prove that they were raped. We still have so far to go before mentalities change.'

He shakes his head and keeps his eyes glued to the Formica table.

'For more than three years now, there's been no statute of limitations for the rape of a minor, Lukas,' I say to give him a nudge. 'You must know that. Erik Brink, Peter Lind and Mikkel Martinsson could have been brought to justice.'

'Oh, really? How? It was their word against Sarah's. And Sarah would never have given evidence. Never. She told me so. On the basis of what proof, then? Jenny and Wilma are dead. But let's assume those three did go down for what they did. How long would they have spent behind bars? Twenty months? Probably not a single day for our high-and-mighty mayor's husband. She would have played the political card and called it a witch hunt.

No, the justice system would never have delivered fair or proportionate punishment to Martinsson, Lind or Brink for the seeds of torment and death they sowed. All three of them were living their lives regardless, trampling the dead bodies of my family with every step they took. Every smile they smiled. Every little victory they celebrated. Every new life they brought into the world. Every moment in life they were so fucking entitled to.'

The door to the interview suite opens.

Jasmine comes in and puts a jug of water and three paper cups on the table, then leaves the room.

I fill the three glasses.

Lukas takes his and drains it slowly. He licks his lips between sips, making me think of a child enjoying a sugary drink.

'Do you realise what you have to look forward to, Lukas? What you can expect when you're in prison? You're a child killer.'

The lawyer is about to voice an objection, but Lukas puts his arm across the table.

'I'm not afraid of what lies ahead. I feel freer than I ever have. I'm free from my tormentors and I'm happy they got what they deserved. Those men took everything from me. It was only right for me to take everything from them, too. For me to take their children like they took my family. I want them to live through the hell of every day I've suffered since I was nine years old. I want them to live with the unbearable weight of the double guilt, knowing that they sacrificed their children to atone for their sins, knowing that their children died as martyrs, like Saint Lucia. My mother and Wilma died of grief. My father plunged into a depression so deep, he lost the strength to look after me. At ten years old – ten, Commissioner,' he says, stabbing the table with his index finger, 'I was taken into foster care in Stockholm, then when I was eleven, I went to a foster family in Västervik. When I was nearly twelve, I started wetting the bed. And every time it happened, the mother of that family would hang up my dirty sheet in the living room to make an example of me. She thought that if the other kids saw it, their teasing would stop me from doing it again. At thirteen, I was kicked out of a perfume shop. They thought I was messing with all the tester bottles out of mischief. But I was desperate to find my mother's smell, Commissioner. So I wouldn't be afraid anymore.'

He hangs his head for a moment, then looks up and locks his pale eyes to mine.

'I've spent the past twenty years trying to rebuild what those men destroyed. Twenty years is a long time, Commissioner. And as you can see, I failed. Those men took everything away from me, all for a few seconds of their own pleasure.'

He leans forwards, puts his forearms on the table and interlaces his fingers.

'Do you realise how absurd this whole thing is, Commissioner? All for a few fleeting seconds of pleasure.'

57
Maïa

26 December 2023

Comfortably seated on the sofa in Sophia Akerman's living room, I can barely distinguish the dark sea beyond the reflections in the bay window. Darkness is the layer of choice in Sweden's winter wardrobe. For a few hours at most, the day shrugs off that layer, revealing a little sun, then dons a cloak of shadows once more.

I savour a sip of *glögg*, the Christmas mulled wine my hostess has just served me. I wonder if maybe, just maybe, this is my first taste of the after-time. At long last.

Sophia is alone today. No family, no housekeeper.

'How has your Christmas been?' she asks, offering me a plate of cinnamon biscuits. 'You were with Christian, weren't you?'

Much better than last year, I think bitterly. The fact of the matter is, I simply don't remember the Christmas holidays last year. Those first few weeks after Ebbe's death, not long after Alice passed, were a long, painful journey. Days melted into one another. Time was blurred by my tears.

This year, I needed to break from tradition. No turkey for three. No *smörgåsbord*, either – the traditional Swedish Christmas buffet I would always help my mother-in-law to prepare. There was no sense replicating those family rites on my own. Honestly, I would have preferred to ignore Christmas completely, but it's everywhere and I didn't have the strength to go to the ends of the earth to avoid it.

When Christian asked me what I wanted, I just told him I didn't want to cook. So, he invited me over to his place to sample some oysters and enjoy a good steak and some fine wines. And while he busied himself in the kitchen, I found myself in a whole new situation for six o'clock on Christmas Eve: I was sitting down on the sofa. Yes, sitting down. With a glass of Barolo, no less. Gazing out at the frozen inlet and the ice-locked wharves of central Stockholm, with the incredible feeling that comes with being a part of delivering justice by unmasking the abusers and acknowledging the victims.

The day after tomorrow, Aleks will be back from visiting his parents. He's invited me to join him and the team down at the station for some belated Christmas drinks. They were busy all the way up to Christmas Eve tying up the loose ends of the case. Hardly surprising, given the ramifications that went back more than twenty years. I still don't know what I'm going to do for New Year's Eve. Christian's insisting I join him at the Grand Hôtel Stockholm, a stone's throw from his place, where a friend of his organises a *soirée blanche* every year. We'll see.

'It was painful,' I eventually admit, surprising myself with my honesty.

There are, it seems, some thoughts that I tame and control. And there are others, more raw and authentic, that I share with Sophia Akerman.

At least I've managed not to wear myself out trying to fill the void left by Alice and Ebbe. They were there with Christian and me, around the table set for two. They put in the odd appearance in between words, mouthfuls, images. And eventually, I understood that it's far more difficult to fear what's missing than to live with it.

'Your Christmases will never have the same flavour they did before, Maïa, because the holidays always point to those who are absent.'

'And those who are guilty.'

Sophia probes me with her gaze. I let mine wander out over the bay.

'I've been thinking about the woman who crashed into Alice and Ebbe and killed them. I've been thinking about her more than ever. About her family. About her children.'

'And has that made you less angry at her?'

'Hell, no. Even more, I'd say.'

Sophia smooths her lips into a smile. 'That's a natural part of the grieving process. We start by directing our anger at those who left us, then we turn it on ourselves before directing it back at others. For some, the resilient ones, the anger eventually dissipates. For others, the ones who dwell on it, it keeps metastasising all their lives.'

Sophia turns her gaze out to sea. Mine drifts back to her. To her profile and the wrinkles that take nothing away from her beauty. I wonder where she fits into that picture. Is she one of the resilient ones, or one of those who dwell on their grief?

'There's an advantage I have over you, Maïa,' she says. 'Anna wanted to die. The problem is, she did not go silently. She had to make a scene and caused suffering, like she always did.'

Sophia closes her eyes and shakes her head, as if to contradict what she's just said. Then she straightens up, stretching her dancer's back, and reopens her eyes. They seem more grey than blue in the pale light of the living room.

'I received a letter,' she tells me, with strength in her voice. 'Just before Christmas. Two days after the article about the murders came out in *Dagens Nyheter*. From a mother.' Sophia sweeps a liver-spotted hand across her face. 'Sorry, that was a silly assumption to make. The writer wasn't necessarily a mother – or a woman, for that matter. I just jumped to that conclusion because she, or he, criticised my role as a nurturing mother. That person suggested I ask myself what share of the blame was mine.'

'Your share of the blame for the murders?'

'That too. By extension. That person pointed to the "original sin", she says, miming air quotes around the words. 'To the fact that I gave birth to and educated a suicidal, unstable and neglectful daughter, who in turn became a mother to a rapist and a murderer.'

'Those are terribly cruel words, Sophia. I'm sorry.'

'But those words are true, Maïa. That person was only stating the facts. The undeniable facts.'

I move closer to her on the sofa and take her hands in mine. They're cold and soft. I wrap my palms around them, the way I would do a child's.

'You're not responsible for your grandson's actions, Sophia. And you're not to blame for your daughter's death. Our children's choices don't belong to us.'

'That's the power of words for you, Maïa. Or rather, the power of their absence. The power of silence.'

She turns her gaze to the bay window.

A few seconds tick by as I continue to warm her hands in mine. Still, in spite of the intimacy of the gesture, there's something awkward – unpleasant, even – about this moment. We're like second-rate actors in a theatre, going through the motions of a scene that ends up feeling more forced than authentic.

Suddenly, Sophia pulls her hands free from mine and gets up with the energy of her lost youth. My whole body tenses. There's a heaviness to the atmosphere. A sheen of apprehension.

'Come with me,' Sophia commands, but in a faltering voice, as she steps around the armchair she was sitting in.

I feel a growing sense of unease as I follow her down a vaulted corridor with tall, pale-wood doors that seem to pulsate in the glow of the chandeliers.

Sophia pushes the third on our left, which opens to reveal a small room with a desk facing the same view as in the drawing room: the sea, the beach and the bay, all black as night.

Sophia walks to the desk covered in leather- and canvas-bound books, faded by time and arranged in stacks of various heights. She sits down, moves two stacks to one side and pulls a tape recorder towards her. Then she presses the play button.

I

I ... I've decided to talk to someone about all this.

And I've understood that I had to start with the only person who knows, even though they're not here anymore: you.

I have no idea how many ... I don't even know what to call it ... how many episodes, let's say, I'm going to record. Anyway, this is the first.

I'm fifteen years old. I'm at a party, on a beach, in Värmdö, and I've had too much to drink.

I'm not old enough to be at this party, and I'm not old enough to drink either, obviously. I'm supposed to be sleeping over at my friend Magda's, the one you call a scatterbrain. But I was hoping I'd get to spend the night with the boy I'm crazy about, the boy I came here with, but now he's forgotten all about me. I don't even know if he's still here.

I'm not drunk to the point of being sick, at least I don't think I am. But I'm drunk enough that I couldn't fight anyone off if something happened to me. You know Mum. She's always bending my ear about precautions and being prepared for the worst. And for once, I wish I'd listened to her.

I can't call her. She would fly off the handle. The next bus isn't for another four hours or more, and as you know, back then you couldn't just call a taxi in the middle of the night to take you to Lidingö.

So you're the one I call. I tell myself, so I don't feel guilty, that I'm in danger, and that's what you're there for: to protect me.

'I'm in Värmdö and I'm drunk,' I told you.

You started laughing, and you told me you'd done a lot worse.

You came to pick me up. I fell asleep on the way back. I didn't want to go home. I was supposed to be sleeping over at Magda's. So you took me home with you, to your apartment in Stockholm at 7

Strandvägen. You suggested I take your bed. You would sleep on the sofa in your office. I went to sleep without even getting undressed.

I wake up to a wave of pleasure. Caresses. On my breasts, between my legs. I don't know how long I stay in that semi-sleep, still hazy with alcohol, before I'm conscious that I'm not sleeping anymore. That I'm not dreaming, and that it's your hands that are on me.

The pleasure turns to horror. Horror and fear. I'm paralysed. I can't move my legs or my arms. I can't make a single sound. Not even a 'no'. Because I know I can't say no to you. After all, you love me. Do you say no to the first man who ever loves you? To the man who is everything all at once? Where's the line between loving someone and being a lover? From cheek to mouth, it's only a few centimetres. Such a fine line, don't you think?

I force myself to close my eyes. I persuade myself that this is love. It must be, I tell myself, even though deep inside myself, I know those thoughts are wrong. But I sugar-coat them with your love. I brush them with all the devotion you've given me since I was born. I rewrite the definition of your caresses with the ink that's flowed between us over fifteen years.

And I distance myself from us. From this room where it all starts – no, actually, where everything ends. I travel back to that forest, near Woodstock, in 1952. I take refuge in that theatre to listen to the wind, the rain and the benches creaking. To forget the sounds of you and the scars of my silence.

58

Sophia stops the recording. She lays her hands flat on the desk, one on either side of the tape recorder.

The silence is buzzing around us.

I don't recognise the voice I've just heard. Clear, composed. But the obvious conclusion makes me nauseous.

'It was at 7 Strandvägen that the great poet Rasmus Akerman had his bachelor pad,' Sophia blurts with bitterness, without taking her eyes off the tape recorder.

'Your father,' I whisper, incapable of moving a muscle.

'Anna's beloved grandfather. Her substitute father.'

The horror sinks in. I stifle the urge to vomit.

'After I discovered Gustav's letter inside *Scars of Silence*, I kept on looking through those boxes of Anna's belongings. I came across these cassettes. I started listening to one, then I stopped. A bit too quickly, I dismissed them as the result of my little lost daughter going on a feminist rant.'

She presses her lips together. She puffs out her chest. She clenches her fists.

'And then I received that letter accusing me of being a bad mother. A dangerous, destructive mother. And I ... I decided to have a closer look at the books from Anna's shelves, the ones I never would have bought myself, the ones I would have teased her about. I decided to listen to her cassettes, too. All six of them ... none of which are dated, by the way. I have no idea when she recorded them.'

Sophia draws a hungry gasp of air. The kind of breath that saves someone from drowning, or keeps them going between floods of tears.

She turns to face me, a weeping veil of grief covering her eyes.

'Putting a man on a pedestal makes him a statue, a god to be adored. Rasmus Akerman was the very picture of the ideal father. But it turns out, he was quite the Pygmalion. It's my fault, Maïa. It's all my fault. And if anyone's ever going to dethrone him, it has to be me. The sender of that hurtful letter was right: I am the original sin. I threw my daughter at my father like a piece of meat. And while he got his teeth stuck in, I spent my life taking it out on her. Like a child who tears a doll to shreds only to moan about it being broken.'

I want to say something, but I can't. I think about Anna and her desperation as a child, then as a mother, when her son turned into a copy of her own tormentor.

'My father never...' Sophia's voice trails off for a moment. 'My father never laid a finger on me. But how ... could I not have known he was raping my daughter?'

She unclenches her fists and brings her hands together in prayer.

'It's impossible not to know, Maïa. It's not that you don't know it. You just refuse to see it.'

I place my palms on her shaking shoulders – a comforting gesture my father often modelled when there were no words to bandage my wounds. What happens to you, I wonder, when your father, your hero, changes face and turns trust into torment? What happens to the admiring child inside you? I suppose it's just another thing to prey on and tear to shreds too.

'Needless to say,' Sophia goes on. 'I realised why Anna kept Gustav's confession letter inside *Scars of Silence*. My daughter locked both of her tormentors away in the same box.'

59
Maïa

1 March 2024

It's the middle of the afternoon and the sun's preparing to set over the greyness of the sea in this never-ending winter.

Aleksander stops the boat and gives me a smile. The roar of the engine surrenders to a gentle lapping of water against the hull.

My house is just a dot on the bay, tickled by the bulrushes swaying in the breeze. This evening, Sophia Akerman is coming here to dinner for the first time. It's been nearly a month since she spoke out on the national evening news on SVT1. Sitting in my living room, Aleks and I watched her go to battle and make a lot of noise about all the things that silence had destroyed.

Sophia stated the facts in their brutal simplicity. Her father, the great poet whose work was celebrated across Scandinavia for almost a century and taught in schools and universities, was a child sex offender who raped his granddaughter, Anna, for years.

'I always thought of my father as the tree of life. The sap of that tree nourished our dynasty and nurtured the spirit of Akerman Editions,' Sophia said on live TV. 'But all along, that tree was diseased. It was rotten to the core. And the only thing to do with a tree like that is to chop it down.'

The interviewer asked her how she was coming to terms with the revelations. She wanted to know if the new light that had been cast on Rasmus Akerman's life made him seem more like a monster now than a father to her.

'My father wasn't a monster. He was a man,' Sophia replied.

She paused, one hand suspended in midair as if to trace the

contours of an abandoned thought. The interviewer didn't dare to fill that silence. The camera, however, held her in its sights and captured the fire in her hypnotic blue stare. As if the cameraman was just as captivated by her as the viewers at home.

'The terror and horror of a rape are cloaked in normality, not monstrosity.'

In the weeks that followed, Sophia gave one interview and speech after another, absorbing the shocks and deflecting the criticism firmly, yet gracefully. After Anna's accusations against her grandfather were made public, more reports of rape and sexual assault followed. Fourteen, that's how many victims of Rasmus Akerman have come forward so far. Twelve women and two men. They are all survivors.

I asked Sophia, during a morning walk, if speaking out had felt liberating. 'Certainly not,' she replied. 'But I hope that my actions will be liberating for others.'

Silence is consent. I've been thinking a lot about that old proverb recently. Silence is *not* consent. Sometimes, silence is the only weapon, or the only shield, within reach.

'Look,' Aleks suddenly says, pointing to the sky ahead of us. It's so majestic, adorned with so many colours – stripes of yellow and orange, with a band of pink hovering over the sea, like the horizon is blushing, having been kissed by the night.

Aleks and I have been working together to hone the art of being alone. He's restitching the parts of his life his wife tore apart. Meanwhile, she's living across the bay in Stockholm, with her daughters half the time – but without her lover, the mayor, whose career is in tatters.

The urn containing Ebbe's ashes is sitting in my lap. I'm cradling it like a shivering child. The anguish feels like a stone in my heart.

This is the hardest thing I've ever had to do.

This urn, I've carried it around the house the way the cast of a vaudeville show would. I've talked to it like someone who's losing her mind – or someone who's seen the light. But I was only a partner. His partner, for twenty-five years. And right here, right now, I must let him go.

Aleksander smiles at me, but leaves me the space I need for one last tête-à-tête with this history of mine.

Ebbe told me one day that he'd like to be laid to rest as near to me as possible. And I want to keep finding him everywhere – in this stunning sunset and this sea of steel.

I stand up, take the lid off the urn and pour his ashes into the water. They tumble with a whisper that sounds like a fluttering of wings.

A wave carries them away.

An image of that empty chair floats into my mind. The idea of keeping a chair free for an unexpected guest. And I think, that's exactly what I've just done.

The void has not devoured me. I've transformed the emptiness into a new space, a garden where I can sow the seeds of a new life.

Acknowledgements

All my inner revolutions have been sparked by reading. This particular revolution was twofold: first I read *Not That Bad*, by Roxane Gay, who gives rape and sexual assault survivors a voice. Then I watched the series *Unbelievable* starring Toni Collette.

An immense sense of indignation began to grow in me. A cry from the heart.

Maybe now that I'm approaching my fifties, I'm giving myself permission to scream and shout. Maybe I'm daring to say no to the aberrations of a system that makes me irate. Maybe I also feel invested with a duty to speak up for those forced into silence. Maybe all that at once. In any case, the first ink of these *Scars of Silence* flowed from tears of incomprehension and an infinite sadness.

First, I'd like to thank my French publisher, Caroline Lépée, for giving this novel a whole new direction with the talent of an artist who can paint not only a scene but also a whole era and drama with three strokes of a brush. How lucky I am to work with you, Caroline!

Thank you to everyone else on the teams at Calmann-Lévy who carry my stories to readers with such energy, passion and good humour. It's a joy for me to be a part of your publishing house.

Thank you to the wonderful team at Orenda Books: my publisher, Karen Sullivan, with her extraordinary energy and passion for books and stories, West Camel, my brilliant editor, Cole, Anne, Danielle and our Fairy-Mary, for making my novels reach my English-speaking readers and my characters travel so many miles.

Thank you to my amazing translator, David Warriner, who manages to capture my voice. It's such an honour to work with him.

Thank you to my father, my first reader, without whom it's unthinkable for me to write.

Thank you to my mum, who's with me every step of the way, and my sister, whose own experience is woven into these lines.

Thank you to Mattias, for holding the fort with so many smiles and words of encouragement in spite of all the Lego explosions and tantrums about having to finish a delicious bowl of broccoli soup.

Thank you to Thomas, my partner in crime, for his unfailing availability and his precious help with my research into the Swedish justice system.

Thank you to Lilas, my writing fairy godmother, without whom this path would not exist.

And thank *you*, my dear readers, for welcoming my stories so warmly. I'm so, so lucky to write for you.